R R

U.S. MARSHALS' FLIGHT 407
PASSENGER MANIFEST

Equipment: ___727___

Pilot: ___Jensen___
Copilot: ___O'Connor___

Number of non-prisoner personnel: ___13, including marshals, staff___
(one nurse), pilot, copilot

Number of convicts: __95*__
  *All convicts must wear shackles and leg irons.

Total passengers: ___108___

EXERCISE EXTREME CAUTION WITH FOLLOWING INMATES:

Carl Hart—Convicted of kidnapping ex-wife, Kelly Jackson. Formerly assigned to Marion, Illinois, correctional facility. Bureau of Prisons approved relocation request after trouble documented between Hart and notorious Marion prison gang.

Ryder Hamilton—Former owner, Hamilton Oil and Gas (Fortune 500 company). Doing time for oil lease scam. Claims frame-up. Considered very intelligent and resourceful. Has flown single-engine Piper Cherokee.

Dear Reader,

The year is ending, and as a special holiday gift to you, we're starting off with a 3-in-1 volume that will have you on the edge of your seat. *Special Report,* by Merline Lovelace, Maggie Price and Debra Cowan, features three connected stories about a plane hijacking and the three couples who find love in such decidedly unusual circumstances. Read it—you won't be sorry.

A YEAR OF LOVING DANGEROUSLY continues with Carla Cassidy's *Strangers When We Married,* a reunion romance with an irresistible baby and a couple who, I know you'll agree, truly do belong together. Then spend 36 HOURS with Doreen Roberts and *A Very...Pregnant New Year's.* This is one family feud that's about to end...at the altar!

Virginia Kantra's back with *Mad Dog and Annie,* a book that's every bit as fascinating as its title—which just happens to be one of my all-time favorite titles. I guarantee you'll enjoy reading about this perfect (though they don't know it yet) pair. Linda Randall Wisdom is back with *Mirror, Mirror,* a good twin/bad twin story with some truly unexpected twists—and a fabulous hero. Finally, read about a woman who has *Everything But a Husband* in Karen Templeton's newest—and keep the tissue box nearby, because your emotions will really be engaged.

And, of course, be sure to come back next month for six more of the most exciting romances around—right here in Silhouette Intimate Moments.

Enjoy!

Leslie Wainger

Leslie J. Wainger
Executive Senior Editor

Please address questions and book requests to:
Silhouette Reader Service
U.S.: 3010 Walden Ave., P.O. Box 1325, Buffalo, NY 14269
Canadian: P.O. Box 609, Fort Erie, Ont. L2A 5X3

SPECIAL REPORT

MERLINE LOVELACE,
MAGGIE PRICE,
DEBRA COWAN

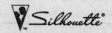

INTIMATE MOMENTS™
Published by Silhouette Books
America's Publisher of Contemporary Romance

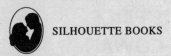 SILHOUETTE BOOKS

ISBN 0-373-27115-8

SPECIAL REPORT

Copyright © 2000 by Harlequin Books S.A.

The publisher acknowledges the copyright holders of the individual works as follows:

MIDNIGHT SEDUCTION
Copyright © 2000 by Margaret Price

COVER ME!
Copyright © 2000 by Debra S. Cowan

FINAL APPROACH...TO FOREVER
Copyright © 2000 by Merline Lovelace

This edition published by arrangement with Harlequin Books S.A.

® and TM are trademarks of Harlequin Books S.A., used under license. Trademarks indicated with ® are registered in the United States Patent and Trademark Office, the Canadian Trade Marks Office and in other countries.

Visit Silhouette at www.eHarlequin.com

Printed in U.S.A.

CONTENTS

MAGGIE PRICE turned to crime at twenty-two. That's when she went to work at the Oklahoma City Police Department as a civilian crime analyst. During her tenure at the OCPD, Maggie stood in lineups, snagged special assignments to homicide task forces, established procedures for evidence submittal, even posed as the wife of an undercover officer in the investigation of a fortune teller.

While at the OCPD, Maggie stored up enough tales of intrigue, murder and mayhem to keep her at the keyboard for years. The first of those tales won the Romance Writers of America's Golden Heart Award for Romantic Suspense. Maggie invites readers to contact her at 5208 W. Reno, Suite 350, Oklahoma City, OK 73127-6317.

Like many writers, **DEBRA COWAN** made up stories in her head as a child. Her BA in English was obtained with the intention of following family tradition and becoming a schoolteacher, but after she wrote her first novel, there was no looking back. An avid history buff, Debra writes both historical and contemporary romances. Born in the foothills of the Kiamichi Mountains, Debra still lives in her native Oklahoma with her husband and their two beagles, Maggie and Domino. Debra invites readers to contact her at P.O. Box 30123, Coffee Creek Station, Edmond, OK 73003-0003, or via e-mail at Harlequin's Web site at www.eHarlequin.com.

MERLINE LOVELACE spent twenty-three exciting years as an Air Force officer, serving tours at the Pentagon and at bases all over the world before she began a new career as a novelist. When she's not tied to her keyboard, she and her handsome hero, Al, enjoy traveling, golf and long, lively dinners with friends and family.

Merline enjoys hearing from readers and can be reached via www.eHarlequin.com. Be sure to watch for her next books: *The Spy Who Loved Him,* January 2001 Intimate Moments, and *The Horse Soldier,* January 2001 Mira Books.

Midnight Seduction

Maggie Price

A special thanks goes to my coworkers at Will Rogers World Airport in Oklahoma City, Oklahoma, for their inestimable expertise, support, help and encouragement.

Books by Maggie Price

Silhouette Intimate Moments

Prime Suspect #816
The Man She Almost Married #838
Most Wanted #948
On Dangerous Ground #989
Dangerous Liaisons #1043
Special Report #1045
  "Midnight Seduction"

Chapter 1

Arriving in the teeth of a predawn storm wasn't something Christine Logan had planned for the second day of her new job. Rain sluiced over her vehicle's windshield. Wind buffeted the airport-issued Bronco as if it were a child's toy. The jagged spear of lightning that, seconds before, cracked the inky sky had locked her fingers onto the steering wheel in a death grip.

Still, it wasn't the prospect of getting fried by lightning or the probable storm-caused chaos awaiting her as Whiskey Springs's new airport director that had pinpricks of nerves crawling the back of her neck. It was the thought of facing Quinn Buchanan, the one man who could suck the air out of her lungs faster than any natural disaster.

He'd always had that effect on her, from the instant his brother introduced them, to the moment Quinn ended their relationship. Even now, three years later, just thinking about the chemistry that had sizzled between them seemed to thicken the air inside the Bronco.

"Get a grip," Christine muttered. Granted, fate seemed to have spun her life in a full circle by putting her back in Texas and in Quinn's path. But, things had changed in the past three years. The terrible guilt she'd felt over Quinn's brother's death had eased. Even the desperate pain that had come when Quinn turned away from her no longer rose up to grip her by the throat. She'd healed. Gotten on with her life. And had adamantly refused to ruminate about Quinn Buchanan.

Until yesterday, when she had no choice but to let thoughts of him rush back. That was when her secretary handed her the roster for today's staff meeting. To her dismay, Christine had discovered that Quinn was now Captain over the Whiskey Springs Police Department's airport division. He didn't work for her but, since security was top priority at any airport, her former lover was destined to be a part of her new job.

He hadn't been on-site yesterday. She'd found out he'd been at the police pistol range for annual requalification. At least she hadn't had to deal with seeing him her first day on the job. Still, knowing Quinn would again be a presence in her life, albeit her *professional* life, had put a knot in her belly that had nothing to do with new-job jitters. She hadn't slept a wink last night. Hadn't managed to eat.

WSPD had at least twenty-five captains. Why, out of all of them, did Quinn have to be the one assigned to *her* airport? When she'd left Whiskey Springs to take a division head's job at L.A. International, he'd been a sergeant, working undercover in the Vice Detail. Now he wore captain's bars. His brother's death hadn't slowed Quinn, career-wise.

It was the only thing that hadn't suffered.

Peering through the watery windshield, Christine chided herself that what had happened between her and Quinn no longer mattered. *Now* mattered. Snagging the director's job at Sam Houston International Airport had been a great career move, one she planned to parlay into further advancement in the aviation industry. The fact that her new job involved Quinn was the one dark cloud on her horizon.

A conference table, she thought, flexing her fingers on the steering wheel. Her first dealings with him in three years would be across a conference table, with her staff seated around them. *She* was in charge of the airport, she could make sure she and Quinn didn't wind up alone together, at least not until she had a chance to steel herself against his presence.

That last thought had her frowning. After so much time, seeing Quinn shouldn't even put a blip on her internal radar screen. Yet, more than just a blip was going on inside her, she conceded. It felt as if a jet engine was revving in her chest.

A sudden boom of thunder shook the Bronco. Rain hammered the roof with vicious fists. Squinting out the windshield, Christine steered around a corner; headlights licked across the chain-link fence that marked the airport's north perimeter. The four-lane street that funneled traffic to the sprawling terminal was covered with a wet sheen that reflected the brake lights of the morning traffic.

The next instant, lightning bolted beside the Bronco, illuminating the landscape like a camera flash. Christine yelped as sparks flew and a thin sapling toppled onto the fence.

"Holy…" She grabbed the microphone off its clip on the dash. "Airport Three, this is Airport One."

"You're on the air early, boss."

Despite the tension that had her spine stiff, her lips curved. After her dad became Whiskey Springs's airport director he'd hired Pete Jacobs, a born troubleshooter, as his maintenance manager. Now, she was Pete's boss.

"What do the weather gurus say about this storm, Pete?"

"That it's wound tighter than a Harley on nitro." As he spoke, Christine pictured the burly, gray-haired man with an ever-present cigar jammed in one corner of his mouth. "We've just gone under a tornado watch," Pete continued. "Which is a regular occurrence around here each April."

Christine gave thought to the airline delays that always accompanied storms. That meant a terminal filled with prickly travelers, piles of luggage and overwhelmed concessions. "What's going on with the airlines?"

"Everything's on schedule so far."

"If the tornado watch gets upgraded to a warning, how long will it take to get everyone in the terminal to the pedestrian tunnel?"

"Five minutes, give or take one."

"Okay. Stay with the weather data and let me know what's happening." When the Bronco topped a small rise, the lights of the gleaming glass and chrome terminal came into view. "By the way," she added, "a sapling just went down on the north fence."

"I thought you were on your radio at home," Pete commented. "It's barely six-thirty. You're not due in until eight."

"I decided to come in because of the weather." She didn't add that the prospect of seeing Quinn had kept her up all night.

"You and Buchanan," Pete commented. "He had the police dispatcher call to let me know he'd be in early, too."

"I'm going straight to my office," Christine said, trying to sound as if Pete's news hadn't just locked her jaw. "Call me there."

"Ten-four. You know, Christine, I'm glad to have you back working here, as director this time. You've got your dad's style. It's nice to know a Logan's running this airport again."

"Thanks, Pete." After signing off, she snapped the microphone back onto its clip and let out a slow breath. She'd find out soon enough if she had what it took to run the airport with her late father's efficient precision.

Minutes later, Christine steered onto the drive that led to the employee lot. Braking at the gate, she rolled down her window and slid her ID card through the slot on the reader. The process took mere seconds, but when she jerked her arm back inside the window, the cuff of her red silk blazer was soaked.

"Great." She shook her head, giving thought to her raincoat, still packed in who-knew-which of the crates the movers had stacked in every room of her new apartment over the weekend.

Water sprayed beneath the Bronco's tires as she pulled into her parking space. Umbrella ready, she shouldered the door open against the wind, then plunged into the storm.

Water slapped at her like an angry demon. The wind tossed rain under the umbrella, snapping its metal ribs straight up. By the time she raced through the door into the terminal, her red silk suit was drenched and she was soaked to the skin.

"Wonderful," she muttered, cramming her ruined umbrella into a trash can. With a sigh of resignation, she slicked her damp, blunt-cut hair away from her face and regarded her surroundings.

Even at this early hour, the terminal was bustling. A

bedlam of voices mixed with the light rock playing from the speakers recessed into the ceiling. Customers lined up at the various rent-a-car service counters; travelers crowded one of the baggage claim areas, collecting luggage off a churning conveyor belt.

As Christine moved, the cool air prickled her damp flesh and she gave silent thanks for the change of clothes she'd brought in yesterday with her boxes of personal office paraphernalia. The jeans, chambray shirt and tennis shoes were more appropriate for trips out to the airfield, but they were at least dry.

Just as she reached the staircase that led to the third floor offices, the siren outside the terminal blared. Seconds later, a woman's calm, recorded voice sounded on the PA system.

"Attention in the terminal. Due to a weather emergency, please proceed downstairs to the pedestrian tunnel."

Dread settling in her stomach, Christine clipped her ID card to her wet lapel. While she threaded through the crowd, she silently blessed Pete Jacobs for cueing the PA announcement.

"Please go to the tunnel," she repeated as she moved, pitching her voice over the din of the still-howling siren.

As voices rose with urgency, Christine caught a glimpse of WSPD's gray uniform. Her heartbeat hitched, then leveled when she realized it wasn't Quinn approaching. The uniform was worn by an officer she'd met the previous day.

"Officer Sheridan will escort you to the tunnel," she stated to the people nearby. Leaving Sheridan to deal with the baggage-claim crowd, Christine moved to the nearest rent-a-car counter.

The PA announcement replayed.

By the time she'd made her way past the counters and

bag carousels, the first level was cleared. She dashed up a staircase to where restaurants, shops and airline passenger counters were normally crowded with customers at this hour.

There, a blue-shirted man from Pete's maintenance division waved stragglers toward an escalator. Noting he had things under control, Christine veered toward the nearest concourse.

Outside thunder crashed; rain pelted the floor-to-ceiling windows. Lightning streaked across the horizon, silhouetting a 727 parked at one gate. At the entrance to the concourse, the security checkpoint workers had secured the sliding gate to bar access before leaving their post.

"*¡Madre de Dios!*"

Her heartbeat spiking, Christine spun around.

"*¡Mi hija! ¡Mi hija!*"

Shoving her damp hair off her cheek, Christine stared at the short, Hispanic woman who clutched a blanket-swaddled infant while flapping her free hand at the gate. A small boy stood beside the woman, gripping her skirt.

"*¿Hija?*" Christine asked, struggling to recall her high school Spanish. "Your daughter?"

"*Sí.*" The woman waved her hand toward the concourse. "She lost! Maybe down there."

"I'll find her," Christine said, digging in her tote for her master key. Just then, the maintenance worker she'd spotted earlier dashed around the corner, keys jangling from his belt.

"I've got an emergency," Christine stated. "Unlock this—"

"Listen, lady, everybody's supposed to be in the tunnel," he stated. "My boss told me to make one last sweep—"

"I am your boss," Christine said, flashing her ID. "A

little girl's lost, maybe in this concourse. Open this gate, then take this woman and her children downstairs.''

She saw the flicker of recognition in the man's eyes when he read her name. ''Yes, ma'am.''

He jerked a key ring off his belt, had the gate unlocked and shoved open in seconds. When he turned back, his gaze shifted across Christine's shoulder, then he said, ''We've got a problem, Captain.''

''What's going on?''

The familiar deep voice that came from behind her had Christine's pulse shooting from high gear into frenzy. Blood pounded in her cheeks; her hand trembled once on the strap of her tote. She let out the breath that had caught in her throat, then turned and met Quinn Buchanan's impossibly blue eyes.

''A little girl's lost, maybe in this concourse,'' she said, thankful her voice at least was steady. ''I'll look for her while you—''

''I'll go.'' For the space of a heartbeat, Quinn's eyes lingered on her face. The look he gave her was so direct, so intense, that her palms began to sweat.

He turned to the woman who now had tears streaming down her cheeks. ''Ma'am, what's your daughter's name?''

''*¿Qué?*''

Quinn raised a dark brow. ''*¿Cómo se llama su hija?*''

''*Maria,*'' she sobbed. ''*Maria Hernandez.*''

''*¿Cuántos años?*''

''*Tres.*''

With ease of habit, Quinn spoke into a handheld radio as he stepped around the gate and headed into the concourse.

The instant Christine caught up with him, his shoulders went rigid beneath his dark suit coat. ''Dispatch says we could have a tornado on the ground any minute," he said, flicking her a grim look. "This concourse is nothing but glass walls," he added, his searching gaze sweeping from side to side. "Go to the tunnel, Christine. *Now.*"

Although she bristled at his curt order, she acknowledged his concern was warranted. The same glass and gleaming chrome that made most airports impressively spacious turned them deadly in the face of storms and bombs.

"It's a big concourse," she said, taking two steps to his one. "Two can search in half the time."

"Can't argue that. You take the east side. Try to stay clear of the windows," he added across his shoulder as he headed in the opposite direction.

Christine veered toward a departure gate, its padded seats and passenger service counter deserted. Hiking the strap of her tote up on her shoulder, she bent and peered below the seats.

"Maria?"

Christine spotted a few paper cups, a carelessly tossed aside newspaper, but no little girl. After checking behind the counter, she moved to the next departure gate.

She was aware of the storm roaring outside. Cognizant of the howling wind and rain lashing against the glass that might shatter and turn lethal any minute. Yet her thoughts, as she continued her harried search, centered on Quinn.

He had changed, she thought as she checked the lock on a door leading to a jetway. His thick black hair no longer lapped carelessly over his shirt collar the way it had when he'd worked undercover. He now wore his hair short and brushed back from a straight hairline. His handsome face had thinned, accenting sharp cheekbones and those off-the-chart blue eyes that, with just one look, could make a woman shudder.

She had. God, she had. More times than she could count.

She had also wept, mourned, and longed for Quinn. Then she'd gotten over him.

Because she had, she knew that whatever she felt inside was anything but yearning. She would never again let herself yearn, not for this man who had walked away when she needed him most.

Her breath coming fast, Christine shouted Maria's name as she dashed through the next two departure gates, then checked the darkened entrance to a grab-it-and-run hot dog concession.

Outside, thunder crashed. The wind picked up, wailing like a lost soul. Rain battered the windows.

"Christine!" At the sound of Quinn's voice, she raced into the center of the concourse. Her hope that he'd found Maria faded when he dashed around a newsstand holding only his radio. "Maria's been found."

"Thank good—"

"There's a twister on the ground. We're in its path." As Quinn spoke, the wind calmed. The rain stopped abruptly. The air inside the terminal seemed to take on weight. An ominous silence descended around them.

Terror consumed Christine. "We won't make it to the tunnel."

"You're right." He clamped one hand on her elbow. "There's a private handicapped rest room just past the coffee shop."

The sound of their heels echoed like gunshots off the waxed tiles as they raced down the concourse.

Quinn jerked open the door to the rest room; Christine darted inside just as a deafening roar blasted around them.

"Get in the corner!" he shouted, slamming the door behind him.

Diving for the corner, Christine wedged her back against

the wall. Her mind registered the coolness of the tiles against her damp, hose-clad legs. Quinn hunkered down to face her, then wrapped his arms around her, his body a protective barrier over hers.

Fear…and a mix of emotions had her heart hammering. The storm's roar intensified, sounding like a train speeding through a tunnel.

When Quinn's arms tightened around her waist, Christine closed her eyes.

"It'll be okay," he murmured, his breath a warm wash against her temple.

With him crouched over her, prepared to take the brunt of the storm, she felt protected and safe. Oh God, she felt…

His arms. They wrapped around her like a lover's, holding her in an achingly familiar embrace that made her pulse throb, hard and thick.

His chest. Her face was turned to the side, one cheek cushioned against the broad range of muscles while the remembered scent of him seeped into her lungs. She heard the strong, steady beat of his heart while her own pounded painfully. Dragging in a ragged breath, she catalogued the sinewy feel of the chest that she knew sported a crisp mat of dark hair that she had swirled her fingers through more times than she could count.

His thighs. He had one knee wedged against the wall; the inside of his thigh rode atop hers. The power, the press of muscle, the strength in the legs that had straddled her body in another lifetime sent a shiver up her spine that had nothing to do with the prospect of being hurled into oblivion by a tornado.

The ceiling tiles above them lifted, then smashed down. Seconds later, a flurry of snowlike pieces of foam floated around them. Outside the door, glass shattered; something heavy slammed into the wall behind Christine.

"God…" She was trembling, shaking. Against her ear, Quinn's heartbeat remained steady.

The lights flickered, dimmed, then went out, plunging the small room into pitch darkness. Then everything went silent.

Christine dragged in a ragged breath. "Quinn?"

"We made it."

For the space of a dozen heartbeats, neither of them moved. The warm press of his body against hers shot unbidden thoughts through her brain. Thoughts of all those nights they lay together, sated and unmoving, their arms and legs tangled, their flesh slicked with sweat.

Her throat closed and she shoved away the memory while blinking back a rare swell of tears that stirred her temper.

She'd been determined to control their first meeting in three years. Positive that when they faced each other, a conference table would separate them, a representation of the distance that existed between them. Now, here she was, huddled on the floor with Quinn's arms around her and not enough space between them for even one splinter off that damn table!

Stiffening her spine, she placed a palm against his shoulder and pressed him back. "It's over, Quinn."

"Yeah."

He shifted his weight. Seconds later, she heard a click. A weak ray of light from the thin flashlight he held in one hand illuminated the rest room in silver light and shadows. Christine felt the press of his hand on her shoulder. "You okay, Slim?"

"Yes." She tried to ignore the blood pounding in her

cheeks from his use of his private nickname for her. "You?"

"Still in one piece."

She stared up into the face she knew so well, his eyes an almost transparent blue in the uncertain light. For a brief instant she felt it, that instinctive pull that had existed between them since the moment Jeff Buchanan introduced them. In another lifetime, she had wanted this man more than she'd wanted to breathe.

She kept her eyes level with his. That other lifetime had passed. "Do you always carry a flashlight?"

"I heard the weather forecast, so I grabbed it on my way out the door."

"Good, it will make it easier for us to get out of here," she said as they rose in unison. "I need to find out what's happened to my airport."

"So do I." The light bobbed against the tiles as Quinn moved to the door. The lock gave a soft snick when he turned it, then he gripped the knob and pushed.

Nothing happened.

Christine blinked. "What's wrong?"

"The door's blocked." He put his shoulder against the door, then shoved. Still nothing. A second attempt failed to nudge the door even a fraction.

Quinn turned to face her, his eyes cool, unreadable. "The good news is we're alive. The bad news is we're stuck here."

"We *can't* be stuck," Christine stated.

Quinn leaned a shoulder against the rest room wall, studying her through the flashlight's weak beam.

Her dark hair was damp and slicked back, emphasizing high cheekbones, whiskey-colored eyes and full lips. His gaze slid down her throat to her shoulders, then lower. The red suit molded wetly against curves he'd memorized a lifetime ago. They had shared some unforgettable times in a shower's steamy haze while a mix of slow need and urgent lust drove them to mate. On a silent curse, he pushed away the unsettling image. He didn't need a reminder of how good Christine Logan looked wet.

And of how she felt. Which was what he'd gotten a few moments ago. Even with a tornado ripping overhead, the feel of her breasts locked against his chest and one trim, endlessly long thigh riding the underside of his had sent a familiar awareness through him.

"We *can't* be stuck in here, Quinn."

Focusing his thoughts, he glanced toward the rest room's entrance. "The door's blocked." Pushing back the flap of his suit coat, he rested a hand beside his holstered Glock. "We're not going anywhere until someone springs us."

"Then we need to contact somebody about doing that."

He held up his radio. "Dead. The storm must have gotten the repeaters on the communications tower. Maybe the tower."

"People might be hurt. I need to talk to Pete Jacobs so I'll know what needs to be dealt with." Turning, she walked to the corner, snagged her bag, pulled out a cell phone and crammed it against one ear.

Moments later, a crease formed between her brows. "Circuits are busy." Her mouth set, she slid the phone into her pocket.

"Dispatch will reroute through the emergency operations center. Hopefully that won't take long," he said, tamping down on his own need to see to the injured, then make sure the airport's security was intact. "Problem is, nobody knows we're here. Until communications come online, we have no way of telling them. Even then, getting us out will be second to tending the injured. We might be here awhile.''

She closed her eyes, opened them. "Wonderful."

Had he not been watching her so closely, Quinn would have missed the quiet shiver that went through her. "You're cold."

"I'm okay."

"Your hair's wet. So are your clothes." Leaving the radio and flashlight on the sink, he pulled off his suit coat. "You'll have enough to deal with when we get out of here without getting sick."

"I'm fine...."

Her voice drifted off when he settled the coat around her shoulders. As he shifted the lapels, he caught a whiff of rain mingled with her soft vanilla scent. Gazing down, he watched the way the dim light cast shadows over her face, highlighting her eyes, sharpening her cheekbones, softening her skin.

Like a phantom stroke across his flesh, he again felt the soft press of her body against his. His hands tightened on the coat's lapels as he forced back emotions that seemed to have gone haywire. She was no longer his. Why then, for a fleeting instant, did he feel her slipping through his fingers all over again?

He dropped his hands just as his radio sputtered to life. "Victor Ten?"

He took a step back, snagging the radio off the sink. More than anything, he needed to rid his lungs of that soft vanilla scent. "Victor Ten, go ahead."

"Ten-twenty?" the dispatcher responded.

"I'm in B Concourse, south end."

"Ten-nineteen."

He raised a brow. He *wished* he could return to his office. "The airport director and I took refuge in the private handicapped rest room. Debris has us blocked in."

"Roger, Victor Ten, is anyone in your party hurt?"

"Negative. Do you have a status report on injuries?"

"A parking attendant is down. EMTs are on the scene."

Quinn met Christine's waiting gaze. He had the sense that she was holding her breath. "What about on the airfield?"

"No injuries reported. An MD-80 parked at Gate 4C sustained damage, resulting in a fuel spill. Fire crews are there."

"What about the airfield? Can the tower give us their view of any damage?"

"The tower doesn't respond to calls. It might have gotten hit. A unit is en route."

"Dear Lord," Christine groaned and closed her eyes.

"Have you let headquarters know we need backup?"

"Ten-four. The twister cut a slash through the city. Headquarters says we're on our own for a while."

Quinn issued instructions to the dispatcher then added, "The cell phones are out. The director needs to talk to Pete Jacobs. Have him radio her on this channel."

Christine shook her head as Quinn signed off. "If the MD-80 has electrical damage, one spark could ignite the fuel. The crew working there…" Her hands curled into fists. "I feel so helpless."

"So do I."

With silence settling around them, Quinn watched her pace, her long, slender legs taking her from one side of the small room to the other. Three years ago, she had not deserved to be shackled to a guilt-riddled cop who could no longer put their relationship first, so he'd walked away. It had taken time, but the guilt had subsided and he'd forgiven himself for the part he'd played in putting Jeff in harm's way. Not until then had he realized that, by letting Christine go, he'd cut out his own heart.

"Airport One?" Pete Jacobs's voice boomed through the radio. "This is Airport Three."

Quinn handed the unit to Christine. "Airport Three," she responded. "Pete, what's the status of the damaged MD-80?" As she spoke, she knelt beside her bag and retrieved a notepad and pen.

"Debris punched a hole in a fuel tank." The maintenance chief's gruff voice battled against the sound of heavy rain and wind. "A hazardous materials crew is foaming the spilled fuel."

"Any word on the control tower?"

"From what I can see, looks like the upper cab is gone. The phone lines are down, so we don't know what damage was done to the lower part of the building. The police are checking it out."

"This airport's shut down until the FAA gets the tower back in operation," Christine stated. "Radio our Ops Division and tell them to initiate a NOTAM," she added, referring to a "Notice to Airmen" issued by the FAA to redirect air traffic.

"Roger."

Crossing his arms over his chest, Quinn studied the woman sitting on the floor, who was scribbling notes on the pad propped on the top of one thigh. In the semidarkness, her expression was serious, but not fearful. It reminded him of the calm, inner strength that had attracted him to her when they'd first met.

When Jeff died, she'd stayed strong. It had been his brother's devastated widow and young daughters who'd needed him most. And because he'd talked Jeff into working in his place that fateful night, Quinn could do no less than make Rebecca and the girls his priority. Now, Rebecca was married to a man his nieces adored. Life had gone on.

"I'll hold a staff briefing in a couple of hours." With brisk efficiency, Christine continued to jot notes while working the radio. "By then we should know where we stand on damage."

"Roger. I take it the captain can hear me?" Pete asked.

When Christine confirmed, Pete continued, "Might be something going on with the marshals' plane that was due to take off around the time the storm hit."

Quinn frowned. A prison that served as the national processing and transportation center for federal inmates was located on the airport's south boundary. The U.S. Marshals Service operated the various aircraft that continually shuttled prisoners all over the country.

Christine handed him the radio as she rose from the floor.

Quinn keyed the microphone. "What sort of something?"

"Don't know," Pete responded. "The plane's sitting on a taxiway near the prison with a couple of vans surrounding it. Debris has the plane blocked so it can't taxi back to the transfer center. Seems to me, since that plane isn't going anywhere, they'd have started off-loading those prisoners by now."

"Seems that way." After signing off, Quinn met Christine's gaze. "If something happened on board the marshals' aircraft, we may be dealing with more than just tornado damage."

"That's all we need." She shoved a hand through her hair. "A crisis situation on a plane filled with prisoners right on the heels of a tornado."

"My thoughts, exactly."

Easing out a breath, she pursed her lips and studied the notepad.

The gesture reminded Quinn of how seductive that mouth could be.

He jammed a hand into his pocket. Seeing her, touching her, made him think of things he'd forced out of his mind. Things that now flooded to the surface. He'd forgotten nothing about her, he realized. Not the expressive sable-brown eyes, or the silky dark hair that framed her face, or her cool, vanilla scent.

For months after he let her go, he had lain awake nights, tormenting himself with thoughts of her. The only thing that had kept him from going after her was the knowledge that he'd made the right choice. Right for her sake, as well as for the people Jeff had left behind. Over time, he had even managed to nudge Christine into a place in his mind where he no longer hungered for her.

Or so he'd thought.

The moment he saw her today, *touched her,* every feeling he'd ever had for her had come rushing back, stronger than ever.

Quinn set his jaw. Nobody had to tell him that having Christine Logan back in Whiskey Springs was going to cause him to lose even more sleep.

Chapter 2

Two hours after they dove into the rest room for cover, Christine and Quinn walked out.

"Watch your step," Pete Jacobs cautioned as glass crunched sickeningly beneath their shoes.

Christine's throat tightened when she saw that the storm had shattered every window in the concourse. Ragged pieces of glass glinted from walls, planters and the padded seats toppled throughout the passenger boarding gates. Gleaming shards hung like stalactites from the ceiling.

Outside, rain fell in a torrent. Damp gusts blew through the open panes, chilling the air. Christine's flesh prickled beneath the coat Quinn had draped over her shoulders.

"Does the terminal still have its entire roof?" she asked.

The maintenance manager nodded. "Damnedest thing I've ever seen, especially when you consider we've got fencing, oil well rigs, baggage carts, roofs off a couple of hangars and other debris scattered across the airfield. We found the upper cab of the control tower sitting in the middle of runway three-five-right.''

Christine shook her head. ''Did all the controllers make it out in time?''

''Yes, lucky for them.''

Quinn glanced sideways. ''I take it that's what had us blocked in?''

''Roger, Captain,'' Pete said, his gaze following Quinn's to the chairs, a phone card vending machine and two crumpled newspaper racks piled beside the rest room door. ''Last time I saw that vending machine it was up by security screening.'' He paused to touch a match to the end of a thick cigar. ''Good thing you folks took cover. If you hadn't, you'd have been cut to pieces.''

''Good thing,'' Christine echoed. She slid a look toward Quinn when he stepped away to respond to his dispatcher's call on his radio. After their initial contact with the outside, there had been little for them to do while they awaited rescue, so they'd sat in silence a few feet apart on the tiled floor. With each minute that passed, her system had grown more unsteady.

After years of hurt that had slowly transformed into dragging regret—and a final knowledge that she'd gotten over him—how could his presence still make a direct assault on her nervous system? *How?*

Reaching up, she fingered the gold hoop in her right ear. From the moment Jeff Buchanan introduced her to his kid brother, the chemistry between her and Quinn had sizzled. Even now, that clearly hadn't changed. She scowled. So, fine, he was still pulse-stoppingly handsome, and she was still physically aware. All she had to do was ignore her hormones and get over it.

Pulling her gaze from Quinn, she studied the destruction around her. As perverse as it seemed, she was glad of the more immediate problems that faced her. They would keep her thoughts off Quinn until she got that treacherous awareness under control.

Turning back to confer with Pete, she determined the injured parking attendant had been transported to the hospital.

"I'll have Ula check on her condition," Christine stated, referring to the efficient secretary she'd inherited from the previous airport director. "Pete, I want to inspect the airfield before I hold a staff briefing. Can you get away to take me?"

"You're the boss," Pete stated. "You say go, we go."

Just then, Quinn rejoined them, his mouth set in a grim line. "One or more prisoners have taken control of the Marshals Service Flight 407."

Christine's mouth went dry. "Is anyone hurt?"

"That's unknown. There's an alarm in the cockpit that sends an emergency signal. The pilot managed to hit the button and radio to the transfer center that a prisoner had a gun. After that, all communication from the plane ceased. The FBI's sending in a negotiator and hostage rescue team by helicopter. The weather's playing havoc with their ETA." Dipping his head, Quinn met Christine's gaze. "Until they get this hijacking resolved, your airport essentially belongs to the feds."

She lifted her chin. "We'll cooperate fully with law enforcement, Captain, but Sam Houston is *my* airport."

He flashed a grin. "That's what I expected you to say."

Quinn's grin had always done devastating things to her. It still did, she discovered when her heart jammed against her ribs. Swallowing hard, she looked at Pete. "I need to find some rain gear before we go out on the field."

"What we've got down in the maintenance office isn't fashionable, but it'll keep you dry."

''That's all I ask.'' Shrugging off Quinn's suit coat, she handed it to him without meeting his gaze. ''Thanks for the loan, Captain.''

''You're welcome.'' When he took the coat, she felt the glide of his fingertips across hers. A frisson of heat shot up the back of her neck. Her gaze rose slowly to meet eyes as blue as a cool, calm ocean.

The tornado, she assured herself when her clenching stomach shot a skitter of panic through her system. This was the second day of her new job and she had just survived a tornado that had devastated her airport. She had a hijacked plane filled with federal prisoners parked on one of her taxiways. *Those* were the reasons her emotions teetered on a wild pendulum. *Those* were the reasons the air around her was so thick she couldn't seem to drag enough oxygen into her lungs. Quinn's presence had nothing to do with it. *Couldn't* have anything to do with it. He had loved her, then walked away. She had put him behind her long ago and gotten on with her life. She was a professional, she could work with him. That was all that was required of her. Nothing more.

She would do nothing more.

Her staff briefing ended, Christine gathered her pad and pen off the conference table. After answering a few last questions from the airport's public information officer, then the fire chief, Christine entered the hall that connected the conference room with her office. Thick, dove-gray carpet muffled her steps as she passed the small sink, counter and refrigerator nestled near the closet where her hopelessly wrinkled red silk suit now hung. After inspecting the airfield, she'd taken a quick shower in the private rest room that adjoined her office, then pulled on her chambray shirt, jeans and tennis shoes.

Turning a corner, she entered the roomy office that had once belonged to her father. The boxes stacked in one corner contained items that would put her own personal stamp on the office where rich wood covered the walls and an oriental rug pooled soft color across the floor. Stacks of reports, files and printouts awaiting her review sat on top of the big mahogany desk positioned in front of a wide window.

After dropping her pad and pen in the center of the desk, Christine checked her watch. She had maybe ten minutes until Quinn arrived with the FBI agent in charge of the hijacking operation and the U.S. marshal whose men were now held hostage on Flight 407.

Ignoring the paperwork on her desk, Christine turned and looked out at the rain-soaked airfield. Her gaze tracked an airline van headed across the apron to a maintenance hangar that had lost most of its roof in the tornado. Quinn had left the staff briefing early to set up an emergency command center. Because her spine had stayed ramrod stiff the entire time he'd sat across the conference table from her, she had welcomed the page on his beeper that had summoned him to meet the feds.

Not for the first time, she wondered what their lives would be like now if that one long-ago night had never happened. Would they still be together if she hadn't cajoled Quinn into accompanying her to a benefit when he'd been scheduled to work an off-duty security job? If he had asked any cop other than his brother to work in his place? If, while she and Quinn sipped cocktails, that drug-crazed robber hadn't shot Jeff point-blank in the chest?

So many *if's,* Christine thought. And never any answers. After Jeff died, the grief and guilt had been overwhelming. She'd suffered with the knowledge that *she* was responsible for his working in Quinn's place. Battled even more guilt by giving thanks that it hadn't been the man she loved who had died. Even as she stood at Jeff's grave beside Quinn, she'd sensed his own ragged-edged guilt distancing him from her. Guilt that he should have been the one working the job that night. Guilt that Jeff's wife was now a widow, his two young daughters forever fatherless.

There had been so much guilt. And pain.

Christine closed her eyes against the memories that sliced at her heart. She had ached for comfort, had been desperate to give Quinn the comfort she knew he needed. Yet, whenever she reached for him, she met the wall he'd erected around his emotions. The last time she'd tried to step into his arms, he'd turned away, telling her he had nothing left to offer her, that he needed to give everything he had to Rebecca and the girls. The torment in his eyes had told her the wall he'd put up around himself had become impenetrable. There was nothing she could do but watch him walk away.

"Christine?"

With her mind filled with thoughts of Quinn, the sound of his voice coming from the doorway was like a bullet to the heart. She gripped the back of her leather desk chair and turned.

Quinn stood just in front of two other men. The one wearing a navy suit matched Quinn in height and build; he had dark hair and sharp blue eyes in a handsome face. The second man was small and stubby with a wide, lined face and thinning brown hair. His brown suit was as rumpled as the small paper bag that dangled from one hand.

With the rawness of her memories still churning inside her, Christine pulled in a deep breath. Somehow, some way, she had to get a grip on her emotions. Had to separate the man who was once her lover from the cop who now headed security at her airport. The baffling flood of longing that had swept through her when he'd held her while the tornado raged was something to be suppressed and ignored.

And forgotten.

Watching her, Quinn narrowed his eyes. "Ula's not at her desk, or I'd have asked her to call to let you know we were here."

"It's all right." Avoiding his gaze, Christine moved toward the front of her desk. "Come in."

Quinn angled his head in the direction of the older man. "Christine Logan, this is FBI Special Agent Mason Taggart." Quinn gestured toward the second man. "Marshal Spence Cantrell."

Christine shook hands with both men, indicating they take a seat in the twin leather chairs in front of her desk. As she settled behind her desk, she noted Quinn had ignored the other chairs dotting the office and opted to rest one shoulder against the wall that displayed a large aerial photo of the airport.

"I can have one of the clerks bring in coffee," she offered.

While Quinn and Spence Cantrell shook their heads, Taggart opened his bag. "I'll pass." The FBI agent had a Texas drawl as thick as cold molasses. "My wife's made me give up caffeine and nicotine. Now, my one vice is macadamia nuts." Leaning forward, he offered the open bag to Christine while studying her with an intensity that left no room for doubt he was sizing her up. "Join me, Miz Logan?"

"No, thank you. Agent Taggart, I want to assure you that the FBI has this airport's full support and cooperation during this crisis situation."

He dipped his head. "Nice to get something handed to you instead of having to pry it loose."

"Because lives are at stake," she continued, "Flight 407 has priority."

"We're on the same wavelength, Ms. Logan." Taggart's brows slid together. "From what I saw when we helicoptered in, you're dealing with some major damage that's going to keep your airfield closed for at least a few days."

"Correct. Already, I have seven local airline managers and their corporate offices wanting to know when the airfield will again be operational. The FAA is arranging to bring in a temporary control tower. They need a timetable as to when I foresee the airfield will be ready to handle commercial and general aviation traffic."

Taggart's gaze leveled on hers. "That, along with a hijacking, is a lot to have on your plate, this being your second day on the job." The edge that had settled in his voice was in direct contrast to the man's laid-back manner.

"Whether I've occupied this office two days or two thousand is not the point," she countered, unsurprised that the FBI agent had checked out who he'd be dealing with during the crisis. "The point is how I deal with what's on my plate."

"True," Taggart agreed, then popped a nut into his mouth. "What's your plan on getting back in operation?"

"I'll clear the debris from the east runway." As she spoke, Christine rose and moved to the aerial photo. There, she tapped a fingernail on the runway that lay on the opposite side of the airfield from where the marshals' hijacked plane sat. "The airlines will have to juggle schedules, but we can get them back in operation at Sam Houston using only this one runway." She shifted her finger on the map, much too aware that Quinn's gaze never left her face. "The other half of the airfield can remain closed for as long as it takes you to resolve the hijacking."

Taggart's eyes narrowed. "Do you have the manpower and heavy equipment on hand to clear the airfield?"

"No, but a local construction company does. They began working on a pavement project here last week so they're on-site. I've already contracted with them to bring in more crews and the equipment to remove the storm debris. I wanted to coordinate with you before I issued a notice to proceed with the job."

"Good." Shoving his bag of nuts into his pocket, Taggart leaned forward in his chair. "I need you to have that construction company add even more crews and equipment to the job."

Christine tilted her head. "Why?"

Taggart exchanged a look with Cantrell. "I've got a hijacker by the name of Carl Hart demanding I remove debris on the taxiway around 'his' plane. He also wants the runway nearest the plane cleared."

Christine blinked. If that happened, there would be little to stop Flight 407 from taking off. "You're sure you want *that* side of the airfield open, too?"

"No, ma'am, I don't, but Mr. Hart does," Taggart replied. "I need time to figure out what he's up to, so I'll buy that time by trading him concrete for hostages." The agent inclined his head toward the aerial map. "Start the crews working at the end of the runway farthest from where Flight 407 sits. That way, Mr. Hart will see I'm making a good faith effort to meet his demands."

"I understand."

Taggart met Quinn's gaze. "Captain, I trust I can count on you to make sure every man on that crew knows the taxiway where Flight 407's parked is off-limits. Those three snipers watching the plane won't take kindly to anyone drifting too close."

Quinn nodded. "My troops will take care of perimeter security for as long as you need them."

"How many people are on board the plane?" Christine asked.

"One hundred eight, counting Hart," Spence Cantrell responded. "Ninety-five prisoners. The rest are marshals, a few staff members, one pilot and a copilot."

Christine nodded. "Do you know how Hart gained control of the aircraft?"

"Not yet," Cantrell answered. "We operate our planes like flying prisons. All inmates wear shackles and leg irons. Before boarding, everybody gets frisked for weapons. None of the cabin crew or marshals on board the flights carry firearms because of the risk that they could be overpowered and those weapons taken away." Cantrell's mouth tightened. "We think Hart has an accomplice at this airport who smuggled a weapon on board the plane."

Christine went rigid. "One of my operations people?"

"It's possible," Quinn stated. "More likely, it's one of the private ground crews that service the plane. A fueler. Maybe a mechanic. Could be someone who works for one of the airlines."

"Even so, I intend to review the files of all my personnel."

"So do I," Quinn said. "My people are rerunning background checks on everyone who's been issued an ID card to access the airfield over the past year. That includes everyone on your staff."

"Fine." Christine remet Taggart's gaze. "Has Hart made other demands?"

"Yes. He wants his ex-wife brought here."

"Do you know why?"

"Not yet," the agent responded. "Hart's doing time for

kidnapping her, so it sounds like he has some sort of
agenda involving the woman. She goes now by the name
of Jackson, Kelly Jackson. Lives two hours from here in
Ryan, Texas. Since Marshal Cantrell has had dealings with
her in the past, he's heading for Ryan in a few minutes.''

Christine almost missed the flicker of emotion in the
marshal's blue eyes. Curious, she wondered what past
dealings Marshal Cantrell had had with the hijacker's ex-
wife.

Taggart rose. ''Call me before you put those crews to
work on the runway, Ms. Logan.''

''Count on it, Agent Taggart.''

''You did good, Slim,'' Quinn said after Taggart and
Cantrell left her office.

Christine turned. Quinn still stood where he'd been
throughout the meeting—one shoulder propped against the
paneled wall near the aerial map of the airport. ''I pre-
sented a plan that works for both of us, is all.''

''And proved to Taggart you can handle this job.''

''I didn't know I had to prove myself.''

''Not to me, you don't,'' Quinn said, giving her a long,
steady look. ''I found out a long time ago you can do
anything you set out to do. This job isn't any different.''

When he shifted away from the wall and moved toward
her, she took a step back. *Business.* She intended to maintain a strictly professional relationship between them.

''Before you go, Captain, I'd like your opinion on the
best site for the FAA to locate its portable control tower.''

He arched one dark brow. ''Sure.''

Seated back at her desk, Christine sorted through stacks
of file folders until she found the one she'd had Ula bring
in earlier.

''Here's an exhibit of the five-story parking garage,''

Christine said, pulling the legal-size paper out of the folder. "I think the top deck of the garage is the best place for the tower."

As he studied the exhibit, Quinn placed a palm on her desk and leaned in. "It'll take months to repair the actual tower, so the portable one will have to handle traffic on both runways," he commented.

"That's right." She tapped a finger on a spot on the exhibit. "This location should give the air traffic controllers as clear a view as possible of both." As she spoke, Christine's gaze slid to Quinn's hand splayed against her desk's dark wood, a hand that had once conjured magic against her skin. The spicy scent of his cologne that she would forever associate with hot, intimate sex slid into her senses, making her throat go dry. Her heart gave one thump before she quashed the flicker of desire.

"I agree." Quinn slid a fingertip across the exhibit. "We'll set up a perimeter of cement barricades along here to keep security tight."

Christine opened her mouth to reply, but no words got past the knot in her throat. What air was left in her lungs had thickened.

She needed space. Lots of space.

She rose so suddenly that her shoulder caught Quinn's. The impact knocked her off-balance.

"Easy," he stated, gripping her forearms to steady her. His eyes seemed to intensify in color as he stared down at her. "What's wrong?"

"Nothing." He was so close she could see the dark flecks in those stunning blue eyes, each individual long, sooty eyelash that surrounded them. "I just remembered something I need to take care of."

"You have a million things to take care of." As he

spoke, his hands slid slowly down her arms to circle her wrists. "What specific one are you talking about?"

His face was only inches from hers, his mouth close. *So close.* For one moment, one very dangerous moment, her brain simply clicked off. All she knew was that she was suddenly desperate to find out if he tasted the same after so long, if his mouth still fit so perfectly, hotly against hers.

She felt the pulse hammering at the base of her throat, saw that Quinn's gaze had lowered, settled there.

"Quinn, let go."

"No." His fingers tightened on her wrists. "Not just yet." His eyes rose, dark and intense, to lock with hers.

"Quinn—"

"Slim, we need to talk."

"No." Panic overwhelmed desire. What was she going to do? How could she want this man, *this man,* after he'd turned his back on her? How could she feel desire while warnings flashed like neon in her brain? *Be careful. Don't touch. Don't let him close. Not again. Never again.*

If she could put some distance between them, she was sure she could come up with viable reasons to heed those warnings.

Self-preservation had her pulling free of his hold, had her backing away, gaining distance.

"Christine...."

"Don't." She held up her palms to ward him off. She had to breathe. Dammit, she couldn't breathe. "We have jobs to do, a million details to see to. We don't have time to deal with anything else."

His eyes narrowed. "That's not all that's going on here."

"Nothing—"

"Up until a few minutes ago, I thought it was just me,

but I was wrong. We've both got things to deal with that have nothing to do with our jobs.''

She dropped her hands, curled them against her jeaned thighs. ''Other than the running of this airport, you and I have nothing to talk about.'' Her voice was steady, despite the old cravings his presence had forced through a door she'd slammed and locked years ago. Those cravings were dangerous. Painful.

''I had my hands circling your wrists, Christine,'' he said, his voice as soft as a caress. ''Your pulse was off the chart. Do business matters often have that effect on you?''

She raised her chin. ''I have work to do.''

As she dropped back into her chair, Quinn's pager beeped. With hands that weren't quite steady, Christine pushed papers into whatever file folder was closest.

Shoving back one flap of his suit coat, he unclipped the pager from his belt and checked the display. ''My chief's downstairs.''

''I'll let you know what the FAA says about that location for its tower,'' she stated as he turned.

''Fine.'' From the corner of her eye she saw him hesitate, then he turned back to the desk. Reaching down, he put one finger beneath her chin, prodded it up until her gaze met his.

''We're going to have that talk, Slim. I promise you that. Someday soon, we're going to talk.''

Chapter 3

"Give me your best estimate, Pete," Christine said several hours later while she and the maintenance manager stood on the grassy area at the edge of runway one-seven-left. The swirling dark clouds and torrential rain of that morning had been replaced by hazy evening sunlight that peeked through thick clouds. "How many lights did we lose in the tornado?"

The burly maintenance manager swept his gaze down the length of the runway while he pulled a thick cigar from the pocket of his blue work shirt. "Best guess is about two hundred edge lights—that's the total for both runways. Twice that number of taxiway lights."

Christine nudged back the hair that a gust of humid wind dashed into her eyes. The wind and the strident grind of a bulldozer's engine as it shoved rubble off the runway's surface nearly obliterated Pete's response.

The owner of the construction company she had contracted with earlier in the day had been as good as his word. One hour after she'd phoned and given him notice to proceed with the job of clearing the rubble-strewn airfield, a fleet of dump trucks, front-end loaders, cranes and flatbed trucks with bulldozers piggybacked onto them arrived at Sam Houston. Per Agent Taggart's request, she had called the command post to let him know the equipment was on-site. Taggart advised her to have the dozers driven to where they could be seen from the hijacked plane, but to hold off all work until she heard back from him.

A half hour later, the self-contained steps built into the hijacked plane's aft lowered. Per the deal Taggart had struck with Carl Hart to trade human lives for cleared runway, five of the prisoners taken hostage that morning shuffled down the steps, wariness flashing in their eyes. Marshals, clad in bulletproof vests, riot helmets and armed with twelve-gauge pump shotguns, waited behind prison vans parked on the taxiway. After herding the inmates into the vans, the marshals transported them to the nearby transfer center. Taggart then called and gave Christine the go-ahead to start clearing the runway nearest the hijacked plane.

Now, she and Pete stood near the runway's end farthest from Flight 407. Sitting nearly two miles away, the plane and seven-story prison looked almost toylike. In the distance, she could see the FBI's portable command post on the outskirts of the security perimeter that law enforcement had established around the 727.

The plane's stark-white body reflected the last rays of the sun that slowly slipped toward the horizon. Christine gnawed her bottom lip, feeling a now-familiar rush of anxiety for the hostages still aboard that plane. No one knew for sure what Carl Hart had planned for the plane and those he held captive. Since one of his first demands was that the taxiway and nearest runway be cleared, it was obvious he intended to force the pilot to put the plane into the air. Whether Agent Taggart would allow that, Christine couldn't guess. All she knew was that the lives of some or all of the people aboard Flight 407 might depend on how fast she cleared the runway on which she and Pete now stood.

"We also lost airfield guidance signs," Pete added. With lighter in hand, he cupped a palm around the end of the thick cigar. "Replacing those'll take another hefty chunk out of the budget."

"I've already gotten this airport approved to receive federal disaster funds." Out of the corner of her eye, Christine noted that a red maintenance van displaying the logo of one of the airport's fixed base operators had parked several yards from where she and Pete stood. The driver, a tall, thick-bodied man wearing jeans, a dark work shirt and a ball cap with the FBO's logo on its front had alighted from the van and was now conversing with several shovel-wielding crew workers.

"I'll worry about the budget," Christine continued, picking up the thread of conversation as she looked back at Pete. "You concentrate on getting this airfield back in service."

"You got it, boss," Pete said, his gaze following hers to the far-off hijacked plane. "Speaking of that, before I drove out here to meet you, I got a call from the FAA." He inclined his head toward a cement block structure that sat in the distance. The antenna toppled against its roof was bent like a crooked finger. "They'll have a crew here first thing in the morning to start repairs on their navaids," he said, referring to the various FAA-owned flight navigational instruments that dotted the airfield.

"Good." Christine glanced at her watch, saw it was

nearly seven o'clock. "I need to touch base with the supervisor over this construction crew." Her gaze sought, then settled on a man wearing a white hard hat from which curly gray hair sprouted around its rim. He was currently overseeing the positioning of several portable trailers that held large generator-powered spotlights. "I want to make sure he understands they're to leave the taxiway untouched until he hears different from me. After that, I'm going to drive home and get a couple of changes of clothes. Grab some dinner. I'll sleep on the couch in my office until this airport is back in operation."

"My wife already brought me some extra clothes," Pete said, the wind grabbing the stream of gray smoke he exhaled. "If you need me to take care of something during the night, I'll be bedded down at the field maintenance compound."

Christine touched a hand to his thick forearm. "Thanks, Pete. I don't know what I would do without you."

He dipped his head. "You'll do the same thing your dad would have done. You'll manage. You'll manage just fine, boss."

The low rumble of thunder that sounded from somewhere over the horizon had Pete scowling. "Dammit to hell, more rain's the last thing we need. These crews can't work through the night if we get deluged."

"Let's hope the storm stays to our west," Christine said, even as the fresh smell of rain drifted on the air. She didn't want rain, she thought, glancing up at the clouds scudding across the slate-blue sky that edged closer to twilight with each passing minute. She wanted the crews working throughout the night, wanted the hijacking crisis resolved, wanted her airport in operation, wanted *everything* back to normal.

Her emotions, included.

We're going to have that talk, Slim. I promise you that. Someday soon, we're going to talk.

No. Christine flexed her fingers, unflexed them. She and Quinn weren't going to talk, not about anything other than issues directly relating to the airport.

I had my hands circling your wrists, Christine. Your pulse was off the chart. Do business matters often have that effect on you?

She closed her eyes. It didn't matter. Didn't matter if Quinn's very presence drew her like a divining rod to water with the same force it had when they'd first met. Didn't matter if he felt that searing attraction just as surely as she. Didn't matter if he *knew* what she felt…which he did, thanks to her traitorous pulse. None of that mattered because she had no intention of acting on that attraction. Three years ago, when Quinn turned away, knives had slashed into her soul. It had taken her what seemed like a lifetime to get over the pain. Over him. No matter that the hurt had faded, no matter that she now understood he had handled his grief over Jeff's death the only way he could, no matter that she'd forgiven Quinn for that hurt. None of that mattered.

What mattered was that he *had* hurt her. Desperately.

She had trusted him with her heart and he'd broken it. The thought of handing him her heart a second time had fingers of panic clawing inside her belly. She would never again put herself on such thin ice where Quinn was concerned. She knew with certainty she couldn't survive it shattering under her again.

A second rumble of thunder, closer now, jerked Christine's thoughts back to the present. Taking a deep breath, she turned to face Pete. "Instead of hoping we don't get rain, maybe we should hope there's not another tornado mixed with that rain."

"You have a point."

Keeping one concerned eye on the darkening sky, she headed across the runway toward the crew chief.

With police traffic quietly crackling on the in-dash radio, Quinn parked his unmarked cruiser on a grassy patch beside Christine's Bronco. As he watched her walk away from Pete Jacobs, Quinn's throat tightened. He had always admired the way she moved with an athletic and economical grace that wasted neither time nor energy. That grace was now enhanced by the snug denim that encased her endlessly long legs and curvy bottom.

Sensing he wasn't the only male admiring the view, Quinn slid his gaze sideways. Two men holding shovels had their gazes glued to Christine's butt. A third guy, wearing a ball cap with an FBO's logo, stood with his head cocked and mouth pursed, apparently appreciating the entire nifty package.

"Damn," Quinn muttered, as a muscle in his jaw began to work. He'd been so sure he'd finally gotten over her. During the past year, there had been entire days when he didn't think about her. Nights when memories of her no longer drifted in to haunt his dreams. Weeks when he gave no thought to the engagement ring he'd bought the day before Jeff died or the proposal he never made.

When he'd first laid eyes on Christine this morning, it was as if he'd suddenly jolted out of some sort of limbo. A limbo, he now realized, he'd been caught in for the past three years. He had gotten an even bigger jolt a few hours ago in her office when he'd felt the pulse in her wrists hammering like mad beneath his palms. *Hammering for him.* The mix of wariness and confusion and desire swimming in her dark eyes had knotted his gut. Until that instant, he hadn't known he was ready to resurrect the part of himself he'd buried with Jeff.

Hadn't known he was still in love with Christine Logan. Had never stopped loving her.

Now he knew.

"Holy hell."

When she left Texas three years ago, she'd taken a job at L.A. International, started a new life fifteen hundred miles away. He would bet—just bet—that somewhere in those unopened boxes stacked in her office was a frame that held the photo of the current man in her life.

Scrubbing a hand across his face, Quinn shifted his gaze back to Christine. She stood talking to the construction foreman, her eyes serious, her stance all-business as she pointed toward the distant hijacked plane. Watching her, Quinn acknowledged how comfortably she carried authority on her shoulders. *Smooth, shapely shoulders.* The little licks of fire that ignited inside him had him stifling a groan. It would be a hell of a lot better for his blood pressure— and easier to think—if he didn't know just how soft those particular shoulders felt against his lips.

And tasted.

Quinn knew the knots in his gut were the least of his problems. Somehow, some way, he had to convince Christine to let him back into her life. He would crawl if he had to. Beg, if that was what it took.

"Might as well start now," he muttered. Grabbing the small blanket and brown paper bag off the seat beside him, he shouldered open the cruiser's door.

Christine's steps slowed when she spotted Quinn sitting on a blanket spread across the hood of an unmarked police car. The strengthening breeze ruffled his dark hair. Since she'd last seen him, he had stripped off his navy suit coat and tie; his white dress shirt was open at the neck, its sleeves rolled up to expose tanned, corded forearms. A holstered weapon was clipped onto his waistband beside his gold badge. A brown bag that sported the name of the hotel on the airport premises sat beside him on the blanket.

"I remember how you get so focused on a job that you forget certain things," he said, his gaze following hers to the brown bag. "One being to eat."

Christine ran her hands down her jeaned thighs. "I haven't had time to think about food."

She wanted their relationship to be strictly professional, but how could it when their pasts were so intertwined? She checked her watch, then inclined her head toward her Bronco. "I'm going to drive home and get some clothes. Fix a bite to eat there."

Quinn gave her an easy smile. "Why take the extra time when your dinner's already delivered?" As he spoke, he pulled two thick, plastic-wrapped sandwiches out of the bag, followed by lidded foam cups.

The rumble of thunder had her glancing up at the gray, swirling clouds. "It could start raining any minute."

"Then we'd better eat fast." He dipped his head toward the spot beside him. "Take a load off, Slim. It's been one hell of a long day."

"True," she agreed, silently acknowledging the dragging fatigue that had settled in her legs and back. Quinn couldn't possibly know that her long day had started nearly twenty-four hours ago when raw-edged anticipation over seeing him had kept her tossing and turning all night.

She also hadn't eaten a thing, not since lunch yesterday. Which, no doubt, was the reason that the sight of the sandwiches had her empty stomach growling.

Shifting her weight, Christine looked across her shoulder. An engine droned as a bulldozer's blade scraped debris off the runway's surface onto the grass. Crew members walked at a safe distance behind the dozer, shoveling aside smaller pieces of debris left in the bulldozer's wake. Out on the grass, a front-end loader spilled a clattering heap of rubble into the back of a dump truck.

She looked back at Quinn. With his presence sending ripples of unease down her spine, having an audience was probably best while they shared their first meal together in three years.

She gave her shoulders a restless move. "I never was one to turn down food."

"That's another thing I remember about you," he said quietly.

Hating the fact that his reference to the past made her pulse jump, she slid onto the cruiser's hood. "You've got a lot of unimportant facts cluttering your brain, Buchanan."

"Let's see how unimportant you think these are." His gaze locked with hers, he handed her a napkin and one sandwich. "Mustard, not mayo. Dill pickles instead of sweet. Cheddar cheese, not Swiss. Hold the tomatoes." Reaching behind him, he snagged one of the foam cups. "Unsweetened iced tea with two lemon wedges."

"Thanks." She lowered her gaze, concentrating on unwrapping the sandwich. The fact that he recalled her exact food preferences was convenient, nothing more.

"You're welcome."

She tasted her sandwich, her brows sliding together while she chewed. "You're supposed to track down Carl Hart's on-ground accomplice. Shouldn't you be rerunning background checks on everyone with airfield access?"

"I *am* rerunning background checks," Quinn answered before taking the first bite of his sandwich. "Which, by the way, also include you and all of your department's employees," he added after a moment. "The National Crime Information Center's computer went down about an hour ago. My dispatcher has instructions to let me know when NCIC comes back online." He shrugged. "I hadn't eaten, so I figured this was as good a time as any."

After the first two bites of her sandwich, Christine discovered she was ravenous. While she ate, her gaze drifted to the hijacked plane. "Do they have food on board?"

"Box lunches," Quinn said, his gaze following hers. "The prison kitchen loads one for each person listed on the itinerary onto the plane before each flight. Each box has a couple of sandwiches, something to drink. According to the men he released, Hart passed the food out to the other prisoners around lunchtime." Quinn's eyes narrowed. "He also fed the pilot and copilot, but not the marshals or other staff members."

"If this situation lasts much longer, Hart's going to want more food."

"He made that demand about three hours ago."

Christine looked back at Quinn. "Will Taggart give him more?"

"Like everything else, he'll use food as a negotiating tool. If Hart gives up more hostages, he'll get food. Each time Hart demands something, Taggart will insist he release a few hostages. Doing that won't get everyone on board freed, but some are better than none."

Christine chewed in thoughtful silence. "What about the plane?" she asked finally.

"What about it?"

"Hart wants this runway and the taxiway around the plane cleared, so it's obvious he intends for it to take off after he talks to his ex-wife. What will Taggart do about that?"

"Hard to say. Right now, he's made it clear to Hart that

if the plane moves, the hostage rescue team will stop it. Taggart's got three of his HRT men armed with shotguns positioned about fifty yards away from the plane. It starts rolling, the snipers shoot the tires out. If the plane's got four or six flat tires, it can't roll and can't take off. Hart would only have made more problems for himself.''

"If the plane's fired on, Hart might start killing hostages.''

"Yeah.'' Quinn wadded his napkin and the plastic wrap off his sandwich into a ball, then dropped them into the paper bag. "There's no way to predict what Hart might do. To save lives, Taggart might have to let the plane take off. If that happens, you can bet there'll be a shadow plane in the air that'll keep Flight 407 on radar but stay out of visual sight. No matter how long it takes, no matter where that plane winds up, the feds won't back off from getting Hart, the other prisoners and their own people back.''

Sandwich finished, Christine dropped her trash in the bag then swept her gaze across the debris-littered airfield. While they'd eaten, the sun had lowered, the air had thickened. The spotlights on the portable trailers were now on, illuminating the runway where the bulldozer continued its slow, grinding progress.

"I've got serious problems to deal with,'' she said. "But I'll take being airport director any day to heading a hostage rescue team.''

"I know what you mean,'' Quinn said, wadding the bag in his hands. He remained silent for a moment, then said, "Tell me about the last three years, Slim.''

When she turned her head to meet his gaze, the wind dashed her hair against her cheek. "What about them?'' she asked, hooking the loose strands behind her ear.

"I'd just like to know what you've been up to.''

''Work,'' she answered. She'd been thankful the position at LAX had opened when it did, grateful she'd had somewhere to run after Quinn ended their relationship. ''I've mostly concentrated on my career.''

''You've got your own airport now so it looks like all that work paid off.'' His hand flexed against the wadded bag. ''What about the other parts of your life?''

''What about them?''

''Is there a man in the mix somewhere?''

Christine shifted her gaze back to the airfield. ''There was for a while. Things didn't work out.'' Steve had been gentle and caring and had wanted to marry her. Although she had tried to love him, in the end, her heart hadn't cooperated.

''Too bad,'' Quinn murmured.

Because she couldn't help but wonder, she remet his gaze. ''What about you? What have you been doing the past three years?''

''Working. Spending time with Allie and Sara.''

His reference to Jeff's daughters tightened Christine's throat. On the night their father died, the two little girls had sat on Rebecca's lap, clinging to her, doing their best to comfort a grief they could only dimly understand.

Christine pulled in an unsteady breath. ''How are they?''

''Great. Allie's into ballet. Sara's on a swim team.'' Quinn's mouth curved. ''Both are growing like fertilized weeds.'' He paused. ''Rebecca remarried nearly a year ago.''

''I hadn't heard.'' Christine swallowed around the lump in her throat. ''I hope she's happy. She deserves to be happy.''

''She is. Paul's a great guy. The girls are crazy about

him, and he feels the same about them." Quinn raised a shoulder. "It feels right that he and Rebecca are together."

Christine fought an instinctive urge to reach out and touch Quinn's hand. "What happened to Jeff wasn't your fault." She wasn't aware she'd put her thoughts into words until a shadow of old hurt flickered in Quinn's eyes.

"It took me a couple of years, and a few sessions with the department shrink, but I finally figured that out." He lifted a hand, shoved it through his dark hair. "After Jeff died, there were a lot of things I should have said to you, but didn't. I never meant to hurt you, I hope you know that."

The ache in her heart was like a burning. Closing her eyes, Christine fought off a wave of emotion. She could not, *would not,* allow Quinn to sneak past her defenses. She had to remember how badly she had hurt when he walked away. Had to remember the long days and even longer nights she'd spent agonizing over him, wanting him. She'd put her broken heart back together and there was no longer any room in it for him.

"I don't…" Her voice hitched and she dragged in a breath. If the air had been heavy before, now it was unbreathable. "It would be best if we leave the past where it belongs."

He stared back at her, his eyes unwavering. "I'm not so sure about that."

"I—"

A crash of thunder splintered the air; lightning broke open the sky. Rain fell in sheets, hard and vicious.

Yelping, Christine jumped off the hood, dashed around the cruiser, jerked open the back door and dove in. She didn't know Quinn had followed her in until she twisted around, intending to pull the door shut and met a wall of muscle.

"Lord." Inching back, she shoved her sodden hair off her face, then glanced down. Her chambray blouse was plastered to her flesh, her jeans and tennis shoes soaked. "This is the second time today I've gotten drenched."

Slicking back his wet hair, Quinn glanced out the rear window. "If this keeps up, you may make it to three."

"Not if I can help it." Using a palm, she squeegeed water down one arm while easing forward to peek into the cruiser's front seat. "I don't suppose you have a dry towel handy?"

"Sorry, towels aren't on the police equipment list."

She gave him a dark look through wet, spiky lashes. "I knew you were going to say that."

Using a forearm, he swiped water off his brow. "To be honest, I can't say I'm all that sorry about not having a towel."

Christine took in his soaked shirt and slacks. "Why?"

"Because you look real good wet, Slim." His mouth curving, he leaned and nudged an errant strand of hair off her cheek. "Always have."

Her spine stiffened when his fingertips lingered against her flesh. Stiffened even more when those fingers began a soft massage that rolled her heart over in her chest.

"Quinn..." Silence hung between them while rain drummed the roof of the car, washing over the windows like a roaring river, turning the evening gloom to a faded gray. Static crackled faintly from the radio in the dash.

When his palm moved to cup the side of her throat, heat shot through her veins.

"Don't," she said, even as the desire that had settled in his eyes sent a raw echo of need through her. Raising a hand, she curled her fingers on his wrist, yet she couldn't bring herself to shove him away.

It took her a moment longer to realize she was simply clinging to him. The awareness had her nerves snapping. She understood it was not him she fought against, but her own needs.

His palm moved against her throat. "Your pulse is off the chart again."

Her stomach muscles clenched. "Quinn, we can't...."

"Yes, we can." His hand slid to her nape as he leaned to nip her bottom lip. "I'm going crazy wondering if you taste the same, Slim."

Before she could protest, his mouth was on hers, covering and conquering. Her heart kicked in her chest, driving the breath out of her body. The smell of rain on his flesh, mixed with the same spicy male scent that had heated her blood in another lifetime crowded her senses.

Mistake. Even as her lips parted beneath his in avid invitation, the word was like a warning strobe in her brain. Yet already his kiss pulled her from the edge of logic.

His familiar taste swamped her with memories of when she'd reveled in his kisses while they lay sprawled together, arms and legs tangled, their flesh slicked with sweat. A bittersweet, undeniable longing had her body straining against his, no longer stiff but eager.

His other hand dove into her hair. The upholstery gave a whisper as he nudged her back against the seat.

Hunger came in swift, sharp waves that made her shudder. Heat raged through her veins like a firestorm. Her fingers tightened on his wrist. Her free hand rose to splay against his chest; beneath her palm she felt the tensed ripple of muscle, the thunder of his heartbeat through his wet shirt.

"Christine...."

As his mouth continued its tormenting, enticing assault of hers, his hand slid from her throat to cup her breast. A soft, yielding murmur escaped her lips when his thumb began circling her already budded nipple.

Had she really forgotten how just the feel of his lips could shoot annihilating sensations throughout her entire body? Had she ever really believed any other man could make her melt so slowly, so luxuriously against him?

No, she realized as her fingers curled into his shirt. She had forgotten nothing about Quinn Buchanan. Not the way he could seduce with just one graze of his mouth against hers. Or the hard feel of his body covering hers on soft, cool sheets.

Nor had she forgotten how much he'd hurt her.

She had loved him beyond reason. She had loved him and he'd left her and she'd died on the inside.

"Quinn, no," she managed against his mouth.

"Yes," he corrected. The hand in her hair slid to the back of her neck and held her still with firm, determined fingers. Angling his head, he deepened the kiss.

Panic scrambled inside her as she felt him pulling her toward a clawing desire against which she had no control.

"Quinn." She pulled back far enough to see his face while she fought to regain both her breath and sanity. "I want you to stop," she said, her voice shallow and ragged. "We have to stop."

"All right." His breathing as unsteady as hers, he loosened his hold minutely. He remained where he was, leaning over her, studying her face with blue eyes that had gone as dark as smoke. "Christine—"

"I can't," she blurted. "I don't want any part of this."

Before she could react, his palm settled against her chest. "Your body's sending a whole different signal."

Jerking sideways, she slid across the seat until she reached the door. Her breasts ached from his touch, her thighs trembled. She had to get away from him. Had to have time alone to gather her wits. Turning to the window, she could barely see the outline of her Bronco through the gray sheet of rain. She was about to get drenched for the third time that day.

"I don't care what signal you think you're getting." Looking back at Quinn, she curled her fingers around the door handle. "I don't want a personal relationship with you. We had one. It didn't work. Period. I make it a point to learn from my mistakes."

He leaned back against the seat. "So do I," he said softly.

The glint of determination in his eyes closed her throat. "And not repeat them."

"I'm with you there, too."

"Fine. Then we agree this won't happen again."

"No," he said mildly. "My mistake was letting you go, Christine. I didn't know how big a mistake that was until I saw you this morning. I know now. That's a mistake I don't intend to make again."

"Your thinking's twisted, Buchanan." She shoved an unsteady hand through her wet hair. "You can't let go of something you don't have."

Emotion flickered in his eyes. "That's another mistake I'd like to correct," he said, his voice a soft, intimate glide against her damp flesh. "You could give us another try, Christine."

She felt regret for what might have been creeping inside her and forced it back. "I could also try jumping off what's left of the control tower. Either way, I risk a few breaks.'' She shook her head. ''Nothing's going to happen between us, Quinn. You need to accept that.''

He dipped his head. ''Now that we both know where the other stands, Slim, what are we going to do about it?''

''Not a damn thing.'' Shoving open the door, she dashed through the downpour toward her Bronco.

Chapter 4

Before dawn the following morning, Christine walked into the one airport restaurant that had remained open after the tornado hit. Already the place was crowded and noisy, its air thick with conversation and the smoky smell of bacon frying. Though the airport was closed, the crews working to repair the airfield and terminal building needed quick access to food. Yesterday, she had arranged with the concessionaire to keep the restaurant in operation for the duration.

She filled a mug with black coffee, then made her way past the crowded tables. At the rear of the restaurant she slid into a booth.

She needed caffeine and solitude.

After spending the night with thoughts of her damaged airport, the hijacking crisis…and Quinn keeping her tossing and turning, she doubted either caffeine or solitude would do her much good.

Now, sitting alone in the booth, she allowed thoughts of Quinn to overshadow all others.

It had been bad enough losing sleep over him after she'd learned they would be working together. At least then she'd been dealing only with memories whose sharp edges had been dulled by time. The moments they'd spent last night in the close, intimate confines of his cruiser had left her with all new memories, ones that had twisted her insides into a knot.

What in heaven's name was she going to do?

She could no longer deny that the chemistry between her and Quinn was as strong as before. Even so, it was wrong. *All wrong.* Despite the fact that she understood the reasons he had walked out of her life—understood intimately the guilt that had motivated his actions—he had walked all the same. Could she ever again completely trust him to be there when she needed him?

She didn't think so.

Closing her eyes, she sipped the hot, potent coffee while fighting back a wave of emotion. Last night when Quinn's mouth took hers so relentlessly, she had been close—*so close*—to being swept away. Desire for him had sparked inside her with such staggering speed that she now knew the flame that had once burned between them had never been completely extinguished.

She had never known desire could be so painful. Or make her feel so off-balance. So vulnerable.

No, she thought, tightening her fingers on the mug's handle, she was vulnerable only if she allowed herself to be. Desire, after all, was simply an emotion. As was regret. Where Quinn was concerned, she had lived with both for a long time. Just as she had let neither of those emotions

control how she'd lived her life for the past three years,
she would allow neither to motivate her now. What had
been between her and Quinn was in the past. That was
where she intended it to stay. They would share no more
clenching embraces. No more lung-searing kisses. From
now on, all dealings between them would be strictly business.

Glancing up, she spotted Quinn striding through the restaurant's entrance. Instead of a suit, he wore a black polo
shirt open at the neck, well-washed jeans that molded his
long legs and scuffed boots. His gold badge and holstered
weapon were clipped to his belt. The instant longing that
shot through Christine weakened all the vows she'd just
made.

Her fingers trembled against the mug while her heart
pounded. She was realist enough to know that, at this rate,
she would find herself involved with him whether she
wanted to be or not.

What in heaven's name was she going to do?

Quinn scanned the restaurant's interior, his gaze meeting
hers. For a brief instant, his eyes probed her face with such
intensity that she felt as if she were not being looked at,
but into. Then he glanced across his shoulder and spoke
to FBI Agent Mason Taggart who had ambled in behind
him. Taggart, dressed in the same rumpled brown suit he'd
worn the day before, inclined his head in her direction.

Christine dragged in a deep breath while the men went
through the service line. Even as she tried to placate herself
with the knowledge that she wouldn't have to face Quinn
alone this morning, the tide of uneasiness that had been
with her since he'd kissed her brainless rose a little higher
inside her.

Carrying a glass of ice and a plastic bottle of orange

juice, Taggart settled on the opposite side of the booth; Quinn slid in beside her.

She could smell his soap, his skin, the spicy cologne that had made her senses swirl only hours ago.

"Morning, Miz Logan," Taggart said in his thick Texas drawl.

"Good morning." Christine gave the man a slight smile, then met Quinn's gaze. "Captain Buchanan."

Blue eyes met hers over the rim of his coffee mug. "Morning."

"The Captain and I thought this would be a good time to update you on a few things," Taggart stated as he twisted off the container's lid and poured orange juice over ice.

"I'd appreciate that," Christine said, forcing her thoughts firmly to business.

"I'll start with what we know about our hijacker's background," Taggart said. "For years Carl Hart was president of a bank his family owned in Oklahoma City. Kelly Jackson went to work there and caught his eye. Not long after that they married and she quit her job. Apparently, the honeymoon hadn't been over long when Hart started abusing her. She finally walked out and moved to Ryan, Texas, where her mother lived. Hart hunted down Kelly and dragged her back to Oklahoma. He'd crossed the state line with her—that constituted kidnapping so the feds got involved. Hart was tried on kidnapping charges and convicted. He was in the county jail in Oklahoma City awaiting sentencing when he managed to escape."

Christine shook her head. "Did he go after his ex-wife?"

"He was on his way to Ryan when he got picked up," Taggart answered. "In the meantime, Spence Cantrell headed there to advise Jackson of her ex-husband's escape and offer her protective custody. That offer turned out to be unnecessary since Hart was captured shortly after Cantrell arrived in Ryan."

Taggart paused to sip his juice. "That was eighteen months ago," he continued. "Since then, Hart's been in the federal prison in Marion, Illinois. From his first day there, he's stirred up trouble between himself and members of a prison gang. The trouble escalated, so when the Bureau of Prisons received a recent relocation request from Mr. Hart's lawyer, the request got quick approval." As he spoke, Taggart pulled the small rumpled brown bag he'd carried yesterday out of his suit pocket and offered it across the table. "Have a macadamia?"

Both Quinn and Christine shook their heads.

"As you both know," Taggart continued, "located on this airport is the only federal prison transfer center in this country. Any inmate entering the federal system, or being transferred, spends time at the PTC. That's not a secret. Mr. Hart came here after his kidnapping conviction and before his transfer to Marion. It's logical to think he knew he would return here for a few days, maybe a week, if he got himself reassigned to a different prison."

Christine blinked. "You're saying Hart purposely caused trouble with the gang in Marion so he would wind up back here at the PTC?"

"That's how I see it," Taggart answered. "Like I said yesterday, Mr. Hart's ex-wife, Kelly Jackson, lives only two hours away. He's adamant she make an appearance here."

"Have you found out why?" Christine asked.

"Not yet." Taggart's eyes narrowed. "I expect we'll know more when Marshal Cantrell gets her back here."

Christine frowned. Cantrell had left for the woman's

home in Ryan, Texas, after their previous day's meeting. "They're not here?"

Quinn shook his head. "When Cantrell got to Ryan, he found out Kelly Jackson went on vacation. She told her neighbors she was heading wherever the road took her, so they aren't sure where she went, or when to expect her. They think she'll get back in the next couple of days. She better. Cantrell put an APB on her vehicle. And he's keeping tabs on her home." A line formed between Quinn's brows as he stared into his coffee. "Everything we've come up with on Kelly Jackson points to her being squeaky clean. Even so, I'll feel a lot easier after I get my hands on whoever planted the gun on board that plane and know for sure she's not somehow involved in this hijacking."

The mix of fatigue and frustration in Quinn's voice pulled at Christine. "Did the NCIC computer come back with anything last night?"

"No." He shoved a hand through his dark hair. "So far, we haven't found a link between anyone with access to the airfield and Hart. I had the PD's Special Projects Unit go over the list of personnel with access. Projects didn't spot anyone known to do business with local bookies and who might be in the market to make some fast money to cover gambling debts. A credit bureau check shows a few of the people on the list are overextended, but no one owes enough money to make you think they'd risk sneaking a gun on the plane." Quinn shrugged. "That's supposing Hart has money stashed somewhere to pay his accomplice."

"If he does, we'll find it, Captain," Taggart said. Settling back in the booth with his glass, the FBI agent switched his gaze to Christine. "How much of a delay did last night's storm cause for the crews clearing the runways?''

"A few hours," she replied, keeping her thoughts firmly off the personal ramifications of the sudden deluge that drove her and Quinn into the back seat of his cruiser. "I'll have both runways cleared by nightfall. First thing tomorrow morning my operations people will conduct an inspection. If all debris is gone and there's no pavement damage, they'll open each runway." She glanced at her watch. "The FAA's portable control tower is due in this morning. Installation and hookup of equipment take about twelve hours."

Ice rattled as Taggart sipped his juice. "This afternoon, I want you to order the construction crew to start moving some debris off the taxiway around the plane," he said finally. "Tell them to work at a slow pace, and I damn sure don't want all the debris cleared. Not now, anyway."

Christine exchanged a look with Quinn. The grimness in his eyes told her Taggart's request didn't come as a surprise. "You really may have to let the plane take off?" she asked carefully.

"Mr. Hart insists that's the only way to keep those on board *his* plane alive. Keeping them alive is, of course, what I want."

"Of course." Christine shook her head. "I wouldn't want your job, Agent Taggart."

"I've been in this business a long time, Miz Logan. I learned early on to prepare for any eventuality. Mr. Hart wants that taxiway cleared. I'm willing to accommodate him if he gives me more hostages. So far, he's given me thirteen—five so I'd start clearing the runway. Another eight to get more food delivered to the plane. Counting Hart, that leaves ninety-five on board. I intend to get as many released as possible." Taggart raised a shoulder.

"Meanwhile, I've got three sharpshooters who guarantee that plane won't move one inch unless I let it."

The now familiar sense of dread for those held aboard the hijacked plane resettled in Christine's stomach. "If you do let it take off?"

"We go to Plan B," Taggart replied. "The minute this hijacking went down, I put the Bureau's Gulfstream six-passenger jet on alert status. It'll set down here as soon as your east runway opens. Suzanne Delachek, one of the FAA's most senior flight check pilots, will be on board." Taggart pursed his lips. "The woman has probably forgotten more than most folks will ever know about a 727. If circumstances require that I let Flight 407 get airborne, Ms. Delachek and I—and a few others—will be shadowing the 727 in the Gulfstream." Taggart's hand clenched on the brown bag. "I guarantee you, Miz Logan, whether it happens here in Whiskey Springs or somewhere outside this country, Mr. Hart will eventually be mine."

At that instant, a soft beep sounded. Quinn and Taggart reached for their pagers the same instant Christine pulled hers off the waistband of her slacks.

"Mine," Taggart said, regarding his pager's display. "The FBI director wants an update on our status." Nodding to Christine and Quinn, Taggart stuffed the small bag of nuts into his coat pocket and slid out of the booth.

Christine watched the FBI agent thread his way past the tables and booths that had filled to capacity while they'd talked. Her gaze settled on a man wearing a dark work shirt who sat alone at one table. His thick hands wrapped around a mug, his gaze tracked Taggart's progress toward the restaurant's door. Furrowing her brow, she tried to remember where she'd seen the man before, but nothing came to mind.

"Is coffee all you're having for breakfast, Slim?"

"Yes," she said, turning her attention back to Quinn. "I notice you're having the same."

His mouth curved. "Yeah, but I'll remember to eat later. I can't say the same about you."

Now that Taggart was gone and she and Quinn were alone in the booth, her nerves began to tangle. Was she destined to feel forever as though she'd just run a marathon whenever he got near?

"Have you changed your mind?" he asked.

The sudden softness in his voice put an instant wariness inside her. "About what?"

"Last night. Still think what happened between us was a mistake?"

Lowering her gaze, she stared into her coffee's murky depths. It wasn't enough just to want, she reminded herself. She had wanted this man before, and when he'd walked out of her life she thought she might die from the pain. Had wanted to die.

Still, there was something about Quinn Buchanan that would always make her want to tempt fate. That was exactly what she'd done last night when she'd let him kiss her.

She jolted when the pager she still held in one hand sounded. Grateful for the interruption, she checked the display.

"I've got to go. The FAA's portable tower just arrived."

Quinn nodded, then slid out of the booth. He waited until she'd risen, then turned to face her, his blue eyes inscrutable. "I'll be sure to ask you that same question some other time, Slim."

Sixteen hours later, Christine stumbled into her office, swinging the door closed behind her. After leaving the restaurant that morning, she'd liaised with Pete and the FAA reps responsible for placement of the temporary control tower. That done, she'd driven downtown where she spent several hours giving in-person reports on the airport's status to the city manager, the mayor and all three airport trustees. The remainder of the day had involved meetings with airline managers, operators of other on-airport businesses and her own staff.

Now, the FAA's control tower was in place and ready to start operation. Both runways were cleared. The taxiway on which Flight 407 sat had, according to Agent Taggart's instructions, been partially cleared of debris.

She had done everything in her power to help keep the hijacked passengers alive.

Right now, there was no more for her to do. No more urgent calls to make or return. No meetings to attend. No more checks of the airfield, not until morning when the airport resumed operations. The only thing she had to do right now was be available.

She could be that while she slept.

Her body spent with fatigue, she headed for the small bathroom off her office, washed her face and brushed her teeth. Snapping off the light, she walked to the couch, toed off her shoes, then dropped like a stone facedown onto the cushions.

She was asleep in thirty seconds flat.

So far, all the checks Quinn had run on individuals with access to the airfield had been a wash. He'd had every undercover cop in WSPD's Vice Detail question snitches about anyone on the street with knowledge about the hijacking. Nothing. He and his troops had checked the welfare of everyone with a current airport ID on the off chance someone had wound up murdered and their ID stolen. Another zero. He'd scoured the list of people who had signed in to visit prisoners housed at the PTC the same time as Hart. The hijacker-to-be had had no visitors, and Quinn could find no connection between Hart and anyone who'd had contact with any other prisoner. Or guard.

Now, as he strode through the dimly lit reception area that led to the airport's executive offices, Quinn bit back a vicious case of frustration and the beginnings of a headache. Someone on the ground had smuggled a weapon on board Flight 407. That someone had to have authorized access to the airfield. If it was the last thing Quinn did, he was going to find that someone.

His steps slowed when he neared the closed door to Christine's office. He frowned when he saw no thread of light coming from under the door. She had notified his dispatcher nearly two hours ago that she would be working in her office in case she was needed.

With concern spiking through him, he tapped lightly on the door. When he got no response, he turned the knob and swung the door open. The dim light coming from behind him wedged into the dark office as he stepped inside.

Crossing silently to the couch, he gazed down at Christine's sleeping form. She lay on her stomach, her head turned toward him, one arm and one bare foot dangling off the cushions. Her lips were slightly parted; her dark hair spread like smooth silk across a cheek that looked impossibly sculpted in the dim light and shadows.

Emotion tightened his chest. Had he ever really believed his life could be complete without her?

Quinn scrubbed a hand across his face. Time had eased the guilt, faded the vicious grief he'd felt over Jeff's death. Yesterday he had discovered what an empty shell of an existence he'd been living. He wanted to be whole again.

He couldn't—would never be—unless he had Christine Logan back in his life.

The problem was, she had made it clear she didn't want him back in *her* life.

Muttering an oath, he walked across the office to the small closet, opened the door and pulled out a blanket. Maybe she had yet to figure it out, but she wasn't going to slip though his fingers again. He'd be damned if he would let her.

Christine dreamed she was floating in a pool of warm, soothing water. Suddenly Quinn was beside her, his hands roaming across her damp flesh while his mouth moved on hers in a moist, deep, sumptuous kiss that went on endlessly, endlessly until she was as pliant as melted wax.

"Quinn...." His name escaped her lips on a moan of pain mixed with pleasure.

"I didn't mean to wake you, Slim."

His voice was so soft, so close, so real. *Too real.* Her eyelids fluttered open. Disoriented, she rolled onto her back, trapped between the dream and the present. "Quinn?"

"I brought you a blanket."

Her blood seemed to thicken, as if his very presence had slipped into her body like a drug. "A...blanket...?"

He was crouched beside her, the light angling through the open door of her office shadowing his face as he leaned in to tuck the blanket beneath her shoulders. With that gesture he closed her off with him, shut out everything in her world but him, just as he'd been all that existed for her in the dream.

"Didn't want you getting cold."

She doubted she would ever be cold again, not after the way she had melted in his arms.

Soft as a whisper, his fingertips nudged her tumbled hair off one cheek. "Go back to sleep, Slim. I'll see you in the morning."

A deep, almost desperate longing for what they once shared gripped her. Would it be wrong, so wrong, to experience again all they'd lost? To block out all the past hurt, all the regret and share this one moment in time? This one night, she could keep the want and need separate, she told herself. She wasn't ever going to *need* him again.

When he started to rise, she snagged his hand. "Quinn?"

His fingers slid between hers, linked. "Yeah, Slim?" In the dimness his eyes looked as soft as fog.

"Stay. I want you to stay with me tonight."

His hand went still against hers. "Why?"

"Because…" She cupped her palm against his cheek, felt the stubble that covered his jaw. "Just because," she murmured, bringing her lips to his.

His mouth was warm and soft and infinitely more potent than any dream could ever be. As their lips moved together, her breath shuddered out to merge with his. His taste, his scent filled her system, swamping her with memories, filling her with an ache only he could ease. Just as her arms rose to slide around his neck, Quinn drew back.

"You're sure this is what you want?"

She let the clogged air slowly out of her lungs. He had walked away from what had been, and what might have been between them. Because of that, she wasn't sure she could ever trust enough again to consider a future together. Didn't know if she wanted one. All she knew was that tonight she desperately wanted to push away all the doubts and misgivings…and logic. Right now, the ragged desire she felt was all that mattered.

"I'm sure this is what I want right now."

"Well, that's honest." He stared gravely back at her, his mouth set. "I'll be honest, too, Slim. I want you now. Tomorrow. Forever. For the rest of my life, I want you."

Without waiting for her reply, he rose and crossed to the door. He swung it closed, blanketing the office in black, velvety shadows. A heartbeat later, she heard the lock engage with a quick, deliberate snick.

Then Quinn was back, crouching beside her, cupping his hand at the back of her neck, his mouth claiming hers as he dragged her and the trapped blanket onto the floor with him.

The kiss was exactly what she wanted. Needed. Hungry and fierce and mindless. Her back pressed into the soft carpet as his mouth crushed down, hot and hard to devour hers. Her heart hammered against her ribs as she gave in to the kiss with a mindless frenzy where desire ruled all thought and blood roared over reason.

She tugged his shirt free of his waistband, then jerked it over his head. Her exploring fingers grazed over the remembered contours of flesh and iron-hard muscle while she breathed in his spicy scent. Her nipples burned against the restriction of her bra; the soft, wet pulse between her legs pounded. He was the only man who had ever made her want so quickly, so completely, so utterly.

Pushing her blouse open, he shoved it off one shoulder and replaced fabric with his teeth. Minutes later, the remainder of their clothes lay heaped around them on the floor.

His mouth traced the contours of her breast, then settled as he used teeth, tongue and lips to feast on one nipple. His fingertips took a slow journey down the flat planes of her stomach, then slid lower until his palm settled, cupping her.

Her heart bounded into her throat.

As he continued to suckle at her breast, his fingers kneaded the most intimate part of her, sending sensation sliding over sensation, building toward delirium. Clutching at the blanket tangled beneath her, she absorbed the first stunning waves of pleasure.

Her muscles tensed, then went lax.

"I'm not done with you," he murmured, then shifted his clever, dangerous mouth to her other breast. His lips fed, his fingers moved, driving her up again until her nerves snapped like a whip and her entire body pulsed.

His name tore from her lips in a mindless moan of pleasure.

Lifting his head, he dragged his hands through her hair, fisted them there. "I'll never be done with you, Christine. Never."

The greed in his voice broke through her already reeling senses. Wanting to feel that greed, she arched her body up, offering more of herself as her nails dug into the hard ridges of his shoulders. She hadn't known she could want so much, that the need for one man, *this man,* could be so sharp, so potent.

So terrifying.

His mouth moved to savage her throat, her shoulder. The office was dark, yet lights danced with brilliant color behind her eyes. With each gasping breath, blood pumped harder beneath her sweat-slicked skin, pushing her system closer to that teetering edge of insanity until she was ready to beg for release.

He entered her in one hard, welcoming stroke. She felt his body shudder as hers took him in, tightened around him. Her hands clenched in his hair; his mouth crushed down on hers as they plunged blindly into the kiss while their bodies moved together, fast and hard.

Breathing labored, flesh quivering, they tumbled over a jagged brink into unspeakable pleasure.

Chapter 5

Day 3

Later, much later, they found the energy to crawl onto the couch. Sitting with his spine wedged comfortably between the upholstered arm and cushion, Christine's bare back snuggled against his chest, Quinn knew he could die right there a satisfied man.

The fact that one of them had left the light on in the small rest room adjoining her office only notched up his level of contentment.

She couldn't know how enticing she looked, he thought, propped against him, her long legs twined with his, her skin still flushed and warm with the afterglow of their lovemaking. She had her head turned toward the wide window behind the desk where the first thready light of dawn seeped through. In the pale light her tousled hair looked as dark as midnight against her cheek.

"Quinn, I have a feeling something terrible is going to happen on that plane," she said quietly.

"Yeah." The urgency he felt to unearth Hart's accomplice churned in his gut like acid.

"What if the request you sent to the Oklahoma City PD comes back with nothing?" Christine asked as she shifted against him. "What then?"

"I'll figure something out."

Thirty minutes ago, he had checked with his dispatcher—so far the results of the inquiry he'd sent to the OCPD hadn't come back. Hart had lived in Oklahoma City for over twenty years; he and Kelly Jackson had lived there during their short marriage. Before his arrest on kidnap charges, Hart had been president of a bank. To Quinn's way of thinking, Hart's accomplice might have lived in Oklahoma City, or at least paid him a visit there. Quinn had faxed OCPD a list of all individuals with airfield access at Sam Houston and requested a check of the names against the PD's misdemeanor arrests. Speeding tickets. Littering charges. Anything minor that wouldn't show up on the national computer.

"That plane's been sitting there for two days," Christine said, her gaze still on the window. "The runway's clear of debris now. Most of the rubble on the taxiway is gone. How much longer do you think Hart will wait until he takes some sort of action?"

"Not long." Quinn slid a palm down her silky hair. "The reason I came up here last night was to tell you Hart's drawn a line in the sand."

She angled her head to look across her shoulder at him. "What sort of line?"

"He swears he'll kill a marshal if he doesn't talk to his ex by noon tomorrow." Just saying the words had Quinn biting back frustration. "Dammit, I need to get my hands on Hart's accomplice, take him out of the formula before then.''

Christine nodded. ''Everything's tied to Hart getting to talk to his ex-wife, isn't it?''

''My gut tells me she's the spark that'll set off whatever events that follow.''

''I can't help but think of the families of the marshals on board that plane,'' Christine said after a moment. ''They swore an oath to do their jobs. We both know that oath won't give their families any comfort if Hart starts shooting.''

Quinn closed his eyes for a brief instant. When Jeff died, it hadn't much mattered that he'd been a cop. What mattered was he was dead. ''You're right, we both know that.'' He placed a soft kiss against her hair. ''We both know.''

He felt a quiet shudder ripple through Christine and he could almost hear her mind clicking back into gear. Angling his head, he saw the shadows that had crept into her eyes. He had a feeling those shadows had nothing to do with the hijacking, and everything to do with him.

''Slim.'' Cupping her shoulders, he shifted her around on his lap until her face was only inches from his. ''Talk to me about last night.''

When she shoved a hand through her hair, the dim light glistened off her soft flesh. ''I don't know what to say to you, Quinn.''

''You could say you enjoyed the past couple of hours.''

The mouth that had so recently sent his system into overdrive curved into a tired smile. ''You know I did.''

His palm grazed the small mole on her right hip. ''And that you're glad we made love.''

''I wanted it to happen.''

''Not the same.'' Her warm vanilla scent clung to her

skin, to the air, to his senses. "And now I imagine you're wondering if you want *it* to happen again."

Her gaze traveled to the boxes stacked in one corner of the office, lingered there. "All this has happened so fast. There's so much going on right now, with the airport, the hijacking. You."

He gave her a wry smile. "You cataloguing me as a disaster, Slim?"

She didn't return his smile. "Where I'm concerned, that may be what you are." She shook her head. "I need time, Quinn. Time to deal with things, think everything through."

He used his thumb to stroke the line that had formed between her dark brows. He still had the taste of her in his mouth from their lovemaking. "And decide if we have a future," he added.

Her gaze rose to meet his. "What we had in the past didn't exactly work out."

"My fault."

"No. It was no one's fault. What we felt for each other wasn't strong enough to get us through together when Jeff died." This time, she used both hands to shove her hair away from her face. "I was sure what we had was... I was sure nothing could come between us. I was wrong."

"I did what I thought was best at the time."

She nodded. "Your brother was murdered while working a job in your place. You took total blame for Jeff being in harm's way that night. Rebecca and the girls were devastated, they needed you and you needed to be there for them. You felt you had nothing left of yourself to give to me, to us. I understand all that."

Quinn pinched the bridge of his nose between his thumb and finger. Then, he had thought by distancing himself he could shield her from some of the pain, yet he had only increased her agony—and his own—by letting her go. It was so easy now, he thought. Easy to analyze actions and motives when the passage of three years had smoothed the grief, the agony. ''My life took a detour to hell. I figured that was where it would stay. No way was I going to drag you there with me.''

''I loved you, Quinn. I would have gladly gone to hell and back with you.'' She swallowed hard. ''Now, here you are, telling me you want me back—''

''I do—''

''How do I know you'll stay this time, Quinn? How do I know, if I let myself love you again, that you'll always be there for me? How do I know this time will be different?''

Considering their past, she had every right to ask those questions. And he knew any assurances he made about how things would be different this time would come off sounding hollow. He eased out a breath. They could rehash the past through eternity and never know if or how their taking different actions would have altered things. At this point, that paled in importance to what lay in their future.

Considering the uncertainty he saw in her eyes, he was going to have to do some fast talking to keep her around long enough so he could convince her they had a future.

Settling his hands on her shoulders, he locked his gaze with hers. ''Here's the deal, Slim. You want to take things slow between us, fine—you set the pace. You want to keep things uncomplicated, no problem.'' He would go quietly insane if that was what she chose. ''You decide to see someone else while you're making up your mind about us, I'll handle it.'' As he spoke, his fingers tightened against her bare flesh. If another man touched her, he would rip his lungs out. ''Any limitations you put on us are okay, as long as there is an *us*.''

She blinked. "Are you serious, Buchanan?"

"Deadly." His hands rose to cup her face. "Letting you go was the biggest mistake of my life. I want you back. I *need* you. I'll do whatever it takes to make that happen."

She lifted her hands, curled them around his wrists. "I...can't make you any promises right now, Quinn."

"Then I'll make you one. For the rest of my life, I'll be right there with you. No matter what happens. No matter where you are. I'll be there."

Tears glittered in her eyes as he leaned and placed a light kiss on her forehead. "I love you, Slim. I want you to love me back. Let me into your life again. Please."

After Quinn kissed her thoroughly and left her office, Christine spent the next four hours dealing with paperwork and phone calls. That done, she stopped by her secretary's desk to tell Ula she would be out on the airfield and in radio contact with the tower. Christine then headed for the elevator that would take her to the airfield basement garage where she'd parked her Bronco the previous evening. In ten minutes, her operations division would begin their inspection of the runways and she wanted to observe. Once the inspection was done and the airport back in operation, the FBI's sleek Gulfstream would be the first aircraft to set down at Sam Houston since the tornado ripped through there two days ago.

Two days. Christine's mind reeled with thoughts of all that had happened in so short a time. She stepped off the elevator, her footsteps sounding hollow echoes against the concrete floor as she dug her car keys out of her leather tote. She didn't have time now to analyze all the events. Didn't want to consider the consequences of the hours she had spent in Quinn's arms.

She hadn't wanted to put herself in a position to be hurt

again, yet she was painfully aware she was on the brink of doing just that. She caught her bottom lip between her teeth. How could she want a man so totally when she wasn't sure she could trust him to be there for her when she needed him?

She had no answer to that question, didn't have time to find the answer. Right now, she needed to concentrate on what was happening—and might happen—on her airfield. Carl Hart had drawn his line in the sand; by noon tomorrow he would either speak to his ex-wife, or he would kill a marshal.

And he would use the gun smuggled onto the plane to do his killing. A gun smuggled by someone working at her airport.

As she walked through the garage, dread settled in her stomach. By now, that someone had probably informed Hart that the runway and all taxiways on the opposite side of the airfield from the hijacked plane were cleared and would soon reopen. Hart would know for sure that the rubble still blocking the marshals' plane had been left there by Taggart as a stall tactic. The hijacker's present state of mind was anybody's guess—no one knew what spark would motivate him to kill. So many things could go wrong, Christine thought. Carl Hart and his unknown helper had placed so many lives in harm's way.

Unlocking the Bronco, she climbed behind the wheel. Just as she slid the key into the ignition, the passenger door swung open.

The man who bounded into the seat beside her was big. Six-four, well over two hundred pounds. His muddy brown eyes glinted beneath the bill of a baseball cap as he slammed the door behind him. "Do what I say, and maybe I won't use this."

Panic curled in Christine's belly then shot up her throat as she stared into a gun's dark, lethal barrel.

"I've got you, you bastard," Quinn said through his teeth as he steered his cruiser across the tarmac toward a gleaming maintenance hangar leased to one of the airport's fixed base operators.

Don Post had been arrested in Oklahoma City four years ago while Carl Hart lived there. Post's arrest for drunk and disorderly after he'd refused to leave a bar at closing time was a misdemeanor, so the charge hadn't shown up on Post's background check returned from the National Crime Information Center. After Quinn received the information from the OCPD earlier this morning, he'd called the Oklahoma City Municipal Court, badgered a harassed-sounding clerk into digging through records she informed him were not yet computerized. Elation had stormed through him when the clerk called back a torturous hour later to advise him that one Carl Hart had posted bond for Don Post.

Quinn now had a positive connection between Hart and a man with access to the Sam Houston airfield. That man worked for the fixed base operator who had the contract to perform maintenance on the planes flown by the U.S. Marshals Service. That contract had given Post access to Flight 407, on which he'd planted the gun for his pal, Hart.

"Got you," Quinn repeated as he braked the cruiser near the hangar's front entrance. Out of the corner of his eye he saw the black and white patrol car he'd summoned for backup pull to a halt beside the hangar's massive side doors. Biting back impatience, Quinn retrieved the file folder he'd grabbed as he raced out of his office. Flipping the file open, he plucked out the copy of the photo taken of Post six months prior when he'd hired on with the FBO.

Quinn wanted a picture of his quarry branded into his mind before he walked into that hangar.

The photo taken for Post's security ID was from the shoulders up; still, Quinn could tell he was a big man. Beefy—had to weigh well over two hundred pounds. The eyes that stared out from the jowly unsmiling face looked as hard as dried mud.

As Quinn studied the photo, a sudden realization crept over him. He had seen Post. On the airfield, two evenings ago. He'd worn a ball cap while he stood with two workers from the construction crew. The three men had watched Christine walk across the runway to talk to the workers' foreman. It was Post whose gaze had followed her with a particular intensity.

Quinn muttered a curse and shouldered open the cruiser's door. He was looking forward to meeting Don Post face to face.

"What…do you want?" Dread stormed through Christine's system, making her voice shake like a leaf in a cold wind.

Keeping the gun pointed at her chest, the man licked his lips. "You're going to make a phone call."

She stared into the gun's barrel that looked like a single black eye. Her first crazy thought was that if he had rape on his mind he wouldn't force her to make a phone call. "Who…do you want me to call?"

"Whoever I say, bitch."

Fear ballooned inside her, made her hands tremble so badly she clenched them in her lap. She was conscious of only two sounds: her own terrified heart pounding in her ears and the harsh rasp of the man's breathing.

She swallowed back the terror that came from the knowledge she was trapped inside her Bronco with a man pointing a gun at her chest. She clamped her teeth over her bottom lip to keep from whimpering. Don't feel, she ordered herself. *Think.* Clear your mind and *think.*

Her gaze darted out the windshield. The small garage was dimly lit and nearly deserted of cars. She harbored no hope that anyone would walk by and cause a distraction that would give her a chance to escape.

Stiffening her resolve, she turned her head, made herself look into his face, feeling the gun without seeing it. Beneath the brim of his ball cap, his dark gaze darted out the windshield, came back to her, then he moved in his seat, glanced out the passenger window behind him. Sweat beaded his forehead and upper lip.

She'd seen him before. On the runway two nights ago, talking to some of the construction workers. And again sitting alone at a table in the terminal restaurant the previous morning. She remembered how his hard, narrow-eyed stare had followed Taggart when the FBI agent left the restaurant.

The man used his arm to blot sweat off his forehead, forcing up the ball cap's brim. She could almost smell the desperation emanating from him as he jerked a cell phone from his shirt pocket.

"Call the dozers." He shoved the phone into her hand. "Order them to clear the rest of the taxiway around the plane."

Well, now she knew the identity of Hart's accomplice! She also knew if the bulldozers moved in without Taggart's approval, chaos would ensue, at least for a time. Chaos that would not only clear the rest of the debris blocking the hijacked plane, but provide a distraction for whatever Hart had planned.

"The FBI won't—"

Her words died when he crammed the gun against her

temple. She winced when he angled the barrel and the sight on its end dug into her flesh.

"This whole deal was only supposed to take a couple of hours," he grated. "That damn tornado hit and I've had to hang around here for days while the cops sniff around. The bastards are so close now I can *smell* 'em. I got this one last thing to do, then I got someplace to go." The barrel shoved deeper into her temple; the sight biting into her flesh sent pain grinding down her cheek. The heavy scent of gun oil cloyed in her lungs. "You don't make the call, I'll put the first bullet in your shoulder. You still won't do what I say, the next slug hits your elbow. Three and four go in the knees. None of 'em'll kill you, but the pain will be so bad you'll wish they had." He wiped his face on his sleeve. "You'll be begging me to *let* you make the call."

The air heaved in and out of her lungs in ragged breaths. *Quinn.* She almost moaned his name as everything she thought she knew about herself, her feelings suddenly shattered, crashed. She hadn't wanted to risk, to chance her heart again. The gun jabbing into her temple made her realize she wanted all the chances she could get. And she desperately wanted to stay alive to tell Quinn she loved him. Had never stopped loving him.

"I'll...make...the call." The icy terror avalanching through her system sounded in her voice.

"Big surprise."

She dragged in air. "I don't...know the number...for the supervisor over the dozers. Don't...have it memorized."

The vicious oath he spat increased her trembling.

"It's programmed into my cell phone," she blurted. With the gun lodged against her temple she couldn't move her head so she shifted her eyes downward toward her tote. "In there. Side pocket."

He stared at her for long, silent moments while sweat ran down his temples, dripped off his jaw onto his dark shirt. "You better not try nothin'," he hissed finally. Jamming a hand into her tote, he dug out the phone, tossed it into her lap.

"Make the call, bitch."

Quinn stalked out of the hangar, a mix of anger and frustration burning inside him like a white-hot torch. For the first time since he'd hired on with the FBO six months ago, Don Post hadn't shown up for work this morning. Hadn't called in to explain his absence. His supervisor had been genuinely surprised when Quinn insisted on checking Post's locker in the break room. Nothing. Post had cleared out everything.

Quinn had already dispatched a black and white to the address Post had listed on his job application, but he knew his troops wouldn't find the man. Why had Post disappeared today? Quinn wondered. Hart's deadline to begin killing hostages was noon tomorrow. Why hadn't Post stayed on the job one more day so he could continue to feed Hart information?

Quinn muttered a curse as his gaze swept the airfield. Numerous service vehicles dotted the nearby apron. Post still had his airport ID, which meant he could move freely around the airfield. He could be in any one of the vehicles.

Quinn's eyes narrowed as he pictured again the look in the bastard's eyes as the man's gaze tracked Christine when she walked across the runway. The look took on a new meaning now, one that put a sense of dread into Quinn's stomach.

His cell phone rang; he pulled it from the holder clipped beside his holstered weapon. "Buchanan."

"This is Airport Director Logan."

Quinn's eyes narrowed. Despite the bad connection he could hear the trembling in her voice. "What's wrong?"

"I need you to send in your bulldozers. Clear the debris still blocking the marshals' plane."

Fear for her locked Quinn's jaw. "Where are you?"

"No, I'm in my car, it won't help to call you back to get a better connection. Just send in the dozers. *Now,*" she added before the line went dead.

His breath coming hard, Quinn climbed into his cruiser as he punched in the number for Christine's office. Her secretary answered on the second ring.

"Ula, this is Captain Buchanan." He leaned, twisted the key in the ignition. "Where's your boss?"

"She left here ten minutes ago for her car. Said she wanted to be on the airfield when the Ops Division inspected the runways. She should be in radio contact with the tower by now."

"Thanks." Quinn disengaged the call then reached for the microphone clipped to the dash.

"Tower, this is Victor Ten. Has Airport One made radio contact with you in the last ten minutes?"

"Negative, Victor Ten."

"Ten-four." Setting his jaw, Quinn replaced the microphone. Christine hadn't radioed the tower. Logic told him whatever it was that prompted her to call him had happened somewhere between her office and her Bronco. She had said she was in her car, so he would check the Bronco first.

Shoving the cruiser into gear, Quinn peeled rubber.

The man ripped the cell phone from Christine's hand, lobbed it into the back seat. When the gun withdrew from her temple, she saw its black metal, dark against his chalk-white knuckles.

He pulled his own phone out of his shirt pocket, punched a button and crammed it against his ear. "The bitch made the call," he said seconds later. "You call me in five minutes and let me know if those dozers moved in." Keeping his eyes locked on her face, he clicked off the phone, set it on the dash.

Staring at the phone, Christine reasoned Hart must have taken a phone off one of the marshals so he and his accomplice could communicate.

"If those dozers don't move, you're gonna have hell to pay." As he spoke, he angled his thick wrist to check his watch.

Five minutes, she thought wildly. Would Quinn find her that fast? Would he find her at all?

"What does Hart have planned?" she asked, fighting to keep her voice even. If she could get the man talking, maybe she could distract him, create a chance to escape. *Do something.*

"To get away, what the hell do you think?" He made a small arc with the gun, then snapped it back, aimed at her chest. "My cousin Carl's a smart guy. Ain't nothing gonna stop him, once he sees sweet Kelly and those dozers move in."

A sick feeling flooded Christine's stomach as she watched his gaze dart out the windshield, back to her, then across his shoulder out the passenger door window. The dozers weren't moving in, at least not within the next five minutes. She didn't dare shift her arm to check her watch. How much longer until Hart phoned to tell his cousin that nothing had happened?

A wave of faintness drenched her flesh, her clothes with

sweat. She wondered if the man still intended to put the first bullet into her shoulder, or would he just kill her and be done with it? Swallowing painfully, she dredged up her voice.

"Hart's your cousin?"

"Distant. We been doing each other favors all our lives. Just like now."

"Why does he want to see his ex-wife?"

"Carl's got some things to discuss with sweet Kelly." His lips pulled back against his teeth in a feral snarl. "Personal things. *Very* personal."

Out of the corner of her eye, Christine glimpsed Quinn step around the column nearest the Bronco's passenger side. Her throat closed, her lungs ceased to work. As he crept closer, light glinted dully off the gun he gripped in one hand, its barrel pointed toward the floor.

Her heart drummed impossibly hard, impossibly loud. *Be careful. Quinn, be careful.*

She was alive. The thought echoed through Quinn's brain as he inched forward, his Glock clenched in his hand. Locking his jaw, he angled his body so his reflection wouldn't show in the mirror hooked onto the side of the Bronco. Everything depended on him taking Don Post by surprise.

The bastard had Christine.

His gaze swept the dim area where the Bronco sat, then flicked to the garage's entrance where dazzling April sunlight shone just outside. He saw no sign of the uniforms he'd radioed to meet him.

He was on his own.

He was close enough to touch the handle on the passenger door. Despite the tinted glass, he saw that Christine's face was white with fear, her eyes wide and glassy as she kept them locked on Post's face.

Blood pooled on her right temple.

Quinn narrowed his eyes. He was going to take the bastard apart, limb by limb.

He forced back white-hot fury. He would let emotion brim to the surface later. Right now, he had to get Christine out of the Bronco. Alive.

Edging sideways, he glimpsed the Beretta gripped in Post's right hand, its barrel aimed at her chest. Quinn's stomach churned while he analyzed his options. After he got the door open, he could screw his Glock into Post's ear, order him to drop his gun. Problem was, if Post wasn't inclined to give up the Beretta, it would still be aimed at Christine.

Quinn's own life suddenly passed before his eyes at the thought of losing her again.

He had to take Post by surprise and at the same time get control of the Beretta. Quinn reholstered his Glock. He needed both hands free for his plan to work. God, it had to work.

Wishing Post weighed about a hundred pounds lighter, Quinn dragged in a steadying breath. Eased forward. Curled his fingers on the passenger door's handle. Jerked.

Post jolted. He whipped around, swinging the Beretta as he turned. Quinn clamped his hand over the gun and twisted, aiming the deadly barrel away from Christine and toward the dash. With his other hand, he gripped the back of Post's thick neck.

He heard Christine cry his name as he dragged Post sideways toward the door. In the same instant, she shoved Post's shoulder, forcing him even more off-balance. Digging his fingers into the bastard's neck, Quinn pitched the big man downward out of the car and onto cement.

Post's vile curses echoed in the air. Flailing his free arm, he struggled to gain his feet.

Hand still locked on the Beretta, Quinn crammed his knee into Post's spine, using all his weight to force him down until he kissed concrete. Gritting his teeth, Quinn jerked Post's right arm up high on his back while twisting the Beretta.

Quinn heard the satisfying snap of bone as he wrenched the automatic from Post's grip. The man roared with pain.

"Move a muscle, you bastard, and I'll break the rest of your fingers."

Out of the corner of his eye, Quinn saw Christine scramble across the Bronco's console, over the passenger seat and out the door. "Quinn!"

"Stay back!"

Keeping his knee ground into Post's spine, Quinn stuffed the Beretta into his waistband, grabbed his handcuffs. Metal sang against metal as he braceleted Post's meaty wrists.

Just then, Quinn caught movement at the garage entrance. Two uniformed cops swung in, guns drawn.

"I've got him," Quinn said. Footsteps echoing, the uniforms dashed to their boss's side. "Toss him in a cell," Quinn said as he rose. "Then call Taggart and tell him we've got Don Post, Hart's accomplice."

"Quinn!" Swallowing a sob, Christine launched herself at him, all but burrowing into his arms when he caught her close.

If the uniforms were surprised to see their boss with his arms wrapped around the new airport director, they didn't show it.

"Read him his rights," Quinn said. "I'll meet you at the office in a few minutes."

"You got it, Captain."

From inside the Bronco, a phone trilled.

"That's Hart," Christine said, her arms tightening around Quinn's waist. "Calling to tell Post the bulldozers haven't moved in."

"Let it ring," Quinn said through his teeth. "It'll do Hart good to sweat over what's happened to his pal."

While the uniforms hoisted Post to his feet, Quinn took his first full breath since he'd seen Christine trapped inside the Bronco. "You all right, Slim?" he asked, nuzzling his face in her hair.

"I am now." She lifted her head. "You?"

"I am now." As he spoke, his eyes narrowed and he angled her head to study her temple. Already a bruise darkened her flesh. "You're cut and bleeding."

"Just a scratch from the gun's sight."

He bit back on a sudden rage that made him want to tell the uniforms to hold off while he made good on his promise to break Post's other fingers. "I want an EMT to look at you."

"I'm okay." She let out a long, shaky breath. "Now."

"I want you checked." He cupped his palm against the uninjured side of her face as he stared into eyes that still held the remnants of terror. He knew how she felt—he was still swallowing back the fear for her that had lodged in his throat. "After that, we both need to head for my office and make reports."

"I'm not getting checked." The hand she placed over his was as gentle as her voice. "This is my airport, Captain Buchanan. That means I run things."

His mouth quirked. "You trying to pull rank, Director Logan?"

"Whatever it takes for me to get the next ten minutes alone with you."

He stroked his palm down the length of her hair. "You can have eternity alone with me, if you want it."

She angled her head. "As a matter of fact, that's what I have in mind."

Quinn felt everything inside him go still. "You want eternity with me?"

"Remember I told you I don't like to repeat mistakes?"

"I'm not likely to forget that."

"I understand now that we didn't stop loving each other after Jeff died," she said, her voice soft, her dark eyes eloquent. "We just didn't know how to hold on to each other tight enough. Fate put us both here at this airport, Quinn. We have another chance. I want to hold on tight and take that chance."

"Slim..." He closed his eyes for a brief instant. "You've had a hell of a change of heart from this morning."

"Not a change of heart. You've always been in my heart." She slicked her tongue across her lips. "Staring into a gun barrel puts things into crystal-clear focus. It made me realize I wanted all those years back that we missed together. Sitting in that Bronco, my biggest regret was that you and I weren't going to get a second chance to make things right. I love you, Quinn."

He cupped her face in his hands. "You're sure?"

She arched a brow. "Sure I love you?"

"Sure you won't spend your life wondering if I'll be there for you when you need me?"

"You were there for me today."

He nodded. Before, he had loved her with all his heart. It wasn't even close to what he felt for her now. "And I'll be there for you the rest of your life, if you'll have me."

Her mouth curved. "Oh, I plan on having you, Captain."

He grazed his mouth against hers, felt desire curl inside him. The heat that flickered in her dark eyes told him she was as anxious as he to explore the love they both thought lost. Still, he knew neither of them would breathe easy until the crisis was over.

"We've done our jobs," she said, as if reading his thoughts. "You took down Hart's accomplice and I got that runway cleared. It's the FBI and marshals' operation now. Still, I wish there was something more we could do."

"Like get a handful of Hart and jerk him off the plane."

"Works for me." She glanced back at the Bronco. "Post and Hart are cousins. I tried to find out what Hart wants with his ex-wife. All Post said was that it's personal. *Very* personal."

Sliding an arm around her waist, Quinn pulled her tight against him. He was never going to let her go again.

"Let's hope Spence Cantrell and the FBI have better luck finding out what that something is."

"Let's hope."

"You wanted ten minutes alone with me before we head to my office, Slim." As he spoke, he raked his fingers through her hair, nudged her head back. "You've still got a couple of minutes left. What say you spend that time kissing me?"

Her mouth curved as she rose on tiptoe. "You've got great ideas, Buchanan."

*   *   *   *   *

Cover Me!

Debra Cowan

To Teddy
Thanks for the shoulder, the laughs and the great ideas

Books by Debra Cowan

Silhouette Intimate Moments

Chapter 1

He looked every bit as good as she remembered. Dang.

Kelly Jackson's gaze skimmed over six-foot-plus of solid, rangy muscle standing in her doorway, the well-fitted navy slacks, the crisp white shirt molding a broad chest, the gold badge clipped to his waistband. U.S. Marshal Spence Cantrell's sheer physical presence had caused a hitch in her pulse the first time she'd seen him eighteen months ago. It still did.

And his piercing cobalt eyes still seemed haunted. Dread inched along her spine. There could be only one reason the marshal was in itty-bitty Ryan, Texas. The peace she'd experienced during her stay at Lake Texoma vanished. Finally, she managed to find her voice. "You've come about Carl."

"May I come in, Miss Jackson?" The voice was the same rough velvet she remembered.

"Yes, sorry." Flustered, her dread growing, Kelly motioned him inside the farmhouse where she'd lived most of her life, shutting out the April sunlight, feeling suddenly as if she were sealing her fate somehow. "May I get you something to drink? Iced tea? Lemonade?"

"No, ma'am."

Memories of the last time she'd seen Spence Cantrell crowded her mind. Eighteen months ago, the day after her mother's funeral, he'd shown up with the news that her ex-husband, Carl Hart, had escaped out of a window of the Oklahoma County jail where he was awaiting sentencing.

Through her increasingly horrible marriage, the ordeal of her kidnapping trial, her mother's illness and subsequent death, Kelly hadn't shed one tear. Certainly not when she received the paper in the mail officially reinstating her maiden name. But when Spence Cantrell had suggested she pack a bag and leave her home in case Carl returned, the strain of the previous year had overwhelmed her. To her complete mortification, she'd broken down and sobbed.

If that weren't bad enough, the marshal had drawn her against his chest and held her. She could barely look at him afterwards, though she was more than grateful. In the end, she hadn't gone with him. Carl had been recaptured about an hour after Spence's arrival. Still, he had seen her cry when no one else had, had seen her at her weakest and she couldn't seem to get past that. "Carl's escaped again, hasn't he?"

"No, ma'am." With long fingers, Spence Cantrell slid his cell phone into the pocket of his dress shirt. His seal-dark hair was finger-combed neatly back except for one wayward lock, which fell onto his forehead.

He wasn't handsome in Carl's sleek, perfect way, but

he was certainly more compelling. Where the sharp precision of her ex's features had translated into cunning cruelty, the strong chin, sharp jaw and chiseled planes of Cantrell's face were blunted, as if carved then smoothed by a pair of loving hands. A potent combination of intelligence and gentleness. Blatantly male, yet approachable.

"Please, tell me. If he hasn't escaped, then what?" The man took up entirely too much space in Kelly's small foyer. She moved into the living room, fighting the urge to wring her hands. "Is he dead?"

Cantrell stopped in the arched doorway. "No."

"This news can only get better." Kelly shoved a shaking hand through her hair, then wrapped both arms around her middle. "What's he done?"

Spence glanced away briefly, then leveled his gaze on hers. A muscle in his jaw flexed. "He's hijacked a plane."

She blinked. A small sound of surprise escaped her. *"What?"*

"A federal transport 727, carrying marshals and prisoners."

Ice slithered down Kelly's nerves. "One of *your* planes? A marshals' plane?"

"Yes."

"Where?"

"Sam Houston International Airport in Whiskey Springs."

"Why can't you people keep him locked up?" Fear made her say it, laying bare the terror she'd tried for the last two years to forget.

Spence's jaw clenched.

She closed her eyes, the calm she'd found this past week now a snarl of knots. "I should've stayed at the lake."

"I know you've just returned from vacation and I'm sorry to do this to you, but we need your help."

"I can't begin to guess what he's trying to pull."

"You're the person who knows Hart best."

"You want to ask me questions." The reminder of her life with Carl put a queasy feeling in the pit of Kelly's stomach. She couldn't bear to relive the humiliation, the anger. *The fear.* She couldn't control the tremor in her voice. "When you showed up last time, I had just gotten myself, my life back together. I had to start all over. I'm not doing that again. I don't talk about Carl. To anybody."

"You have to talk to me." Cantrell moved into the room, only a step, but enough to intimidate. "I'm a federal marshal."

"You'd fall into that anybody category." She edged around to the other side of the couch, putting something solid between her and this man she'd thought about too often over the last eighteen months.

"What if he kills people? Takes that plane out of the country? What if you could've stopped him?"

"Don't try to lay that on me." The fear numbed her insides. She heard her voice, but was barely aware of her words. "You guys are the ones who keep losing him."

Cantrell put his hands on his hips, lean fingers splayed wide. His jaw clenched. "I need all the information on him I can get. And on any associates he may have had."

"I don't see how I can help you. Everything I thought I knew about him was a lie."

"Anything you tell me can help me build a profile, try to figure out what he hopes to gain by hijacking a con-air flight. Why would he do something like this?"

"Because he's a wacko, that's why."

"That may be." His eyes darkened, but Kelly couldn't tell whether it was from impatience or amusement. "But it's not specific enough to help me come up with a plan."

She didn't want to think about Carl, let alone talk about

him. But if she refused to help, she couldn't live with the consequences. "How many people are on that plane?"

"One hundred and eight."

Compassion stabbed deep. There were convicts on that plane, but also marshals, men who gave their lives to protect civilians. Men with sweethearts, families. Men who could die if Carl wished it. "Ask me whatever you need to. I wouldn't put it past him to kill someone."

Spence was close, his woodsy scent tickling her nostrils. Her nerves shimmered as she realized she didn't feel physically threatened by him. Emotionally was another matter.

Compassion flashed across the rugged planes of his face. This was the man who'd given her his business card and told her to call, day or night, if she ever needed anything. "I'm going to have to ask you to get some things together and come with me."

"Some things? How many things? Go where?"

"Hart's threatened to start killing marshals if his demands aren't met."

"Why would you come all this way to inform me that Carl hijacked a plane? You could've called me if all you want is information." Kelly went still, apprehension knotting her throat. "What demands?"

"He wants to talk to you."

She swayed, reaching down to clutch at the back of the couch.

Spence's gaze scoured her face and a small frown furrowed his brow. Concern? she wondered vaguely.

"Do you feel faint?"

"No. I don't know," she murmured, her fingers digging into the nubby plaid upholstery. She'd never fainted in her life; for once, she wished she could. Anything to escape this returning nightmare of Carl. "Why? Why does he want to talk to me?"

"I was hoping you'd know."

She shook her head. "I have no idea."

She knew she had to go with Spence Cantrell, but she needed a moment to accept that, to work through the shock that scalded her senses like a live flame. Would she ever be free of Carl?

Cantrell reached toward her, then let his hand drop back to his side. "Miss Jackson, are you all right?"

"Yes." She blinked back tears. She wasn't going to cry in front of him this time, though she couldn't help the longing that stabbed through her to lean against his strong chest once again, to grab the hand he'd nearly offered. "You're not going to make me...see him? Please?"

Cantrell's eyes darkened. "No, ma'am. You don't have to get within a hundred yards of him, but we have to be able to tell him you're on your way. And I do need information from you."

She searched his eyes, her chest aching with the need to breathe. "That's all?"

"That's all," Cantrell said firmly, his eyes turning intense with the promise, masking the shadows there.

She was *not* talking about the physical abuse. In the first place, that kind of information wouldn't help the marshal. In the second place, she felt stupid enough for marrying Carl. She wasn't going to humiliate herself by admitting he'd hit her. Or that it had taken her until the second time to leave.

Numb with shock, she came around the couch and started for the stairs. "I'll get my things."

"I'm not sure how long this will take. Pack enough clothes for a couple of days." His strong fingers closed over her elbow, guiding her steps gently.

Her arm brushed the hard, flat plane of his stomach.

Steadying herself with a hand on the banister, she managed a smile. "I'm all right. Thank you."

She drew away, grateful for the support, but uncomfortable with the feel of his hand on her arm, the silent strength that pulsed from him.

She hurried up the stairs to her bedroom, her emotions seesawing. The marshal scrambled her common sense. She didn't want to be within a hundred miles of Carl. And she didn't want to be this close to Spence Cantrell.

As she threw some things in her overnight bag, Kelly tried to calm the panic that pushed at her like a swelling tide. She knew why she didn't want to go to Whiskey Springs with Spence Cantrell. It was because of the man, not the marshal.

It was the man who tangled her thoughts, caused her pulse to go haywire. The man whom she'd tried to forget since their first encounter. The man whose haunted eyes touched something deep inside her. The man whom she wanted to ask if he'd ever been married. If he had a family.

Invisible walls, perfected by years of practice, snapped up to guard against the dangerous, insistent curiosity she felt. She hadn't been curious about a man since her divorce. Why did she have to be curious about Spence Cantrell?

She felt off-balance and not only because of her loathing to revisit the past. That wounded look in Cantrell's eyes reached deep inside her, stirred feminine impulses she'd managed to repress since Carl.

It wasn't just that Spence was handsome. Or, she admitted with gritted teeth, that she felt attracted to him. But there was a connection. It was the torture she'd seen in his eyes. She knew torture, had survived her own private hell, was still surviving it.

Gathering her bag, she walked into the hall and started

down the stairs. When Cantrell looked up, her steps faltered as those blue eyes bore straight into her soul.

She felt something with Spence she'd never felt with Carl. Safe. And that scared the fire out of her.

She forced herself to descend the next step, then the next. Drawing in a ragged breath, she tried to quell the sudden flurry of anticipation and apprehension in her stomach. Safe, hah. Protected? Those feelings were dangerous. Another time, they'd swept her up like a twister—merciless, fast, hard. She'd gone with her emotions once, listened to her heart instead of her head. Never again.

That was the problem. Cantrell jumbled the signals between her head and her heart. Usually so clear, right now they crackled with static and she had to listen hard. Her heart said she could trust Spence Cantrell; her head screamed *don't.*

As she reached the bottom of the steps, his gaze slid over her. There was no heat in his blue eyes, but an intensity that put a hum in her blood, made her skin tight. As if he were aware of every inch of her beneath the blue silk pantsuit.

Tension stiffened his shoulders, but when he spoke, his voice was neutral. "Ready?"

"Yes." No! Even as she experienced the sensation of stepping blindfolded into thin air, she held out her bag to him.

He took it and she followed him to a dark sedan, then slid into the passenger seat when he held open her door. Muscles rigid, hands clasped tightly together in her lap, Kelly stared straight ahead as he climbed behind the steering wheel.

It was bad enough that she had never forgotten Spence's dark blue eyes or the strength in that broad chest. Now he wanted something from her. Something she didn't want to give.

She didn't like men who were able to talk her into things, badge or not. She'd been taken in by a convincing, trust-me type before.

As much as she hated to admit it, Kelly knew her reluctance to accompany the marshal had very little to do with Carl and a lot to do with the raw-edged vulnerability she glimpsed in Spence Cantrell. Those haunted eyes rocked her to her soul and she knew she couldn't trust that. She couldn't.

Ever since Spence had agreed to this assignment two days ago, he had refused to think about Kelly Jackson. Trusting her neighbors' word that Kelly was due back any minute, Spence had issued a nationwide teletype on her vehicle. He'd managed not to think about her as he'd cooled his heels staking out her home and waiting for word on that teletype. Now, pulling out of the circle drive of the decades-old white farmhouse in Ryan, Texas, he knew by the hard squeeze in his chest that he'd never forgotten her.

Their first meeting eighteen months ago had lasted only an hour, and yet he didn't need the bright midday light sliding over her features to recall the high slash of molded cheekbones, the wide, expressive eyes that were as much blue as gray, the delicately boned nose, the silky tumble of mink brown hair.

He set his jaw. *Focus. Remember Hart, the hijacking.*

Spence and the other members of the hurriedly formed federal task force knew that at any moment Hart might start killing the marshals on board Flight 407 and maybe some of the other prisoners. As Spence waited for Kelly to return home, he hadn't been able to put that grim possibility out of his mind. Or ease the urgency crawling over

his skin. Even though the FBI was in charge of the operation, Spence itched to get back to Whiskey Springs. He'd
advised Special Agent Mason Taggart that Kelly was
scheduled to return from her vacation at any moment. It
was a good thing she had. Hart had issued a deadline for
producing his ex-wife: noon tomorrow.

He merged onto Highway 287 South and accelerated.
Little traffic traveled the state roadway today. At Vernon,
he would take US-183 South. They should easily make
Sam Houston International Airport in about two hours.

"I heard there was a tornado in Whiskey Springs,"
Kelly murmured, staring out her window as she had since
they'd left her house.

"Yeah." He glanced at her. "It took the airport out of
commission for a while, but the airport director is trying
to get things operational again."

She nodded, her thick, brown hair framing a fragile profile. Her vulnerability tugged at something inside him.

"I have a manifest of the passengers on our plane, along
with their pictures. I need you to take a look at those once
we get to Whiskey Springs."

"Is there a picture of Carl, too?"

"Yes." Spence couldn't miss the way fear sharpened
her features, turned her eyes a dusky gray. He told himself
his job was to focus on Hart, but his senses hummed with
every nervous tap of Kelly's finger against her leg. He
couldn't ignore the fact that every mile took her closer to
the man who terrified her.

She smelled soft, subtle, like wildflowers and powder.
Tantalizing. Annoying. Sitting so close to her unleashed
memories of another woman, a woman who would hold
his heart until he died. Spence shoved away the razor-sharp
images that clenched his gut and clouded his focus. He
couldn't think about Anna, not now.

"All right, I'll look at the pictures."

He forced his gaze to the road. Damn, it was hot in here. Wasn't it? Kelly didn't seem bothered, but Spence thought he could feel heat shimmering up from the floorboard. After flipping the air conditioner up another notch, he undid the second button on his now-limp dress shirt.

"Did Carl have any good buddies, relatives maybe, who could be helping him out now?"

"You mean, on the plane?"

"Or on the ground."

She thought for a moment, then shook her head. "He had a hundred cousins, aunts, uncles—you get the picture. Only a few of them came to our wedding. As for buddies, he was good at getting people to do what he wanted, but he was never that close to anybody."

"How did you meet him?" Spence asked soberly.

Kelly shifted and with her movement he caught the freshness of her shampoo, the silky warmth of woman. Her scent settled in his lungs. It had been years since he'd even noticed the scent of a woman. Something about her launched a frisson of restlessness through him and he didn't like it. He wanted to push her away, let someone else talk to her, but there was no one else.

"He was the president of the bank in Oklahoma City where I worked."

Spence could sense her reticence to talk, yet she did it anyway. Impressive as hell. "How long did you know him before you began to see each other?"

"A little over a month. He was very personable. I worked at his bank part-time during college so I knew who he was. Still, he didn't really notice me until I started as a full-time secretary."

"How did Hart approach you?"

"At first he would stop by my desk, tell me I was doing

a good job, but one night I stayed late and so did he. He said since his wife's death, he didn't have much reason to go home on time and we started talking. It went from there.''

"He asked you out?''

"Yes.''

"What was that like?''

"Actually, it was very nice. Carl can be a charmer… when he wants to. I wish I'd known that then." She swallowed hard, her gaze drifting to the horizon. Her fingers curled into a fist on her thigh. "He literally swept me off my feet. Wonderful dinners, surprise tickets to the theater, picnics, flowers. He was very attentive and I was totally snowed." She couldn't keep the bitter edge out of her voice.

Giving Kelly a minute, he let his gaze skim the new green of passing wheat fields, the knee-high corn plants. Angus and Hereford cattle were spots of black and red against the hills that flashed by the car window. "How long before you married?"

"From the time we met until the wedding, about four months. My mother always advocated long courtships. Now I know why." Kelly tried to smile, but he caught the pain in her eyes.

His voice softened. Despite his best efforts, his words came out husky, inviting. "When did the problems start?"

"I guess the first time was about two weeks after our wedding. We'd just gotten back from our honeymoon. It was little things at first. My clothes, then my hair. Then the house. They were never right. *I* was never right."

As far as Spence could tell, she was damn near perfect. His gaze slid over her, taking in the full breasts beneath her silky blue top, her lean thighs encased in the same

royal silk. When he lifted his gaze, she was watching him
steadily.

Something hot and electric passed between them, zinged
Spence right down to his toes. He dragged his gaze back
to the road. ''You quit your job at his bank?''

She chewed her bottom lip and looked out the window.
''After we married, I had to quit since he was the president. It was all right, though, because I'd just learned my
mom had systemic lupus and I wanted to take care of her.''

''What did Carl think of that?''

''It was fine with him. He didn't want me to work anyway, said it made people think he couldn't provide for me.
He paid for a lot of Mom's medical bills, but—'' She
broke off, her voice cracking. ''One day, I brought a dog
home from the shelter. Carl blew his temper.''

''He didn't like that you hadn't asked him first.''

''Right.'' She aimed a wobbly smile in his direction.
''You're getting his number a lot faster than I did.''

The same tight heat he'd felt on his first visit with Kelly
uncurled in his chest. Last time, he'd been blindsided.
He'd arrived with news of Hart's escape only a day after
Kelly had buried her mother. When Spence had informed
her she needed to gather her things and leave, she'd broken
down. Unable to turn away from the raw agony in her sobs,
he'd held her.

Holding her had been as much about steadying himself
as comforting her, but the resulting assault of pure, un-
diluted emotion had suffocated him. He hadn't felt anything in years, hadn't expected to since Anna, and suddenly a wall of compassion, loss, attraction had swallowed
him up like quicksand.

''He was so angry at me, he kicked the dog and—'' She
pressed trembling fingers to her mouth and Spence wanted

to reach across the seat, curl her hand into his. "That's when I left."

Her shaky voice tugged at something deep inside him, igniting…emotion. Spence didn't do emotion. He ran a hand over his face and made himself ask, "Was your dog the only one Carl hit?"

Shock and shame flashed across her features, then her expression tightened with defiance. She tore her gaze away and stared straight ahead. "I came back home, to Ryan. I filed for divorce. When Carl was served the papers, he came after me."

She slid a look at him, like a cornered suspect gauging her chances for escape.

Spence had read the trial transcripts, thanks to his uncle Vaughn, a federal judge. He knew that she'd testified Hart had hit her. He should press her about that, but he couldn't bring himself to do it. After a pregnant pause, he straightened. "He kidnapped you?"

Her movement was small, but he noted how she relaxed against the seat. "Yes."

"And since he took you across state lines, the feds handled it."

"Yes."

He needed for her to tell him about the abuse, needed to know she trusted him. Professionally speaking, of course. But something about Kelly Jackson reached inside him, touched places he'd thought long dead. Places that weren't professional at all and caused the memories he'd worked so hard to bury to surface. Despite his best efforts, thoughts of Anna—vivacious, vulnerable, sweet Anna—wound insidiously into his mind's eye.

He pushed away the images, took a deep breath and gathered his composure. He was damn good at his job, never let sentimentality cloud his judgment. So what was going on? His gaze touched on Kelly again before he dragged it back to the road.

Her skin was smooth velvet, her lips full and kissable—no. He shook his head to clear the thought, forced himself to recall his wife's beautiful face, bloody and battered beyond recognition. Her petite body, limp and broken. Smashed pottery, overturned drawers, scattered cutlery. She'd been barefoot.

Guilt twisted a rusty knife inside him. If only he'd taken Len Rattan's threats seriously. Threats were nothing new to Spence; he'd heard them countless times before, and over the fifteen years of his career no one had acted on them. Not once. Always the threats were ugly, but empty. Until Len Rattan.

Spence had never dreamed the two-time convicted felon would come after his wife, go on a vicious rampage with no purpose other than revenge. He had, with a vengeance.

One night after work, Spence had found Anna beaten unconscious in their kitchen. He'd never again looked into her beautiful, chocolate-brown eyes.

It was his fault she'd been beaten, his fault she'd died. All because of his job. Which was all he had left.

Stay focused, he told himself. Remember Carl Hart. Remember that Kelly Jackson is your job. Her fear moved him, her courage touched him. It shouldn't.

He'd gotten a lot of information, but he hadn't gotten it all. A frustration he rarely felt churned inside him. If he ever had any objectivity with this woman, he was losing it fast.

Chapter 2

After spending the day with Kelly, Spence knew, with a rising sense of panicked confusion, that his barriers were slipping. What was it about this woman that got to him? He simultaneously wanted to push Kelly away and get to know her better.

She was a material witness, not a woman. He had to remember that.

Six hours after they'd arrived by car at Sam Houston International Airport, Spence sat with Kelly in a suite of rooms at the newly constructed airport hotel the FBI had made into one of two working command centers. With the airport closed due to the tornado, stranded travelers had nearly filled the hotel. The task force had commandeered the last few vacant rooms, plus a suite big enough for the task force and all the communications equipment. If they needed to get to the terminal, it was less than a two-minute drive.

FBI Special Agent Mason Taggart had assigned the task

of questioning Kelly about her ex-husband to Special Agent Richard Zajak. In Spence's opinion, Kelly had been more than forthcoming. He'd told himself that in the chaos created by the hijacking, it would be easy to focus on the work, not Kelly Jackson. He'd been wrong.

From his chair against the wall, he slid a look at her, noting the fatigue that tightened her mouth, hollowed her cheeks. Tension wound like a new spring in his gut, across his shoulders. He knew why Zajak kept hammering at Kelly and he wanted to protest that forcing her to admit Hart had physically abused her wouldn't help them that much, but he was well aware they needed all the information she had.

Giving himself a mental shake, he ignored the way her scent slyly settled in his lungs like a sultry summer night. He rubbed the taut muscles in his neck and rose, needing to move.

"Was the trial the last contact you had with Hart?" Zajak's voice lashed the stuffy air in the suite like a whip.

Spence eyed Kelly, who sat at the rectangular conference table with her back to a curtained patio door. She'd sat in the same spot since they returned from dinner to the hotel command center at eight o'clock this evening. Through a slit in the drapes, stars winked in a dark sky.

Closing her eyes, she massaged her temple. "Yes. I've told you that three times."

Spence eased down on the edge of the table; restless energy and dissatisfaction spun through him. Despite the strong, unusual connection he felt to her, he'd insisted on sitting in on the FBI interview. He was glad he had, because he didn't like the way Taggart's man was handling it.

Spence tunneled a hand through his hair, then glanced at his watch. 9:35 p.m. It seemed like days since they'd eaten instead of two and a half hours. Through the last hour and a half of grueling, repetitive questions, Kelly had held out about Hart's abuse.

He thought he knew why she wouldn't admit to it. The shame that had crumpled her features so briefly when he'd asked her that same question in the car had twisted his heart. Spence knew Zajak pressed for the information so they'd know Kelly was cooperating one hundred percent.

"Do you think he was trying to mold you into the image of his first wife?" Zajak fired at her, his eyes hard.

"I have no idea. Because I was twenty-six to his fifty when we married, I know now Carl viewed me as a trophy wife, but I could never figure out if it had anything to do with her."

"How did she die?"

"Heart attack."

"What did you know about him before you married?"

"I *still* only know that his family owned the bank in Oklahoma City." Kelly rubbed her forehead and Spence couldn't ignore the strain in her face. "He'd worked there for twenty-something years. He and his first wife were married over twenty years. He was active in the community and his local church. He was a very affable boss. Nothing like the man behind closed doors."

"How affable?" Zajak's eyes narrowed. "Did he flirt with other women?"

Elbow propped on the table, Kelly rested her head wearily in her hand. "Was he having an affair, is that what you're asking?"

"Was he?"

She leaned forward, her hair falling in a dark curtain across her shoulder. Spence wanted to tuck the silky length behind her ear, smooth away the lines of worry that furrowed her brow. Distance, he reminded himself.

"No, I didn't suspect he had a mistress. No, I wasn't afraid I was going to lose my expensive home, my jewels, my car. That had nothing to do with my decision to leave.

"The local police thought I was a rich, spoiled wife giving her husband a hard time," she said bitterly, clearly conveying she thought the FBI believed the same.

Zajak was getting nowhere. And more importantly, Spence didn't like the harsh way the FBI agent barked every question at Kelly.

Pulling the manila folder containing the Flight 407 information toward him, Spence opened it. "Miss Jackson, would you look at this manifest and these pictures?"

Zajak started to speak, but Spence quelled him with a warning look. Disgust crossed the other man's buzz-saw features, but he turned away.

"All right," Kelly agreed in a voice that was slightly uneven. Apprehension turned her eyes the smoky blue of the sky before a storm.

Spence leaned forward to push the file over to her and his nostrils twitched as he inhaled her floral scent. He immediately drew back.

As she scanned the computer generated passenger list, her gaze faltered once. Maybe she'd seen Hart's name, Spence thought. Then, setting her shoulders, she laid the paper aside and began going through the pictures. Knowing that she would be able to differentiate the marshals' formal suits from the khaki pants and white T-shirts of the prisoners, Spence watched *her*.

Hesitating at one picture, she pushed it toward him. "He looks familiar."

His heartbeat kicked in anticipation as he glanced down at the steel-gray eyes of a dark-haired man. Could they finally have a lead? "That's Ryder Hamilton, used to own

Hamilton Oil and Gas. He's doing time for an oil lease scam.''

"Oh, I remember. The media made a big deal about his arrest."

Spence's heart sank and he pinched the bridge of his nose.

She returned her gaze to the photos. In the next second, she sucked in a quick breath and he saw terror pinch her serene features. She closed her eyes, as if fighting off a memory.

"Miss Jackson?" He waved Zajak off as he started forward.

"I'm okay." She opened her eyes. They were glassy with fear, her face ashen.

No one could fake that color-draining mixture of terror and determination. His gaze went to the picture of Hart that had caused such a reaction. What had that bastard done to her?

"Did you recognize any of those men?" he asked softly. "Perhaps one of them came into the bank while you worked there? Or maybe your home after you were married?"

"Carl. I only…recognized Carl," she said hoarsely. Still pale, she gripped the edge of the table. "And the man named Hamilton, but that was from television and newspapers."

Zajak leaned toward her. "Do you know a man named Don Post?"

Kelly shook her head and Spence straightened, frowning at the unfamiliar name.

"He's a cousin of Hart," the other man explained. "And was his accomplice on the ground. He was captured a few hours ago."

"So, that's how Hart got control of the plane," Spence muttered.

Zajak nodded. "Post is a member of the airport ground crew and he slipped a gun on board."

"Someone helped Carl do this?" Kelly asked, as horror streaked across her face.

"He would have to have help," Spence answered before turning to the FBI agent. "Did Post's capture rattle Hart?"

"Didn't seem to. He's sticking to his noon deadline. No exceptions."

"Damn."

Zajak turned back to Kelly. "Do you have anything to tell us about your ex-husband, Miss Jackson? Anything new?" He plucked up Carl's photo and waved it under her nose.

Defiant tears glittered in her tired eyes. "No, I have nothing new."

"Are you *sure?*" Zajak dropped the picture and picked up a sheaf of papers.

Dread razored into Spence's gut.

"Do you have a hearing problem, Agent Zajak?" she snapped. "I said no. I have nothing new to tell you."

Kelly seemed not to have a compromising bone in her body and Spence couldn't help the admiration that flared. Those soft looks hid a backbone of pure steel.

Zajak's voice cut into Spence's thoughts. "Did your husband abuse you, Miss Jackson?"

"He's my *ex*-husband."

"Did he hit you? Kick you, like he did your dog?"

Kelly's mouth flattened and she stared straight ahead.

Spence ran a hand over his burning eyes. He wanted to urge her to talk, to coax her, beg her—anything—to get the information out of her. He leaned forward. "Zajak, Miss Jackson is a witness, not a suspect."

"We don't really know *how* involved she is, do we?" the other man countered.

"She's not involved." Spence trusted his gut on that.

After a moment, Zajak nodded, his voice less tense. "I have a police report that says you never reported spousal abuse, yet you testified to it in open court. What's the real story?"

"Look at the 911 records," she said tiredly. "My mother called and reported it."

"It says here that Hart hit you."

Instincts prickling, Spence turned toward the other man. Logically, he knew they needed to peel away the layers, to see if they could get anything new on Hart, but Spence's muscles went rigid. His cautionary distance was fading by the minute.

Zajak looked down at the papers he held. "Did you say 'I should've left after the first time, but I believed he wouldn't do it again'? Doesn't that infer abuse?

"Didn't you testify that when you brought home your dog, Hart kicked her, then you. I quote—" Zajak's gaze dipped to the paper as he bombarded her with her words.

"—'He also kicked me because I was trying to protect the dog. He said it was an accident, that he hadn't meant to kick me, but I knew it would only get worse. That's when I left.'"

Kelly looked stricken. Her gaze, tortured and betrayed, sought Spence's.

Fury detonated inside him and he rose from the corner of the table, drawing a startled look from Kelly. He could barely keep a rein on the temper that was searing away his common sense.

"'He broke my finger,' you said. Cut your chin."

Spence's stomach knotted. "That's probably enough, Zajak."

"Question—'How did you get away from Hart?'" Zajak read from the transcript. "Miss Jackson answered, 'He brought a bowl of soup to my room. I threw it in his face and ran downstairs. I got him pretty good in the head with the butt-end of his rifle.' Did you testify to *that,* Miss Jackson?"

Spence wished *he* had the butt-end of a rifle right about now.

Kelly sat motionless, her face chalky. Devastated. A shudder ripped through her and seeing it loosed something dark and brutal inside Spence.

"You said your mother called the police," Zajak continued. "'He knocked me into the wall a couple of times, but the police arrived before he could do much more.'"

Spence's gaze drilled into the cold flint of Zajak's.

"Didn't you say 'I was such an idiot to believe him, but I filed charges after that. Then he went to prison.' Are those your words, Miss Jackson?"

Seething, Spence fisted his hands at his hips, wanting to call a halt, knowing this wasn't his call, but the protective instinct screaming through his body was undeniable. To his left, a crash sounded as a chair slammed into the patio door at Kelly's back and he whipped around.

She stood, eyes manic with desperation. Vivid color flagged her cheeks; her chest heaved. "Yes!" she said in a trembling half whisper. "Yes, those are my words. Yes, I testified to that. Yes, it's true."

Spence didn't want to hear, couldn't bear for her to go through it, but the lives of those men on Flight 407 might depend on any scrap of information about Hart. His gaze riveted on the raw shame in her face. Something hot and fierce burst in his chest.

Her voice gained strength and volume. Resentment glittered in her eyes as she faced Zajak with teeth bared. "It's not enough that you know everything about me! You want me to humiliate myself? You want me to tell you how he kicked me, how he yanked me up by the hair and slammed me into the wall, how I begged him to stop—''

Her voice broke. Her shoulders sagged. ''What can this possibly have to do with the hijacking?'' She momentarily covered her eyes with her hands, then dropped back into the chair she retrieved from its position at the patio door.

''Did he hit his first wife?'' Zajak asked quietly.

''I don't know. Based on my experience, I'd say yes,'' Kelly answered in a wobbly voice.

The defeat, the vulnerability in her posture ripped Spence right down the middle. Silence filled the room.

''It's all right.'' His heart squeezed hard. She shouldn't have to relive this with an audience. She wasn't going to. His gaze leveled into Zajak's. ''This is over. We all need to get some rest.''

''She's telling us what we want to know,'' Zajak argued.

''And I think you got it all,'' Spence said evenly. ''Let's clear out. We could all use a break.''

After a look at Kelly, Zajak tossed the transcripts on the table and walked to the door.

Spence followed him, stopping in the suite's open doorway.

Zajak turned. ''What's going on here, Cantrell?'' he asked in a low voice. ''You got a thing for her?''

''Don't be an ass.'' He glanced across the room to where Kelly sat, her face still cradled in one hand. ''I have a connection to her, is all. Don't screw up what little trust I've established.''

''Seems to be more than that to me.''

''Well, you're wrong. Which proves we're all too tired to think straight.'' He couldn't remember ever feeling such dark frustration and anger, didn't know if it was directed at Hart because of the way he'd abused Kelly or the agent in front of him.

The other man seemed to sense the fine line Spence walked. He held up his hands in supplication. "Sure, I'm going."

Spine rigid, Spence stepped back into the room and pushed the door shut behind him. Taking a few seconds, he tried to diffuse the fury that knotted his insides. Kelly's silent sobs tore at something deep inside him.

He didn't care if it was stupid. He couldn't stand seeing her like this. Walking across the room, he placed a hand on her shoulder.

She sobbed harder, still hiding her face.

"Kelly?" His voice sounded rusty, the words tight in his throat.

She shook her head.

Feeling useless and incompetent, he squeezed her shoulder, wanting to do more, not sure if he should. He eased down onto the table in front of her. "Kelly?"

"I didn't want to talk about that. Can't I forget? Aren't I entitled to that?"

"Yes. Yes, you are." He couldn't imagine having to tell a stranger about his deepest shame, his guilt over Anna. Operating purely on instinct, he cupped Kelly's elbow and pulled her gently to her feet. He pressed her head against his chest and just held her.

She stood stiffly within the circle of his arms, her hips warm and tight against the inside of his thighs. He ignored the low heavy pull in his groin.

She sobbed quietly against his chest for long moments. Hot tears wet his shirt and burned his skin through the damp fabric. Her breasts flattened against him as she finally relaxed, her body curving into his. Lithe, arousing, clutching at a place he'd thought long dead.

His mind hurtled back eighteen months to the first time he'd held her. He'd never forgotten how she felt—her firm thighs against the lean muscle of his, the way her hair tickled his chin. That haunting scent.

He'd dreamed about her for a solid week after that. Hot, erotic dreams that woke him, dry-throated, aching and hard. He'd buried that memory, along with the memories of his wife.

Unable to help himself, Spence rested his head on Kelly's and stroked her hair. He spoke softly, not conscious of what he said. After long moments, she let out a deep breath.

"I must be the queen of déjà vu," she mumbled against his chest. "I promise I don't make a habit of crying on men's shoulders. Crying, period."

Her wry reference to their first meeting curved Spence's lips and he chuckled. She was as emotionally strong as Anna. And they both had the same infuriating stubbornness.

Kelly looked up and smiled shyly, her warm breath drifting against his face.

Spence's heartbeat stuttered. Her mouth was close. So close that he could lower his head just a fraction and touch her lips with his. Taste her. Like he'd wanted to for months, he realized with a jolt. The sudden dilation of her pupils, the oh-so-slight parting of her lips told him she wanted it, too.

No. His muscles locked instantly against the idea.

But she, with a sense of wonder on her face that knotted Spence's gut, reached up and touched his lips. Her finger teased softly. Her breath mingled with his.

He closed his eyes, savoring her touch, yet hurting over it. He loved his wife; they'd had a great marriage. It had been three years since he'd felt anything for *any* woman.

Still, he wasn't going to kiss Kelly. He was going to pull back and—

Her lips brushed his.

Spence's arms reflexively tightened around her, pulling her into the V of his thighs. Fierce, savage need slashed through him, incinerating what little rational thought he had left.

She'd started this, but he quickly took control. Starving, aching. Cupping her bottom in his hands, he pressed her hard into him. His tongue dipped into her mouth, dark and rich like wine.

Hunger hooked into him with shattering force. He wanted to bury himself in her mouth, her body, to feel the cool glide of her skin against his. She wound her arms around his neck, matching him kiss for ravenous kiss.

Driving and desperate, he could not make himself release her. Until somehow a little needle of awareness pricked the bubble of sensation surrounding him. It hit Spence with the force of a body slam what he was doing.

"No." He dragged his lips from her, regret searing him. But was it regret for the kiss or for pulling away? He didn't know. "This isn't…" His voice was rough with need.

She drew back, the hurt in her eyes quickly masked by horrified realization. She touched her lips, moist and swollen from his and the gesture spurred another surge of desire through him. She nodded and stepped away.

He wanted to pull her back to him and his muscles tensed in reaction, but he let her go.

She walked to the door and opened it, her words low and wobbly. "I'll be in my room."

"Yes. Try to get some rest." He wasn't even sure that was his voice, but she nodded and disappeared into the hall.

Spence sat on the table, staring blindly out the window

at the shadowed debris littering the tornado-damaged air-field. Flat-out lust seared him from the inside out. His hands shook. So much for distance.

What in the hell was going on? Spence had no idea how long he sat there—minutes, maybe an hour—before he heard the click of the door. He turned as Mason Taggart walked into the interview room.

Rattled, his thoughts still scattered, Spence pushed up off the table. The hungry slide of Kelly's lips against his, the total surrender in her body still raked through him. He tried to shove the sensations away, focus on the weary-eyed FBI agent in front of him.

Taggart was a walking wrinkle even though he'd discarded his crumpled brown jacket. The sleeves of his limp white shirt were rolled nearly to his elbows. His pants were as crinkled as his face, but those brown eyes were sharp. Alert, despite the weariness dragging at his rounded features.

"Zajak briefed me on his interview with Miss Jackson. Do you agree she's told us all she knows?"

"Yeah." Spence ran a hand over the knotted muscles in his neck. He was glad to hear Zajak didn't want to lambaste Kelly again. "Zajak told us about Hart's accomplice. A cousin named Post."

"Yeah. Buchanan found the connection." The older man lowered himself into a chair, dipping into his ever-present paper bag of macadamia nuts. "Thought I'd bring you up to date. Hart's released eight more hostages in exchange for hot food. With the five he released to get the runway cleared, that brings us to thirteen. Only ninety-five to go. He's still demanding to see his ex by noon tomorrow."

"No." Spence planted his hands on his hips, trying to

think around the tantalizing memory of Kelly in his arms. He didn't know if Taggart would fight him on this, but he was prepared to go to the line if he had to. "I don't care if Hart promises to release the whole damn plane full of hostages. I don't want her near him."

Taggart stopped munching and squinted at him.

Spence hastily corrected, "I don't think it's a good idea. Too much of a threat. Do you know what this guy did to her?"

The other man nodded solemnly. "Bastard."

"On a good day," Spence snarled, wishing he could erase the feel of her body against his, the subtle scent of wildflowers that had invaded his lungs. "I promised she wouldn't have to get within a hundred yards of him."

"I think I can get some more hostages off the plane. I've got three snipers in place, but Hart has the window covers down. They can't even see inside. Agreeing to let him see Kelly might bring him into the open."

"No."

"Just let him see her. Not talk to her."

"No. Stall him. Tell him we're still trying to locate her vacation spot."

Taggart wadded the brown bag shut, a knowing look in his eyes. "Look, Cantrell, I appreciate the position you're in here. You gave your word. You've established trust with this woman."

And contact, Spence thought wryly.

"But we've got to get to this guy. The hostage negotiator is working Hart, but the man wants to see his ex-wife. That's the only reason he's agreeing to anything."

"The negotiator knows what to do. Tell him Kelly isn't an option."

"You know it doesn't work like that," Taggart said sadly. "Hart wants the runway cleared. We did that.

Cleared a portion of the taxiway, too. No sense just letting him drive out of here.''

"That's good."

"But we can only stall so long. Hart keeps volunteering to give up hostages. The negotiator is probably going to agree to let Hart see his ex-wife—"

"You better make it so he doesn't. I promised her."

"Hart's threatened to start killing marshals," Taggart said quietly.

Frustration clawed through Spence. He paced the length of the long conference table, then back, wanting to hit something, someone. Hart. "You should've seen her face when she looked at a picture of the guy. A picture, dammit! I thought she was going to pass out."

"I'm sorry about that, but she's got maximum protection. He can't do anything to her."

Spence hesitated, torn between his co-workers and the woman he'd started to care too much about. "We both know things don't always go as planned."

"They have so far," Taggart said tightly. "I appreciate where you're coming from, Cantrell, but we might have to play this out."

"Find a way that we don't have to."

Taggart's shoulders went rigid at being told how to do his job and Spence reined in his vehement determination. He shoved a hand through his hair. He was tired, frustrated. Damnably aroused. Still. "Please, Taggart. Try to keep Kelly out of it."

If Taggart thought anything about Spence calling Kelly by her first name or actually *pleading* her case, he didn't make any smart remarks like Zajak's. "If my snipers can't get a shot at him, I've got to send someone on board."

"How?" Spence rubbed his neck. "The only place Hart

can't see anyone is down by the cargo hold and there's no way to get from there to the passenger area."

A huge grin split Taggart's face. "I've got a crackerjack FAA Instructor pilot waiting in the wings who says different. Suzanne Delachek has logged more air miles than a flock of Canadian geese and she knows your 727 inside out. She can get a man on board."

Spence froze, adrenaline zipping through his veins. "Let me do it."

"One of the Hostage Rescue Team can do it."

"I'll go. Those are my men, my friends on that plane. And I'm the one who promised Kelly Jackson she wouldn't have to deal with this piece of scum."

It was suddenly worth life and death to keep his promise to Kelly. One woman had died because of his job. He wasn't going to lose another. He didn't know where the thought had come from. Kelly Jackson wasn't his. Still, he couldn't deny the sense of possession burning through him. "Hart doesn't know me. I can sneak on board that plane and take him out."

"We know he had an accomplice on the ground, but it appears he's working alone on the plane, keeping complete control."

Spence nodded. "I'll be careful."

"I don't know."

"Come on, Taggart. Think how good it'll look if our two agencies actually work together instead of both of us marking our territory."

Taggart grinned. "I've always thought cross-departmental politics were BS. All I care about is getting that SOB off the plane without killing anyone."

Spence nodded. He cared about that, too, but he was starting to care more about the woman whose courage still warmed a spot in his heart, the woman whose lips had

branded his. The woman who awakened feelings in him
he'd long ago tried to force out of his heart.

Taggart pushed out of the chair. "If we send you on
board, we'll still need to distract him."

"Surely there's a way we can do that without using
her."

The other man paused, then said quietly, "Maybe we
should let her decide."

No way in hell. But Spence kept his mouth shut. He
had no right to make that call, no rights to Kelly at all.

Taggart stared expectantly and finally Spence nodded.
"I'll tell her," he said through clenched teeth.

The FBI agent nodded and walked out. Spence pinched
the bridge of his nose, his body humming with need, frustration, resentment. He needed to tell Kelly about Hart's
deadline, ask if she'd be willing to see Carl, but he knew
she wouldn't. He didn't want to apply the slightest bit of
pressure about it either.

His need to see her, to reassure her was more than just
to comfort, more than lust. It was something he didn't want
to define. Kelly Jackson got to him in ways no woman had
since Anna. He didn't expect to find such love again, but
he still ached, physically and emotionally, from that kiss
with Kelly.

He couldn't keep her safe if he became emotionally involved with her. But he was afraid it was already too late.

Kelly stood in the middle of her hotel room, her legs
still weak from that devastating kiss with Spence. Wow.
The man was lethal. It wasn't just the way he kissed the
breath out of her, but his gentle ferocity literally made her
toes curl just thinking about it.

She closed her eyes, her belly quivering as she replayed
the hot seduction of his lips. It had been so long since

she'd trusted a man to hold her. So long since a man had held her with tenderness, wanted her with such fierceness. If one ever had.

Kelly could tell herself all she wanted that she'd learned her lesson about trusting people so quickly, so blindly, but that didn't change the fact that she trusted Spence Cantrell. His support against Agent Zajak had sealed that bond for her. No man had ever ridden to her rescue like that.

He was different than Carl. Kelly sensed it, felt it with everything in her, rotten instincts and all. She wished she'd met Spence under different circumstances, wished she knew what put the shadows in his sexy blue eyes.

If only she could forget why she was really here, forget why she'd seen him again, but she couldn't. Walking to the window, she pulled back the curtain and stared out into the settling night. Even in the darkness, the landscape looked as battered as she felt.

Carl was out there, closer than he'd been in years. Waiting for her. Wanting to see her.

A shudder ripped through Kelly and she dropped the curtain, moved back into the room. Why? What did Carl want with her? Why in the world would he hijack a plane, then demand to see her? She had no idea, but she knew it was for nothing good. A queasy lump of dread settled in her stomach.

Exhaustion peeled through her body. Her muscles felt soggy and lax; her eyes burned with fatigue, but she didn't want to go to sleep. For the first couple of months after she'd left Carl, she'd dreamed of his abuse. In her dreams, she ran and ran toward the door, but she could never reach it.

Apprehension and the knowledge that Carl was so near crumpled the shield she'd been able to maintain while awake. But asleep she knew she couldn't guard against the terror, the fear that waited below the surface to swallow her.

She washed her face and brushed her teeth. Watched television for a moment, but the only thing she could find besides the adult movie channel was nonstop coverage of the hijacking. She turned the set off.

Slipping off her shoes, she sank down on the small couch against one window and laid her head back. Staring at the white textured ceiling, she pushed away memories of Carl, tried to blank her mind. But the memory of that kiss with Spence taunted her. So what if she allowed herself to enjoy it? Earlier, fear, exhaustion and stress had toppled her carefully erected defenses like a charred fence. She couldn't allow that to happen again.

Her eyes fluttered shut as she let herself float through the memory of being in Spence's arms. Again she savored the solid strength in those arms, the gentleness in his hands. And his kiss. Hot and hungry, coaxing all resistance out of her...

Kelly succumbed to sleep.

Carl reached for her, his hands biting into her upper arms, bruising.

Never again. No one was ever going to hurt her again. She managed to get one of her arms free and she swung out. It took him by surprise and she pushed at his chest, panic bubbling to the surface. If he pinned her down, he would win.

Frantically, she slapped at him, trying to move off the couch where he had her trapped. Kicking out, she bucked beneath the heavy, masculine weight leaning over her.

"Kelly? Kelly, honey."

The deep voice startled her. It wasn't Carl's.

"Kelly, wake up."

She came awake with a start, twisting violently, trying to escape the arms now locked around her upper body. "Stop it! Stop! I—"

"It's all right. It's Spence. I've got you."

Spence? It all rushed back—where she was, why, who was with her. Choking back a sob, she turned into his chest. "Sorry. I hope I didn't hurt you. I thought—"

"I'm sorry I startled you. I was only trying to wake you."

"Is it over?" She could barely keep a rein on the fear that scraped along her nerves, leaving them raw and cold and numb. "Has Carl surrendered?"

"No, not yet."

She sagged against him. His arms tightened around her. As he settled more fully on the couch, he shifted her onto his lap. For a long moment, he simply held her. His breath teased the hair at her temple.

She knew she should stand up, put some distance between them, but that message was not getting to her legs. She snuggled into his broad powerful chest that at the moment seemed as if it could shelter her from anything.

"Thank you," she whispered.

He nodded, his lips brushing her temple, her cheek. She shifted, and became aware that he suddenly tensed. The muscles in his thighs, the oak-hard belly, his shoulders— all went rigid. And so did something else against her hip.

Her stomach hollowed. Fighting the instincts she'd worked so hard to ignore, she looked up. The hard glitter of desire and uncertainty in his blue eyes started a warmth between her legs. Ignited a longing that had been deeply buried.

"Kelly?"

In that hoarse muttering of her name, she heard everything he didn't say, everything he feared. Knew this was dangerous, unprofessional, incredible. She also knew she needed him in a way she'd never needed anyone before.

His lips brushed hers and his gentle invitation destroyed any distance she'd managed. With a tiny cry, she crushed her lips to his and wrapped her arms around his neck. Strong, warm, virile male pulsed beneath her hands. She melted into him, loving the feel of his solid chest against her breasts, his taut thighs beneath her bottom, his growing arousal against her hip.

Her whole life she'd wanted a man like this. A man whose touch ignited passion, not fear or disgust. A man who wanted her, but who didn't control her. A man like Spence.

She'd learned the hard way to listen to her head, not her heart, but his tongue stroked the resistance right out of her. She didn't want to stop. No matter how much she'd regret it later.

Chapter 3

Spence pulled back, breathing hard. Knocked off-balance by the desire that slammed through him, he shook his head, cupped her shoulders to push her away.

"Spence?"

When she said his name, he felt things he couldn't explain.

"Please tell me you're not married."

"Not married." The invitation in her dusky blue eyes incinerated every bit of common sense he had. Something big and unexpected was happening here and he couldn't walk away.

He hooked an arm around her waist and took her lips again. Fiercely, hungrily, an unfamiliar desperation raking through him.

"This is crazy," he groaned.

"Yes." She kissed him back.

"And unprofessional."

"Yes."

"We should probably stop." He rained kisses on her cheeks, her nose, her forehead before coming back to her mouth.

"Yes," she breathed when they broke apart. "We should stop. We can. *Can't* we?"

Her fingers tunneled through his hair. Just the thought of walking away from her filled Spence with regret, but he needed to remember why he was here. "Kelly—"

"I know." Her hand grazed his hair as she stood. "You're right."

The ragged disappointment in her voice didn't do a damn thing for his resolve. He curled his hands into fists and rose as well, jamming his hands into his pockets to keep from reaching for her. "Are you okay?"

He wasn't sure if he meant as a result of the kiss or the nightmare he'd woken her from.

"Yes." She pushed a few silky wisps of hair out of her eyes. "Has something new happened?"

"Yes. Hart has demanded to see you. By noon tomorrow."

She paled. "Or what?"

He didn't want to tell her. "Kelly—"

"He's going to kill someone."

"Yes," Spence said simply. "Marshals." His muscles locked against the urge to take her into his arms and say to hell with everything.

She turned toward him, avoiding his gaze. He couldn't help but notice that her breasts still rose and fell rapidly. His own heartbeat was off the charts. He cleared his throat. "Taggart's got three snipers in place, but so far they can't get a shot at Hart."

She stilled, those blue eyes trained intently on him.

"He's keeping the window covers down on the plane

and when he shows himself in the cockpit, he's got the pilot or copilot in front of him.''

"Snipers," she murmured.

Fueled by the restless energy surging through his body, the want thrumming like rapid gunfire, he moved around the room.

"So what next?"

"Taggart's going to send someone on board to take Hart out, but to do that he needs a distraction."

"Is he sending only one of his men?" Her voice rose. "You said yourself that Carl could have an accomplice on the plane, too."

"He could. It's risky," Spence admitted, watching her carefully, his lips still burning from hers. "But someone needs to be able to get to him."

"Can't Taggart send more than one man?"

"We have to be careful not to draw too much attention to the maneuver. Carl's demanded more hot food and fuel so I can ride out with the food truck."

"You!" She took a step toward him. "You! Why you?"

"Those men are my friends and…I made you a promise." He stopped, his body rigid, hoping she didn't come closer, needing the distance they'd established.

"But you're risking your life!"

"I'm trained."

"Spence." She shook her head, visibly upset. His heart cracked a little at her concern. "And Taggart wants me to distract Carl while you board the plane?"

"He wants me to ask you." Spence rubbed his neck. "But I told him no, that I promised you that you wouldn't have to get near Hart."

"I can't." Panic darkened her eyes. She moved toward the bed, then toward the window, as if trapped.

Spence ached to reach out to her, but caution held him back. "I gave you my word and I want to keep it."

"What will happen if I don't meet Carl?"

"Taggart will try to come up with another plan."

"What about those guys on board?" Tears welled in her eyes. "I don't think I can do it. What is Carl doing? What does he want?"

Spence could hear the rising panic in her rushed words. "It's okay, Kelly. It's okay." To hell with distance. He snagged her elbow, turned her toward him. "We'll get the bastard. You don't have to see him. We can dress up a policewoman to look like you. By the time Hart figures it out, I'll be on board."

"I just want this to be over. He's ruined enough of my life. Now look what he's doing to those other people." She angrily wiped away a tear. "I'm so tired of him controlling my life, of being afraid of him, but I can't help it." Her voice broke.

The tightrope of stress and anxiety they'd walked all day snapped. Spence pulled her close and angled one arm across her back, surprised at how the feel of her eased something frantic in him.

She lifted her head, her eyes shimmering pools of blue. "Why couldn't I have met you first?" As soon as the words left her mouth, she closed her eyes. "I'm sorry. I shouldn't have said that."

"It's all right." He curled a finger under her chin and lifted her head, losing himself in her eyes. The floor beneath him cracked like thin ice. Watch it, Cantrell. You're about to go under.

A hundred warnings screamed through his brain, but for once he didn't listen. "That would've been nice," he murmured, his thumb grazing her bottom lip.

She smiled up at him. "Really?"

''Really.'' How in the hell had he thought he could ever resist her? ''I know you don't trust easily, Kelly, but you can trust me.''

''I do,'' she whispered, her breasts teasing his chest, her thighs hot against his.

This time when he lowered his head, he knew full well what he was doing. And when her lips parted beneath his, he knew he couldn't stop. Wouldn't.

He only wanted to feel. The way her hair tickled his wrist, the way her lips opened hot and wet under his, the way her hands moved over him with the same near-desperation rushing through him.

For once he shut off his thoughts and just *felt*. The hot velvet of her tongue. The press of her breasts, the eager way she held him to her. If she thought he was strong enough to walk away, she was wrong.

He hooked an arm around her waist. His other hand skimmed the length of her back, curved over her hip and he palmed one round, firm cheek. She made a low sound, both surrender and invitation. At once he felt a release and a tightening low in his gut.

''Are you sure?'' he whispered. For both their sakes, she should say no. That one word from her was the only thing that could stop him from peeling the clothes from her luscious body and sliding into her the way he ached to do.

''Yes,'' she breathed into his mouth. ''Yes. So sure.''

He pulled back, searched her eyes as he stroked a stray strand of hair from her cheek and tucked it behind her ear.

She slid her hands up his arms, onto his neck. The feel of her lean, warm fingers on his skin plucked at his nerve endings. Had he *ever* felt like this? As if he was teetering on the edge of reason and sin.

''I don't want to stop,'' she said in a low voice, her

gaze fixed on his mouth, making his heartbeat skitter wildly. "I want you."

He hauled her to him, his blood pounding at the feel of her full breasts cushioned against his chest, the V of her thighs nudging his arousal. Desire knifed through him, sharp, driving.

The horrible life she'd endured with Hart hovered in the back of his mind. Spence wanted to make it good for her, especially if Hart had treated her in the bedroom the way he'd treated her outside of it. Spence was glad she didn't appear afraid of him.

He raised his head, his heartbeat thundering in his ears. Framing her face in his shaking hands, he skimmed his thumbs over her lips, the satiny line of her jaw. Her eyes darkened with hunger, the same hunger that gnawed at him. But he wanted to go slow. They had time, at least three or four hours while Taggart worked on Hart.

"I won't break," she breathed. Her hands massaged his upper arms, kneading, petting, as she pressed her body full into his.

His smile was wobbly. Swinging her up into his arms, he walked the few steps to the bed and laid her gently atop the pastel-striped cover. Her hands went to the buttons on his shirt and he helped her, shrugging it onto the floor as he leaned over her.

She splayed her hands on his chest, ran them over his pecs and through the hair on his chest. The pleasure that spread across her delicate features tugged at his heart. For a minute, he let her touch him while the anticipation coiled his muscles even tighter.

"I don't want to go too fast or scare you."

She took his face in her hands, her gaze burning into his. "I know who you are, Spence."

She pulled his head down for a kiss, her tongue tangling

with his. Shifting beneath him, she dragged her nails down his back, making him shudder when they skimmed lightly over his flanks. "Clothes," she said huskily. "Take them off."

He raised himself up, fumbling with the small silk-covered buttons on her top, helping her slide the blouse off, then dragging his palm down the velvet of her belly, pushing off the slender silk slacks. Her skin was creamy soft beneath his rough palm. He wanted to taste her.

He could see her pulse beating rapidly in her throat. Pressing his lips there, he rained kisses down to the curve of her breasts that swelled over the top of a barely there lace bra. The urge to rip her panties off and bury himself to the hilt slammed into him. But he wanted to savor this, wanted to know what she wanted, what she needed.

"Tell me how to touch you."

"Just like you are." She took his face in her hands, lifted his face to hers. "Only more."

He kissed her again, drinking from her with a thirst he couldn't imagine ever quenching. Her hands were greedy, something he'd never experienced. It made it difficult to remember that he should go slow.

"You won't hurt me. You couldn't."

"I want it to be good for you."

"It is. It will be." She smiled into his eyes, her hand sliding between them and reaching down to cover his arousal.

His stomach hollowed as she scraped her fingernails along his length. Rolling to his back, he took her with him and lay, muscles whipped tight, as she unzipped his slacks. The whisper slight feel of her hands grazing his arousal pitched his blood to boiling.

He ran his hands up her sides, cupped her satin and lace covered breasts in his palms. She closed her eyes and arched, hot and damp and hard against his erection. He thumbed open the hook on the front of her bra and pushed it off her shoulders, his hands filling with warm, soft flesh. Her nipples were rosy dark and tight. He pulled her forward, taking one in his mouth.

She cried out, holding his head.

"Yes?" He smiled against her breast.

"Yes, Spence. Yes. More."

The way she purred his name had him rocking up against the core of her, wet, hot, ready for him. He wanted to let her call the shots this first time, but he was nearing the edge. Need, urgent and merciless, drove through him like a spike, pushing him closer, closer to a rocky ledge. Still, he was determined to wait for her.

He kneaded her breasts, squeezing, rolling, laving the tips with his tongue. She shifted atop him and her panties landed somewhere near his head. Then her hands were pushing down his slacks, his boxers. Her hand closed over his arousal, throbbing, pulsing in her hand. Spence closed his eyes, fisting the sheets as he savored the feel of her quick hands, then her tongue.

"Kelly, honey, slow down."

"But I want—"

"Me, too." He reached for her, pulling her up, gently turning their bodies so he was once again on top. "I'm on the edge. Don't you want to wait a little longer?"

"No." She stared straight into his eyes, her hands sliding over him, caressing, touching, moving over his back, his arms, his butt. As if she couldn't get enough. "I want you, Spence," she whispered. "I've waited my whole life to say that to a man. I want you now."

He didn't need to hear anything else. Settling into the V of her thighs, he eased inside. That first tight slide had them both catching their breaths. Her hands tightened on his shoulders, moved to wrap around him as she urged him in. She arched her head, baring her throat to him and he bit lightly on the place where her collarbone joined her neck. She wiggled, pulling him deeper, her legs going tight around him.

He lifted his head. "Tell me."

A breath shuddered out of her as she opened those beautiful eyes and stared into his. "Slow and long." A shy smile touched her lips. "Is that all right?"

"It's perfect." He slid deep, fitting his arms under her, stroking in and out of her body with a deliberation that had his muscles quivering, his own body screaming for release, but the look on her face made his wait more than worthwhile.

Euphoria flushed her skin. She stared into his eyes and he swore he was drowning, going down into a well of love where he'd never been before. His throat tightened even as his body did the same. In and out, long, gliding strokes, holding out as long as he could, waiting for her to peak first. And when she did, when she cried his name in a voice raspy with wonder, he let go, pulling her tighter into him, pumping into her with a frantic control.

When his world exploded, her name erupted from his throat.

She tightened her arms around him, her breath warm in his ear. "Thank you, Spence. Thank you."

He lifted his head and smiled down at her. "That goes both ways."

She smiled and they lay there as their bodies cooled. The doubts he'd refused to heed before began to filter in. What had he done? He was involved with Kelly Jackson. Hell, more than involved. He felt something for her, something that might affect his ability to protect her. Trying to soothe her after he'd startled her out of that nightmare about Hart had taken a completely unexpected turn for Spence, but he didn't regret it.

A rush of emotion flooded him—blatant male satisfaction at what he'd just shared with the woman beside him, relief that he welcomed it, and a growing sense of possession. He was no longer able to remain professionally detached, if he ever had been. The first time he'd met her, she'd penetrated the wall he'd built around himself.

He'd never believed in love at first sight, had heard of people meeting and immediately knowing they were meant to be together. His own parents' forty-year marriage had begun after a three-week courtship, but Spence had never bought into it. He couldn't argue since it had worked for his parents, but he'd always thought himself too pragmatic for such romanticism.

He and Anna had been friends first, then it had grown into a strong, unshakable love. Could what he felt for Kelly morph into that?

Spence didn't know. He didn't know a hell of a lot right now. Deliberately he turned his thoughts to the hijacking, to the reason he'd originally come to her room. There was no way Kelly would agree to meet Hart, and Spence knew he couldn't force her. Not after what Hart had done to her. Not after what she and Spence had just shared.

Morning, Day 4

Kelly lay there, Spence's skin hot and supple against hers. She couldn't remember ever being so satisfied, so perfectly matched. She snuggled closer to him, smiling at the steady thrum of his heart beneath her ear. She ran her fingers over his belly in a light circle.

"You all right?" he asked.

"Yes." What had they done? Kelly pushed the little doubt away. She'd wanted this, wanted to enjoy the way

Spence made her feel beautiful and desirable. And she wanted to enjoy this sense of belonging as long as possible.

He knew all about her ugly marriage and she knew next to nothing about him. Sliding a leg between his, she pressed a kiss to his hard, warm chest. "Spence, have you ever been married?"

His arm tightened reflexively around her, his thumb stroking the soft underside of her breast. "Yes."

"You don't have to tell me."

"I want to." He paused. "Her name was Anna."

Kelly turned on her stomach, searching the turbulent shadows in his eyes. "What happened?"

"She was killed," he said flatly. "By a man I'd put in prison."

Kelly drew back at the way his jaw tightened, the emotionless way he'd spoken. Horror and concern mingled. "What happened?"

"After the scumball got out, he came after me. He made threats, but someone was always threatening me." His lips twisted in a grim smile. "I ignored them, until the night I came home to find Anna on the kitchen floor."

His voice turned rusty as he told Kelly how he'd found his wife, beaten unconscious and how she'd never come out of the coma. "She died after two weeks. Because of my job."

"You can't blame yourself." Kelly lifted up on one elbow. "That wasn't your fault, Spence."

He stared blankly at the opposite wall. Kelly wasn't sure if he was talking to her or himself. "It sure wasn't anyone else's and I did blame myself for a long time. I don't anymore, but I regret things. My arrogance, for one. The future we lost. It's been three years since I even thought my future might be something other than the job."

His gaze shifted to hers, deep and thoughtful. He ran

his thumb across her lips, still tingling from his, and her heart clenched at the naked pain in his eyes.

"Did she know you loved her?"

His gaze leveled into hers. "Yes."

"My mother knew I loved her, too. She was sick for a long time and I took care of her." Laying her head back down on his chest, she told him how her mother had suffered with systemic lupus, how Carl paid the bills for her mother's medical needs, but always held it over their heads.

"I felt completely helpless. There was nothing I could do, nothing I could change, but I take comfort in the fact I was with her at the end, that she knew I loved her. I take comfort in those things because they're all I have." She reached up and stroked his hair. "That's all you have, too. Anna knew you loved her, knew you would've given your life for her."

"I would've."

A comfortable silence settled between them before she asked, "How did you meet? Do you mind me asking?"

"No." He squeezed her against him. "We met in college. Dated each other's roommates, then each other."

Kelly wondered if he was aware of the smile in his voice as he talked.

"We were friends first, then fell in love."

Hearing him talk about Anna sent realization knifing through her. Spence and his wife had built a relationship over time, shared experiences, trials, years. Kelly had a relationship with Spence, but was it sex only?

Despite the sharp stab to her heart at the description, wasn't that what it was between them? She'd known him such a short amount of time, how could it be anything else? "You and Anna were soul mates."

"I guess so."

"That kind of love comes along once in a lifetime,"

she said sadly, suddenly wanting to get up, to ask Spence to leave. But she didn't want to hurt him.

"That's what I've always thought," his voice rumbled in her ear.

Hearing about his long courtship, the woman who'd been his best friend and his lover brought slamming home to Kelly how quickly things had moved between them, how quickly *she* had tumbled into bed with him. Even with Carl, she'd never done that. She'd never wanted to share everything with Carl, never wanted to surrender completely the way she did with Spence. It made her sick.

What had she done? Would she never learn? Panic rose in her throat, choking her. She sat up, ignoring the concern in Spence's eyes as he pushed himself to his elbows.

"Kelly?"

"Just want to take a shower." Dragging the light spread from the bed, she wrapped it around her, fighting the urge to stuff her fist in her mouth to keep from crying.

"I'm sorry I went on that way."

"Nonsense. I asked you." So what was her problem? Why did she suddenly feel as if her breath were slowly being squeezed out? "I'll just be a second. You don't have to stay."

She heard him get out of bed. "Kelly, honey—"

"It's all right, Spence." Her voice cracked and she hurried to the bathroom.

He caught her at the door, turning her. "Hey." He nudged her chin up. "I don't make a habit of this. In fact, I've never done this."

She didn't need the flush spreading down his neck to know he was telling the truth. "I know." Which somehow made her even more sad.

He gently fingered a strand of her hair, his knuckle grazing her bare collarbone. "I care about you, as crazy as that sounds." His laugh sounded as hollow and uncertain as she felt. "I know it's been fast and all. Hell, my head's still spinning."

She was afraid she was going to cry. Or scream. Her nerves were stretched taut, humming at a numbing pitch. "This is a weird situation," she said carefully, not wanting to hurt him, but feeling suffocated. And stupid. "I took comfort from you and I appreciate it. Maybe we should leave it at that."

"Maybe." He sounded doubtful.

So was she. The air turned thick, pressed in on her. She reeled with the need to get away. She retreated a step, forcing him to release her hair. "I'd better…take that shower."

He nodded, his eyes dark and shuttered against her now. It broke her heart. She tried to ignore that. And the way her skin still burned with his touch. She gave him a shaky smile and shut the door. Bowing her head against the hard wood, she sucked in a deep breath. Cold sweat dappled her skin.

She waited for him to try the knob, but he didn't.

She was glad. No, she wasn't. Dropping the bedspread, she stepped into the tub and turned on the shower, yanking the curtain closed. Nausea rolled over her in a wave and she braced her hands against the tile, hanging her head.

She blanked her mind, refusing to remember how wonderful it felt to be in his arms, refusing to relive the moment she'd realized that she would gladly surrender anything to Spence. Suddenly she couldn't imagine her life without Spence and that made her angry. She'd fought so hard never to need a man again. Well, she could look at it nine ways from Sunday, but for now she needed Spence. She just had to remember it was only for now.

She stayed in the shower until the blistering water turned tepid. Her hands and feet were wrinkled. Cautiously, she opened the door, hoping he was gone.

He was.

Spence had given her some space, which was what she wanted. So why did she feel as if she'd been kicked in the teeth?

Wrapped in a towel, she sank down on the edge of the bed, surrounded by the mingled scents of their bodies, singling out the spicy scent that was Spence. Her wet hair chilled her bare shoulders. The air conditioner hummed low around her. She was very much afraid she was falling in love with Spence Cantrell, had *already* fallen in love with him.

She closed her eyes against the thought, unable to bear thinking it. It was too fast. Insanely fast. She'd fallen this hard and fast once before; she couldn't afford to do it again. Her heart knew Spence was different than Carl, but even so, where did they go after this? After Carl was captured and sent back to prison. *If* Carl was captured.

She'd been wrong about her feelings before. Was she wrong this time? Had she just made another mistake? Or ruined the best thing that had ever happened to her?

A few hours later, Spence lay in the bed in his own hotel room and stared at the ceiling. Kelly had been shaken by their lovemaking. Hell, so had he, but why had she practically kicked him out? Maybe it was her fear of Hart. Knowing the guy was just across the airfield had to wind her nerves into a knot.

Spence wished he could take away her fear, settle her the same way she'd settled him. She hadn't provided just a much-needed physical release; she'd tripped some emotional trigger inside him. Emotion flooded in, and this time he let it roll over him.

His senses focused with the precision of a laser. His body was sated, but so was his mind. A strange, unfamiliar peace had seeped in, peace he hadn't even realized he'd been missing. And he felt a sense of purpose for the first time in years, something besides just going through the motions.

Oh, yeah, just the thought of his body buried in hers, the tight, secret way her body gripped him made him hard, but it was more than that. Making love with her had shaken him deep inside where he guarded the well of his strength and the most precious of his memories, where he'd built his carefully erected wall brick by scarred brick. She'd penetrated that wall and he couldn't imagine his life without her.

Spence knew that what he felt for her was real. No matter how long he'd known her, his gut told him she was the woman for him and he didn't want to let her get away. The fear in her eyes had unlocked something in him, but it was her courage, her strength that nudged the lock open.

He knew they'd met under unsavory circumstances, knew their emotions were heightened by the hijacking, but that didn't explain why he had this insane urge to wake up next to her every day for the rest of his life. It had happened fast. It made no sense, but there was no denying it.

Spence had fallen for her. What was he going to do about it? He had no idea, but he wanted to reassure her that they hadn't made a mistake by making love, that *she* hadn't made one.

If her feelings right now were anything similar to his, she felt as if she faced the edge of a cliff, surrounded on all sides, pressured to make a split-second decision. Maybe they could do it together.

Remembering the panic that had sharpened her features before he'd left this morning, Spence knew he needed to see her. Needed to let her know that she could trust him. Needed to let her know that when he boarded Flight 407, he had every intention of taking down Hart and coming back to explore what had exploded between him and Kelly a few hours ago.

Foregoing a shave in preparation for his future masquerade as a prisoner, he took a quick shower, brushed his teeth and put on fresh clothes, then started across the hall for Kelly's room.

He gave a sharp rap on her door.

"Cantrell!"

Spence turned to see Taggart moving purposefully toward him, still looking as rumpled and red-eyed as he had last night.

"She in there?" He cocked his head toward Kelly's door.

"I just knocked." Spence raised his hand to knock again, but she opened the door.

Wariness joined the fatigue that hollowed her features. Her gaze shot from Spence to Taggart. "What's happened?"

"Just wanted to give you both a status report," Taggart said.

Kelly nodded and stepped back in silent invitation for them to enter.

Spence's nerves hummed and it wasn't just the fresh soap scent of Kelly curling around him or the memory of being buried deep inside her. The urgency and leashed tension in Taggart's voice had Spence's muscles coiling.

Kelly left the door open and moved into the room. "What is it?"

"Airport Director Logan has a temporary tower in place and she's cleared both runways of debris. At my request, she left some debris on the taxiway that leads to the runway Hart wants to use."

Taggart paused to see if Kelly was following. Spence thought she was probably following all too well.

After she nodded, the FBI agent continued, "Now,

Hart's demanding enough fuel to fill all the tanks and that we clear the taxiway completely. I've gotten him to agree to release eleven hostages in exchange for the fuel and ten more for removing the last of the debris from the taxiway. Once we clear that taxiway, he'll be able to take off. If it comes to that, we've got a chase plane in place off the east runway, out of Hart's sight. My snipers can't get a shot at the SOB, but I think my plan of sending Spence on board while you're distracting Hart might work. We could put this thing to bed." His gaze slid to Spence. "I take it you asked Miz Jackson if she'd agree to be our distraction?"

"Yes." At his sides, Spence's hands curled into fists. "That's not an option."

Taggart glanced at him, then fixed his gaze on Kelly. "I can stall Hart another couple of hours, but that's probably it. I told him you were on your way from Ryan, and he said you'd better make that noon deadline. He's agreed to release twenty-five additional hostages if you'll meet him face to face. That gets fifty-nine people off the plane. We'll outfit you with body armor, put you behind a bulletproof shield. He won't be able to hurt you."

"You'll have to send a policewoman," Spence bit out. "Kelly's not going."

"Yes," she said hoarsely, staring at Taggart. Her eyes were huge in her chalky face. "Yes, I will."

Shock hit Spence like shrapnel. "What! No, you're not. We talked about this."

Her gaze shifted to his. He saw pure terror in the soft blue depths, but he also saw a steely resolve. "Yes."

Chapter 4

In the end, Kelly managed to overcome Spence's objections, convincing him that facing Carl was something she had to do. He reminded himself of that as the two of them silently walked out of the hotel with Taggart and over to the airport. The sun was nearly straight overhead in a calm blue sky that belied the churning tension surrounding them. They had an hour before the noon deadline Hart had set. An hour that Spence wished he could spend alone with Kelly, but time was too tight.

He took her to Airport Director Christine Logan's office, his jaw clenching when Kelly gave him a long look before disappearing into Logan's private rest room with two female FBI agents who would outfit her with body armor, a riot helmet and a bulletproof shield.

The time for objections was past, he knew, but that didn't stop the frustration, the resentment boiling inside him as he strode to the nearby elevator and punched the down button. Thanks to Taggart's timely visit, Spence hadn't been able to find out if Kelly was all right about last night. She'd needed room and so had he, but now?

And never mind about telling her she could watch everything from a safe distance. She was about to be face to face with Hart.

Reaching ground level, Spence strode to the ramp that would take him outside, his shoes clicking sharply against the waxed tiles. The mobile home that housed the FBI's command center was some distance from the terminal in the safety zone around the hijacked plane.

Sliding behind the wheel of his marshal's sedan, he drove away from the terminal. He wanted to stand beside Kelly as she faced the man who'd put her through such hell, but he'd seen a determined strength blazing in her blue eyes. The woman had guts, no doubt about it. And, he told himself, she'd be all right. She'd be surrounded by half the Hostage Rescue Team.

After parking behind the command center, he pulled open the door to the mobile home and stepped inside, trying to focus on his upcoming strategy session with Agent Taggart and Suzanne Delachek. But Kelly was a piece of every breath he took, an ache in every move he made. Despite the way adrenaline zinged through him, he knew he had to strip away all that and concentrate on boarding Flight 407 to take Hart down before he could do any more damage, to Kelly or anyone else.

The mobile home was a nest of humming activity and several degrees cooler than the pleasant spring temperature outdoors to keep the equipment at optimum operating capacity. Besides allowing the FBI to visually monitor the plane and be on the spot in an instant if Hart tried something, this unit was a self-contained home-away-from-home with a small kitchen and rest rooms.

Along one wall were monitors showing the plane from

every conceivable angle. Technicians sat in front of the screens, murmuring into headsets. The other wall boasted more high-tech communications equipment than Spence had seen in a James Bond movie. The stale scent of left-over take-out hovered in the air along with the smell of too many bodies crammed together for far too long.

Receivers and transmitters clicked, hooked into frequencies with the snipers, the Hostage Rescue Team leader, the FBI radios and even one for Quinn Buchanan, captain over the Whiskey Springs Police Department's airport division. People hustled around Spence with quick efficiency.

"Down here, Cantrell." Taggart hailed him from a small table at the opposite end of the trailer.

A leggy blonde stood beside Taggart, a roll of paper stuffed under her arm.

Spence maneuvered his way between back-to-back chairs and tried to push thoughts of Kelly out of his mind. Tried to leash the protectiveness that bordered on possession, tried to calm the swirling fury of emotion inside him. Do the job. Stop Hart before Kelly has to get within fifty feet of that plane.

"Marshal Spence Cantrell, this is Suzanne Delachek." Taggart indicated the woman whose neat appearance and sleekly pinned up silver-blond hair made the FBI agent look even more rumpled. "She's the Senior Instructor pilot for the FAA. She can fly just about anything but a camel."

"Hello, Marshal Cantrell." Her cool blue eyes crinkled as she grinned and shook Spence's hand.

"Spence is fine." He liked her firm handshake and the sharp intelligence that glittered in her eyes.

"Spence is going on board to take down Hart." Taggart crumpled his brown paper bag, now empty of macadamia nuts, into a ball and tossed it into a corner wastebasket.

"I told him you're the one who knows just how to do that."

"Sure thing." With swift precision, Suzanne whipped the roll of papers from under her arm and spread them on the small table in front of them. "These are the blueprints for your 727. What you want to do is go up through the cargo hold."

Spence tried to strip away all but Delachek's expert instruction and his own immediate purpose of getting on Flight 407, but deep down, like the insistent flow of a river, thoughts of Kelly brushed back and forth across his mind. He could—*would*—deal with what was necessary until he was able to get back to her, look into her eyes and convince her there was something special between them, something that needed exploring.

"See these inspection plates in the cargo hold?" Suzanne asked. When Spence nodded, she said, "Take these off to get through to the passenger area. There will be one when you board and one just before you reach the belly of the plane, where you'll need to come up."

"How do I do that? Screwdriver or wrench?"

"Wrench is better. I'd say a Dagen wrench. It's also got a socket end, if you need it."

Spence nodded, making a mental note to call maintenance for the tool when he left here to change clothes.

"We'll be using a Gulfstream III jet as a chase plane," Taggart said. "*If* Hart gets 407 off the ground. Miss Delachek will be on board and so will I, along with backup agents."

Suzanne put in, "We can keep 407 on radar, but stay out of sight."

Spence nodded.

"Even though we have a backup plan, let's try to cut Hart off at the pass." Taggart glanced out the window where the hijacked plane sat without activity at the moment.

"I'll do my best," Spence said. "How many men are you planning to send out with Kelly?"

He thought he saw a flicker of speculation in Delachek's eyes at his mention of Kelly, but he was more interested in Taggart's plans.

"Six. Hart's demanding that she walk out alone."

Spence bit back the curse that rose to his lips. From now on, his job was to try to get to Hart before Kelly did. "I'll take the wrench. I'll also take the handcuff keys and slip them to the marshals." He scratched at his three-day growth of whiskers, wishing for a shave, but if he wanted to blend in with the prisoners on 407, the scruffier he looked, the better. His face itched, his nerves twanged. He was ready to get this finished.

"Thanks," he said to Suzanne before turning to Taggart. "I'll change into the same white T-shirt and khaki pants the prisoners are wearing."

The other man nodded. "According to the hostages released so far, Hart is keeping all the convicts chained up."

"Ah." Spence arched an eyebrow. "He doesn't know who to trust."

"Right," Taggart confirmed. "They never hold prisoners in the prison transfer center long enough for them to get to know each other. Hart's also moved everyone closer to the front of the plane so he can keep an eye on them all."

"So I need to stay behind them," Spence strategized aloud. "We're going to need some weapons loaded onto that food cart. I don't want my men outgunned."

"What about the weapons sensor?" Taggart's beeper sounded and he held up a finger while he reached over and picked up a cell phone, speaking in a low tone.

"You can deactivate that when you remove the inspection plate." Suzanne again unrolled her blueprints, pointed to the drawing of a small box inside the crawlway to the passenger area. "You should be able to get on without raising Hart's suspicions. Like most people, he probably won't think there's any way to enter the passenger compartment from the cargo hold."

"Thanks." Spence gave her a tight smile, nerves coiling. His gaze shifted to Taggart as the man ended his call. "Is Kelly ready?"

"Yeah. She's coming down to ground level as we speak. My agents are bringing her here."

"I want to talk to her before I go out to the plane."

"All right."

"Give me ten minutes to change clothes and get my tools, Taggart. You'll have her wait?"

The FBI agent nodded and as Spence made his way to the rest rooms at the opposite end of the command center, he felt Suzanne's eyes on him with quiet curiosity, but he didn't care if she could see how he felt about Kelly. All he cared about was letting Kelly know she wasn't alone. He hated the idea of her going out to meet Hart, but she wasn't going to go without knowing she had his support.

Spence changed into his prison garb and armed himself with his Glock, the Dagen wrench and the handcuff keys in seven minutes flat. He would go out to the plane dressed in the navy coveralls the food service guys wore and he'd pick those up when he rendezvoused with the food truck. But first he had to see Kelly.

She was waiting outside, behind the command post and out of Hart's view. The warm sunshine did nothing to add color to her pale, drawn face. Seeing her lush curves bulked up by the bulletproof vest, the riot helmet covering her dark silky hair caused Spence's heart to thump hard against his chest. He wanted to take her in his arms, to take her away from here.

She turned and he saw determination fighting the fear in her eyes. A silent message passed between them and he covered the distance between them in two strides. "Everything okay?" he murmured, reaching for her hand.

She nodded, but up close he could see the anxiety dilating her eyes, the waxy sheen of her face.

One of the female FBI agents said gently, "Miss Jackson, we'll wait around the corner. You can have a few minutes."

"Thank you," she said, her gaze never leaving Spence's. She seemed to want something from him and he was all too willing to give her whatever it was. Her gaze skimmed over him, igniting that heat in his body despite the circumstances. "You changed clothes?"

He grinned. "Gotta look like a bad guy."

She reached up and touched his face, her gaze locked on him as if memorizing every detail.

Pressing his hand tightly into her side as if she funneled strength from him, she guided him to the corner of the command post.

Spence stopped, backing into the trailer and pulling Kelly into him. "Are you really all right?"

"Yes." Her hand gripped his tight.

"About last night?"

She drew in a surprised breath, color flushing her cheeks.

"I know it's fast, Kelly, but there's something between us, something special. I've never believed in that love-at-first-sight stuff, but I'm starting to."

She hesitated, folding his hand against her breast, lifting

her other hand to his face. "I told myself I'd never be swept off my feet again."

"We'll go slow. I like slow." His voice lowered. "*You* like slow."

She blushed and he slid an arm around her waist, pulling her close. He rested his forehead against hers, ignoring the hard plastic of the helmet she wore. He savored the subtle floral scent of her, the lithe curves of her body against his. He hated the bulk of the bulletproof vest, hated the helmet that kept him from touching her hair. It only made him doubly determined to get on that plane and squash Hart like the bug he was. "When this is over and I get off that plane, I'd like to take you out."

Her eyes widened. "Like a date?"

"Like a date. We'll go to dinner. Or dancing. Whatever you want."

"You dance?" She tilted her head.

He shrugged. "I will. For you."

She smiled tentatively, looking down at his hand entwined with hers, pressed against her breast.

"What do you say?" He cupped her shoulders, ran his hands up and down her arms. "Something happened between us last night and I liked it."

"So did I," she admitted with a slow smile that wrapped around his heart.

Encouraged, he skimmed his lips over her temple. "We're going to meet back here and I'm going to make you forget you ever knew Carl Hart."

Her eyes welled with tears. "You've got a date."

He kissed her, gently at first, feeling a part of himself break off at the thought of her walking out to meet that monster on the plane. She gave a small sob and her free arm hooked around his neck, anchored her to him as she kissed him hard and fierce. He didn't want to let go of her for even a second, though his hands itched to touch her everywhere. His mind wanted to memorize every inch, hold on to that until he held her in his arms again. But one of the female agents stepped around the corner.

"Marshal Cantrell?"

"Coming," he said harshly, not caring if they could hear the want and frustration in his voice.

Kelly kissed him again, quickly, then swiped at a tear on her cheek. He took both her hands in his, shifted until he was on her eye level. "I'm with you, honey. This is all going to be over very soon."

She nodded, squeezing his hands tight.

"You've got more guts than any woman I know."

That earned him a small laugh. "Right."

He kissed her forehead and walked with her to the back side of the command post, still out of Hart's view. Despite the fact that his heart was tearing in two, he managed to give her a thumbs up as she walked over to the waiting agents. When she waved, he moved to his car and drove across the tarmac to the maintenance shed where he would meet up with the food service truck.

Get on the plane. Get Hart. Get out. Then he and Kelly could get on with the rest of their lives. We *will* do that, Kelly. Spence made a silent vow to the woman whose image grew smaller in his rearview mirror.

Spence was not the same as Carl. What Kelly felt for Spence was different, too, than what she'd ever felt for her ex. More layered, more…certain. Even as she told herself that maybe she shouldn't trust it, it was only the promise of seeing Spence after all was said and done that enabled her legs to work as she stepped onto the expansive tarmac fifteen minutes later after the promised twenty-five hostages hurried off the plane.

Six men, decked out in the same gear she was and then some, formed a V behind her. Men she didn't know, but who were sworn to protect her. Her gaze searched the tarmac, then paused on the food truck heading back from the marshals' hijacked plane. No sign of Spence. He was already on board, maybe even making a move on Carl.

She closed her eyes, taking strength in that remembered kiss, feeling again the steady grip of his hand. Her gaze shot a hundred feet across the tarmac, up the metal steps leading to the open doorway of the white plane. The thin blue stripes down its side wavered in the bright sunlight. No sign of Carl. What was she supposed to do?

"Walk out about fifty feet, ma'am. Let him see you."

She nodded, but she could hardly make her legs move. Shoot, she could hardly breathe.

Carl's voice crackled over the speaker Taggart had told her the FBI had rigged. "Start walking, Kelly, and leave your buddies behind."

From the corner of her eye, she could see the black-suited bodies stop. Nerves pulsing rawly, she took a step without them, then another, holding the clear body shield in front of her as instructed.

"Stop, ma'am," one of the men said and her legs locked as if a switch had been flipped.

Taggart's voice boomed across the tarmac. "She's not coming any closer, Hart, until you show yourself."

Seconds crawled by, tension building on the tarmac, magnified so much that she thought she could hear the men behind her breathing. The sun beat down on her; inside her layers of protective gear, sweat slicked her body which felt numb and weightless. Then someone appeared in the doorway of the plane.

Two people, actually. One almost directly in front of the other, obscuring the second one's face. Sunlight glinted off something at the first man's waist and she realized it was his badge. A marshal. Then she saw the gun, screwed into the marshal's ear.

Carl peered around the marshal's head and it felt as if someone had pulled her heart out of her chest. Images ricocheted through her mind—tearing, painful images. Panic skittered through her. She didn't think she could do this.

She thought of Spence on the plane. In place. Ready to take Carl down.

A sudden click sounded on the still, quiet air, making her jump. Her gaze locked on her ex.

"Get up these steps, Kelly, or I'll kill this man."

She knew he would. Recalling every bit of love her mother had ever showered on her, the new feelings she'd experienced with Spence, she somehow managed to move on wooden legs. Sweat chilled her body.

Spence would jump Carl any minute, she told herself. He just needed her to buy him a little time. She took a step, then another, stopping at the foot of the metal stairs.

The flight of steps seemed horrifyingly short now. Her gaze met the somber one of the marshal, shifted to the gun drilled into his ear. With an eerie realization, she knew suddenly that Carl wanted something from her. Something he couldn't get if she were dead.

Maybe she could talk him out of the doorway. Maybe Spence or the snipers could get a shot at him.

"What are you doing, Kelly? Get up here," Carl snapped, his gaze darting to the HRT team behind her, over to the FBI command center.

"I've met you more than halfway, Carl." Her voice shook, but she forced the words out. "You come out here and say what you want."

"I've got a gun, dammit."

She swallowed hard. She started to take another step, then sucked in a breath when he moved outside. There wasn't a millimeter of space between him and the man he used as a shield, but Kelly kept hoping the snipers could somehow get a shot. "What do you want, Carl?"

"You, darling."

Just the silky way he said it made her skin crawl.

"I've been thinking about you ever since I got stuck in that hellhole of a prison."

She swallowed hard, still could see only one side of her ex's face, the high cheekbone, the cold eye. Swallowing the bile that rose in her throat, she said, "You can't win, Carl. Just surrender before you make it worse on yourself."

She dared not search the space behind Carl for Spence's dark head.

Carl pushed the man in front of him down a couple of steps, his body still completely covered by the marshal's. "Kelly, get your pretty butt up here right now or this guy's dead."

"Carl—"

"No more stalling. Do what I say."

She could tell by the sudden stillness of the marshal that he felt a change in Carl. Shifting to edge up the stairs and still covering herself with the body shield, she put her foot on the next step, expecting to see Spence any minute right behind Carl.

Only three steps separated her from Carl now. A warning flashed in the marshal's eyes a split second before it happened. Kelly didn't even have time to react.

Carl shoved the marshal, who stumbled into her. The body shield clattered to the concrete when she reflexively reached up to break the man's fall. Carl's hand bit into her wrist. She screamed. He dragged her up the steps, folding his body behind hers.

The marshal grabbed at the flimsy rail and tried to keep from pitching headfirst onto the concrete. Kelly screamed again, struggling, lashing out in an effort to hit Carl. Why didn't someone help her? Where was the pilot? Spence?

Pinning her to the front of him, Carl dragged them both up the steps and fell back into the doorway, leaving only her calves and feet visible, his body covered by hers.

"All bets are off, Hart," she heard Taggart bellow.

Carl scrambled for the radio mike, his fingers biting into her shoulder. "Go ahead, Taggart, but if you disable this plane, Kelly's dead. I don't need her alive. I just need her body. And I just gave you another hostage."

Taggart cursed.

"You've got five minutes to get the rest of that damn debris off the taxiway," Carl snapped.

The PA system went dead.

Carl got to his feet, tearing the riot helmet from her head and grabbing a handful of hair as he stepped over her, kicked her feet out of the way and slammed the door shut. "Now."

He yanked at her hair and she scrambled up quickly, using the wall at her back for support. Her scalp burned; tears pricked her eyes.

For the first time in two and a half years, she faced the man she'd put in prison. The man who looked as if he was ready to send her back to hell.

Spence cursed, trying the rusted bolt again. He'd removed the first inspection plate without problem, deactivated the weapons sensor and crawled through the passageway toward the belly of the plane. Now, ready to slip into the passenger compartment, Spence couldn't get this damn bolt loosened.

Sweat trickled down his spine; his heart thundered in his ears. He felt the bolt give, then jam again. Damn! He hoped Hart was still talking to Kelly. Urgency churned inside him. He worked the wrench again, his muscles burning. The dim *whirr* of machinery penetrated his concentration, but he couldn't identify the noise and didn't pause to try. Long, agonizing seconds passed while he cursed the frozen bolt, sweat stinging his eyes. Finally the damn thing gave.

As the plane shuddered and moved slowly forward, he removed the second inspection plate and poked his head through a hole in the floor. He could see straight down the narrow aisle of the passenger compartment. All clear.

He quickly lifted himself out of the passageway and rolled into a dark corner. Easing to his feet, he stepped into a pocket behind the thin, fabric-covered wall. He shimmied out of the navy coveralls, wrapped the Dagen wrench and penlight in them, then stuffed them into the corner.

Now, dressed in the white T-shirt and khaki pants of the other prisoners, he double-checked the safety on his Glock and tucked it into the small of his back. He peered around the corner. Still clear.

Creeping past the back lavatory, the back seat rows, his gaze went first up to the front door of the plane. It was shut and there was no sign of Hart.

The prisoners, roughly a third of the original one hundred and eight, were scattered throughout the front half of the plane. Still shackled, Spence noted with relief. Hart really didn't trust any of them not to interfere with his agenda, whatever the hell it was. Spence quickly counted the additional eleven personnel he could see. Besides eight marshals, it included two legal techs and a nurse. The pilot and copilot up in the cockpit made thirteen. There was no marshal close enough yet for Spence to slip the handcuff key.

The engines' drone rose to a shriek as the plane jerked into motion, steadily notching up its speed. The machinery he'd heard while working in the passageway must have been the dozers clearing the remainder of the debris from the taxiway, per Hart's demands. Spence wished he knew what the hell was going on, but takeoff or no takeoff, his job was to get Hart.

Where the hell was the bastard? What had happened when he spoke to Kelly? Spence was trusting—okay, hoping like hell—that Taggart had kept Kelly safe, that she was back with the HRT guys.

Having no clue where Hart was, Spence moved forward as far as possible, keeping an eye on all the convicts in front of him. He passed empty row after empty row until he reached the one behind the side exit doors. Since no one else was moving around, Spence would be a bull's-eye if Hart suddenly appeared. The plane lifted into the air and Spence slipped into the aisle seat to his immediate right.

Muscles braced, senses heightened against any sudden moves from Hart, Spence took stock of the plane, tried to get his bearings.

A dark-haired man across the aisle slanted a look at him through narrowed gray eyes. Spence recognized him from the pictures he'd pulled on all the prisoners. Ryder Hamilton. Fully prepared to buy the man's silence with his Glock if necessary, Spence leveled a look on the convict. After a long minute, Hamilton clamped his jaw tight and shifted his gaze to the front of the plane, saying nothing.

Spence scanned the rows ahead of him, noting where his men were positioned. Most were in front of, or in the same row as the prisoners, but there were two who sat only three rows up from Spence, in the middle seats on each side of the aisle. All the marshals were shackled with the same belly and ankle chains, just like the prisoners. Until he knew where Hart was, Spence couldn't risk moving to give them a handcuff key, couldn't risk the hijacker stepping out in front of or behind him.

He shoved his gun under the adjoining seat cushion, then took one of the black boxes designed to cover cuffs and prevent prisoners from unlocking them if they happened to get a key. He'd just arranged it over the loosely draped shackles at his wrist when a movement at the front of the plane caught his attention. Arranging his features in the same flat mask as Hamilton's, he looked up. Saw Hart step out of the cockpit. Behind him was—

Spence's heart stopped.

Kelly! What the hell had happened?

Chapter 5

Forcing himself to think, to *breathe* through the crush of fury and disbelief, Spence knew he couldn't make a move. Hart had Kelly right in front of him; she would take the brunt of anything Spence did. As his mind raced through every option he could dredge up, Hart's gaze locked on him like a radar. Hell.

Shoving Kelly down the aisle in front of him, Carl stopped at Spence. Refusing to allow his gaze to linger on Kelly's waxy, drawn features, Spence glimpsed the brilliant relief in her eyes before she stumbled and caught herself. Hart twisted her arm and she winced.

Spence dug the fingernails of one hand into his other palm, remaining in his seat by sheer force of will. He couldn't go for Hart or his gun. Hart, the shrewd piece of scum, was using Kelly as his own personal body shield. Kelly, Spence noted with relief, kept her gaze straight ahead. She was so close Spence could smell her soft wildflower scent, see the way her slender body quivered.

"Who the hell are you?" Carl snarled.

"Cantrell," Spence said in a rough voice, amazed he could get words between his clenched teeth.

"When did you get on this plane? I don't know you."

Kelly's body between them meant Spence couldn't jump the bastard, but it also worked in his favor by preventing Carl a good look at Spence's hastily arranged shackles. He shrugged. "You let more than half of us off the plane. You memorize every one of our faces?"

Hart jammed a .22-caliber Walther TPH pistol into Spence's face.

"Hey, man." Spence drew back. "Take it easy. I got on this plane the same place you did, right back there at the Prison Transfer Center in Whiskey Springs."

"I've never seen you before. Never heard of you either." Hart's eyes narrowed.

The air leaked right out of Spence's lungs as one second scraped by, then another.

Finally Ryder Hamilton broke the silence. "He shared a cell with me at the PTC. Three, four days before we boarded."

Spence fought hard to control his surprise. Hart's gaze cut from Hamilton to Spence. Spence held the hijacker's gaze, his gut caving at the help from Hamilton. Maybe it was the con's word. Maybe it was Spence's beard or the clothes, but finally Hart grunted and thumbed the Walther's hammer back into place. He turned and dragged Kelly with him toward the front of the plane, again keeping her between him and a bullet.

His chest hurt when that first gulp of air crowded in. After seeing the way Carl roughly handled Kelly, Spence didn't care if he took the bastard dead or alive.

At the front row, Hart pushed Kelly into an aisle seat, straight ahead of Spence. Hart placed himself in front of her, his gaze narrowed suspiciously on Spence. Frustration chewed at Spence's gut like acid. No way could he move on Hart now without risking Kelly's life or the lives of the men between him and Hart. He slid his hand under the seat cushion, his hand closing over the reassuring sleekness of his Glock.

Feeling Hamilton's gaze on him, Spence looked over. "Why'd you help me?"

"I've only got six months left on my sentence," the other man drawled in a thick Texas accent. "I'm not screwin' it up for Hart."

Spence nodded, weighing the other man. Finally he nodded. "Thanks. I won't forget it."

Muscles braced, Spence palmed his gun, waiting. Watching. Soon he would get his chance. And he'd be ready.

Kelly rubbed her wrist, her scalp still stinging from the yank Carl had given her hair when he'd first pulled her on board. Relief joined the panic and fear she felt. At least Spence was on the plane. And, she noted, chewing at her thumbnail, Carl hadn't taken his gaze off Spence for more than one second since he'd questioned his identity.

Thank goodness for Ryder Hamilton. She remembered the handsome, former oil executive's picture from the pile of photos Spence had shown her last night. Had it been only last night?

Last night when she'd admitted to the invisible, yet strong-as-steel bond that bound her to Spence? Last night when she'd given him a part of herself she'd thought never to surrender again?

Kelly didn't know why Hamilton had vouched for Spence, but she was going to thank him later. When they got out of this. She refused to consider that they *wouldn't* get out of this.

Do something, her mind urged. She discarded ideas as quickly as they popped into her head. *Jump him.* Ridiculous. *Distract him.* For what? She didn't know what Spence had planned— Wait! She *could* distract Carl. As long as he was studying Spence with the same paranoid intensity he'd always used on her, Spence wouldn't have a chance to make a move.

Her ex's dark good looks were an icy mask of fury and concentration. He switched his gun from one hand to the other and back again. A thick-necked prisoner with a shaved head and swastikas tattooed on either side of his mouth sat directly behind her. Another sat in the same row across the aisle.

She and Carl were right behind the cockpit door, which was open so Carl could keep an eye on the pilot, Jensen, and the copilot, O'Connor. Thanks to the little stainless steel gun Carl kept poking in their faces, the two men obeyed every order without comment. Each also had a wrist shackled to the steering wheel, which explained why neither had been able to help her when Carl had yanked her aboard.

Kelly's nerves thrummed. The hair on the back of her neck prickled. When Carl had walked her right up to Spence, she'd tried not to look at him. Now she had to force herself not to turn around and search for him.

Through her blur of shock and pain and fear, two things became crystal clear. She'd had all of Carl Hart's bullying she was going to take, and she wanted a chance with Spence Cantrell.

Nervous energy rolling off him like a bitter odor, her ex's narrowed gaze returned repeatedly to Spence. A sheen of sweat filmed Carl's upper lip. Stubble dotted his chin, giving his face a dirty pall. She knew he hated being unshaven, hated to be less than immaculately groomed.

She watched him warily. He'd wasted no time getting the protective gear off her. The bulletproof vest and riot helmet lay in the corner where he'd thrown them. His gaze sharpened on her. Satisfaction flared in his brown eyes.

She couldn't believe she'd ever found his coldly handsome, calculating features compelling. She had to get his attention off Spence and on her. "Why did you do this, Carl?"

"I told you, darling. We're going back to Belize." He laughed harshly. "Relive our honeymoon."

The thought of his hands on her made bile rise in her throat. She tried to stay calm. She didn't believe he really wanted her physically. He'd always said she never did that right either.

"I didn't hear from you while you were in prison. Why now?"

Hate frosted his eyes, so frigid that she felt it stroke up her spine. But she held his gaze, her breath aching in her chest.

"I thought about you plenty, darling. About the way you turned on me, about the way you put me in that place to rot."

His own actions had landed him there, but Kelly didn't think now was the best time to point that out. He yanked her chin up. "Remember our time in Belize, Kelly?"

She'd spent the last three years trying to forget it, trying to live with what an idiot she'd been. "But why do you need me, Carl? I'll just slow you down. What are you going to do when you get there? Drive somewhere? Take a boat out to Roitan?"

He raised his hand as if he would strike her and she

pressed into the seat. Bracing herself, she waited as he stared at her, hatred flushing his features.

Finally he lowered his hand, trailed the gun barrel across her collarbone.

Kelly froze. He flashed a smile, a slash of teeth in his cruelly handsome face. "I've got some money waiting for me, darling. Once I get it, I won't need you anymore."

"Money? In Belize? How—" She broke off, a memory surfacing. Not wanting a dime of Carl's money after the divorce, she'd forgotten all about the account he'd opened in the Central American bank. He'd said they would return on every anniversary and he'd deposit money for each year they were together. Mad money, he'd called it. For her to spend as she wanted. On a high from their marriage, he'd been in a generous mood, which he often was when he got his own way. "The only reason you would need me is to access that account you set up for me on our honeymoon."

"That's right."

"But there can't be more than a thousand dollars in there!" Sickened, Kelly gestured at all the people behind her. "You did *this* for a thousand dollars?"

"Hardly. There's between four and five million in that account now."

"What? How on earth!"

"It's quite sad how trusting little old ladies can be," he said chuckling.

It took a second for Kelly to put it together. "You embezzled that money from senior citizens? You were named as trustee for a group of them in the nursing home! Their retirement, their pensions!"

"Not embezzling," he said in a hard voice. "More like…siphoning."

"You're just adding years to your sentence."

He laughed. ''It's easy to doctor accounts, darling. They probably still don't even know the money's gone.''

Anger burst inside her along with disbelief, but what really had her pulse shooting into orbit was the memory that her account could only be accessed with her exact palm print. Carl had set it up that way when he thought he had her under his thumb.

Dread thickened inside her. What reason would Carl have to keep her alive after he withdrew the money from the bank?

He trailed the gun back up her neck, across her jaw. She swallowed, nausea pooling in her belly. Would he ever give her some space? Ever give Spence a window of opportunity to move?

Carl's eyes took on a distant gleam and he fingered her hair. What little breakfast she'd eaten nearly came up. Kelly closed her eyes, swallowing back the bitterness in her throat. If he touched her in a sexual way, she was going to fight him. She wasn't going through that again, especially after experiencing the way a man should touch her.

She tried not to let her mind be frozen by Carl's leer. Relief had her slumping in her seat when he turned toward the cockpit, his eyes narrowed, suspicion tight on his face.

The little bud of anger inside Kelly grew as she watched her ex-husband stalk into the cockpit. He leaned over the pilot's shoulder for a long minute, then he exploded.

''You're going around in damn circles!'' Flinging his arm back, he brought his gun sharply against the pilot's head. ''If we're going to Central America, there's no reason for that gauge to read north-northeast!''

Carl struck the pilot again and a thin line of blood trickled down the man's temple.

Kelly jumped up, screaming, ''Stop it, Carl! You'll kill him!''

Carl hit him again. "Get this plane on course. Now!"

"Carl, stop! Stop!"

Kelly's scream chilled Spence's blood. Bolting out of his chair, he ripped the black box off Hamilton's cuffs and palmed him a handcuff key. "Free yourself and get this key to the marshal in that seat."

He indicated a pudgy, red-haired man three rows up. Hamilton nodded and Spence took off up the aisle. Hart bludgeoned the pilot with his gun, yelling about flying in circles. Kelly was on her feet, still screaming at Carl to stop.

"Kelly, get down!" Spence bellowed to be heard above the noise of stirring prisoners and clanking chains as they all craned for a look. He halted at the cockpit door, leveling his Glock at Hart. "U.S. Marshal. Drop your weapon, Hart!"

The copilot lunged at Hart, swinging at him with the arm not shackled to the wheel. Before Spence could ID himself again, Hart's gun went off in rapid succession. A loud series of pops sounded from the control panel; smoke streamed into the air. Spence fired, too, hitting Hart in the shoulder, taking a bullet himself.

With a bellow of enraged pain, the bastard spun. The plane nose-dived sharply, the motion knocking Spence's feet out from under him. He grabbed the doorframe, his gun flying out of his hand, bouncing across the bullet-riddled instrument panel and disappearing in a tangle of feet.

"Mayday! Mayday!" the copilot yelled. The pilot slumped, blood spreading in a slow stain across his white shirt.

Sharp pain arrowed up Spence's right arm. He'd been hit. He roared and rose to jump Hart, trying to wrestle the

Walther from the convict's iron grip. He nearly had it. Fingers wrapped around the slick barrel, he yanked. Hart broke free, rocked Spence with a hook to the chin. Head ringing, jaw snapping, Spence stumbled backward out of the cockpit. Hart tackled him, grabbed again at the gun.

Kelly jumped on Hart's back, gouging at his eyes with her fingers, trying to wrench him away from Spence. She bit his ear and he roared in pain, bucking violently enough to throw her off. She hit the wall behind her, lying dazed for a moment.

Spence grabbed the gun, Hart's hand closed over his. Dark eyes burned hate and death into his. Muscles popped and both of them grunted with the effort to keep the gun. Spence tried to get a foothold on the floor, tried to brace himself so he could throw Hart off. Pain seared Spence's arm, but he couldn't let go. The plane continued its downward descent; Spence and Hart rolled into the steel frame of the seats, crunched in the narrow aisle.

There! He nearly had the gun turned in his hand—

A gunshot exploded, deafening for an instant. Acrid smoke burned Spence's nostrils.

Absolute silence fell like lead weight.

Then Kelly's wobbly voice sounded in the swollen quiet. "Spence?"

Hart collapsed limply on top of him.

"I'm okay," he grunted, pushing off the hijacker's body and edging into a sitting position. He clamped a hand over his wound and applied pressure.

Two marshals—Lowe and Pendergrass—peered into Spence's face. "You okay?"

Spence nodded, his muscles quivering with reaction, his heart racing.

Lowe leaned down and felt for a pulse in Hart's neck. "Gone," the marshal said.

"We've got the plane back under control. Thanks to Ryder Hamilton." Pendergrass helped Spence to his feet and clapped him on the shoulder.

Spence nodded, caring only about one thing right now. He gestured to Hart's gun where he'd dropped it and turned, catching Kelly with his left arm as she barreled into him.

Relief and euphoria nearly buckled his knees as his body jolted down from an adrenaline high. Burying one hand in her hair, he crushed his lips to hers. She clung to him.

She was alive. He was alive. Hart wasn't.

It felt like hours, but it took only minutes for Spence to have the plane back under full marshal control. And without using the weapons he had brought on board. Despite Kelly's worried urging to immediately sit down, Spence took care of business first. Hamilton had done his part by releasing two marshals, who in turn had released the others. Spence made a mental note to have his uncle Vaughn, a federal judge, give an early review of Hamilton's case. The man had probably saved his life and Kelly's, too.

Kelly stayed close, her hand locked in his. In the cockpit door, he turned to the copilot, concerned about the man who'd seen his partner shot right in front of him. "How're you doing, O'Connor?"

The man's thick gray hair was plastered to his skull and matched the color of his face. Sweat glistened on his forehead and neck. His voice shook as he returned Spence's gun to him. "I'm not hit or anything, but the flight controls are another story."

"What do you need?"

"Another pilot would be nice," the man said drily.

Spence nodded as he tucked his weapon into the small of his back, urging Kelly out of the aisle as two marshals carefully carried out the dead pilot. Two other marshals followed them to the back of the plane with Hart's motionless body. Kelly turned her head into Spence's shoulder.

Setting his jaw against the pain in his other arm, he slid an arm around her waist and pulled her next to him as he said to the copilot, "I'm sorry about Jensen. I know you guys were friends and flew together a lot."

O'Connor nodded, looking dazed and devastated. Streaks of Jensen's blood splashed morbid color on the copilot's white shirt.

"Can you radio the plane behind us?" Spence asked gently.

The man reached for the mike, his hands shaking so badly Spence didn't know if he could push the button.

"I'll try to get you some help in here."

"I'm sorry, sir."

"It's all right." Spence squeezed O'Connor's shoulder. The man had just seen his friend die. Spence wouldn't have been all that steady either.

O'Connor established radio contact with the Gulfstream now following them in plain sight and Spence filled Taggart in. "I'll give you everything in more detail when we land," Spence told the FBI agent. "I need to get some help for O'Connor."

He signed off, then stepped out of the cockpit, his hand slipping into Kelly's. "We need another person in the cockpit with the copilot. Does anyone have any flying experience?"

His gaze went first to the marshals, but they all shook their heads.

Finally, Hamilton spoke up. "I've flown bug smashers."

"Is that a plane?" Spence's system slowed to normal

as he finally allowed himself to savor the relief and gratitude that he and Kelly were all right.

"Little single-engine jobs. I used to fly them around the oil fields of West Texas."

"That'll do." Spence motioned him up.

As Hamilton passed, Spence said in a low voice, "Thanks again for your help, now and earlier. I won't forget it."

The other man's gaze turned speculative. "You're welcome."

After Hamilton moved into the cockpit, Spence glanced around. The prisoners were all still shackled, the marshals again back in control. In the back of the plane, the male nurse was just zipping Hart into a body bag like Jensen's. Even though Spence knew they were lucky not to have lost more men, he hated that Hart had caused the death of a good man, a man who certainly hadn't signed on for gunfire.

A rush of fatigue swept over Spence and his head throbbed.

"Now will you sit down?" Kelly asked, pulling him toward the back of the plane.

"Yes." He allowed her to settle him in a seat, then kissed her again.

"Sir?" the flight nurse quietly interrupted. "Why don't you let me look at that arm?"

Spence nodded and sat quietly, his hand locked in Kelly's, while the man efficiently cut away Spence's sleeve, then cleaned and bandaged the wound.

"Looks like it went in and out."

"Good," Spence said.

"Thank goodness." Kelly settled her head on his shoulder and he shut his eyes as the nurse moved off.

"I was so afraid, Spence."

"Well, you couldn't tell." He opened his eyes and found her staring up at him somberly. "I was damn proud of you."

"You were?"

"Yes." He kissed her, slowly, softly.

She touched his face, wonder coming into her eyes. "We're really okay."

"Yeah. More than okay." He smiled tiredly and when she smiled back, his heart clenched. "Listen, Kelly, about that date—"

"Don't try to get out of it," she teased.

"No chance." He tucked a strand of hair behind her ear. "I love you, Kelly. I know it's fast, but—"

She put her fingers against his lips. "It *is* fast, but when something's right, it's right."

He kissed her knuckles as he took her hand in his. "After my wife died, I shut down, but when I met you, things started happening inside. I don't know how else to put it, but I know it was because of you. I thought I'd never feel about another woman the way I felt about Anna, but I see now that I was just holding on to the love I'd had before so I'd know when, and if, it ever came to me again. I think it has, Kelly. I *know* it has."

Tears glimmered in her blue eyes. "That's the most beautiful thing anyone's ever said to me."

"It's true," he said against her temple, savoring her soft warmth, the peace wrapping around him. "I know how quickly life can change, honey. Anna taught me that. Whatever time we have left, I want to spend with you. If you want some time to think about it, that's fine. But don't think you're going to get rid of me."

She stared into his eyes for a long time, considering. Spence's hand tightened on hers; he was prepared to beg if necessary.

Then a slow smile curved her lips. "You're something else, Spence Cantrell. Since Carl, I haven't trusted my instincts about anything, but this…craziness forced me to. Thanks to you, now I know there are some feelings I can trust. You're one of them."

He grinned. "So, what should we do on our date?"

"Well, you've already given me the ride of my life, Marshal. I can't wait to see what you come up with next."

He nudged her chin up, staring into her eyes. How had he gotten so lucky? "You won't regret it, Kelly," he promised before his lips claimed hers in gentle possession. "I'm going to love you with every breath I take."

She smiled, a brilliant light coming into her eyes and making him go weak inside. "That's funny. I have a feeling you will."

She rested her head on his shoulder and he settled back with his good hand locked in hers as the plane circled round and headed toward Whiskey Springs.

* * * * *

Final Approach...to Forever
Merline Lovelace

Books by Merline Lovelace

Chapter 1

Day 4

"Flight 407, this is Chase One. We didn't copy your last transmission. Say again, please."

Suzanne Delachek pinned her ice-blue eyes on the Boeing 727 streaking through the late afternoon sky a hundred feet off the chase plane's left wingtip. Static crackled in the earphones of her headset. Five seconds passed. Ten. Her heart jackhammering against her ribs, she keyed her mike again.

"This is Chase One, 407." Despite the tension coiled like a snake at the base of her skull, she kept her voice cool and calm. "Repeat your last transmission."

Still no response.

"What's going on?" FBI Special Agent Mason Taggart crowded into the cockpit, hunching down to peer over Suzanne's shoulder at the 727. "Why the hell doesn't O'Connor acknowledge?"

She didn't take her eyes off the other aircraft, all white except for the subdued blue striping on its fuselage and tail fin. She knew the answer to the agent's question as well as he did.

O'Connor was busy—*very* busy!—keeping his crippled plane in the air.

A dedicated U.S. Marshals Service prisoner transport, the 727 had been hijacked three days ago by Carl Hart, one of the convicts on board. The pilot was dead, killed along with the hijacker in a midair shootout that sent bullets smashing into the instrument panel and wreaked havoc with the flight controls. From his last transmission Suzanne knew the thoroughly shaken copilot was now sweating his way through the emergency procedures checklist, trying to determine the extent of the damage.

Suzanne had been talking him through the checklist, step by step. She'd logged more than seven thousand hours in Boeing airframes during her flying career, first as an active duty air force aviator, then as a senior instructor pilot for the FAA. Two thousand of those hours were "PIC" time—pilot-in-command time—aboard a 727. For that reason, the FAA had scrambled a plane and dispatched her to Whiskey Springs, Texas, shortly after the hijacking. She knew exactly what the 727 could do, when it would do it, and how.

What she didn't know was why O'Connor had cut off his last transmission so abruptly.

"Flight 407, please acknowl—"

"This is 407. We got us a problem here, folks."

Suzanne's silver-blond brows snapped together. The speaker's Texas twang identified him immediately. Ryder Hamilton.

The FBI had fed her a quick background brief on the convict who'd climbed into the cockpit to help after the pilot was killed. A West Texas native, he'd parlayed a two-bit oil exploration company into Hamilton Oil and Gas, a Fortune 500 corporation. In the process, he'd scammed hundreds of folks in a get-rich-quick oil lease scheme. He was also the only other person aboard Flight 407 with any experience in a cockpit. Unfortunately, that experience consisted of a few hundred hours in the single-engine Piper Cherokee he once bumped around the oil fields of West Texas. Still, O'Connor had been grateful for even that dubious assistance.

Now, apparently, Hamilton had decided to take a more active role than just reading the instruments for the harried copilot.

"State your problem, 407."

"O'Connor just bought the farm."

Suzanne's heart stopped. Just froze in place for several seconds, then restarted with a painful thump. Praying she'd misheard the transmission, she keyed her mike.

"Say again."

"He just had a massive heart attack." The Texas drawl took on a grim edge. "He clutched his chest and keeled over. Right here at the controls."

Behind Suzanne, Taggart cursed, low and long. She paid no attention to the agent, her every sense riveted on the rawhide-rough baritone in her earphones.

"We dragged him back to the galley," Hamilton relayed. "The nurse is performing CPR, but he says to tell you not to expect any miracles. God knows, we sure could use one right now."

Suzanne allowed herself a short, silent oath. That was all she had time for with a crippled jetliner flying in a huge circle over the Gulf of Mexico, forty-eight desperate souls on board, and a man at the controls who'd never flown anything other than bug smashers.

"All right," she said, infusing her voice with icy calm, "you've got the controls. The aerodynamics for a 727 and a Piper Cherokee are exactly the same. Thrust and drag, Mr. Hamilton, thrust and drag. The jet's just bigger and faster, and—"

"And shot all to hell! Don't BS me, lady. I'm looking at an instrument panel with holes in it big enough to put my boot through."

"We know Flight 407's instrumentation took some hits, but it's maintaining airspeed and altitude. O'Connor put it on autopilot right before his last transmission. We won't disengage until you're ready."

"Until we run out of fuel and fall out of the sky, you mean."

"You're not going to fall anywhere," Suzanne promised, praying fiercely that she was right. "The 727's a forgiving airplane, with big fat wings and a beautiful glide. I know what it can do. Just trust me."

The short silence in her earphones was deafening.

"The last time I trusted a woman, sweetheart, I ended up in leg irons."

Right, Suzanne thought with a flash of scorn. Blame your problems on someone else. That was what all these cons did, including the sleazy contractor who'd convinced her parents to shell out a big chunk of their savings for a new roof, then never delivered so much as a shingle.

Now wasn't the time to challenge Ryder Hamilton's self-delusions, though. Thrusting aside every thought but the safety of the passengers aboard Flight 407, she spoke slowly and calmly.

"I've logged thousands of hours in large, multiengine jet aircraft, Mr. Hamilton. I'm going to walk you through the emergency checklists, step by step. You're going to repeat everything I say, find the appropriate instrument, and repeat the procedure again *before* you twist a single knob or toggle a switch. Got that?''

"Yeah, I got it."

"Ready?"

Across a hundred feet of empty sky, Ryder clenched his sweaty palms around the jet's wheel. Swallowing the Texas-size lump in his throat, he tore his gaze from the shattered instrument panel long enough to shoot a look out the side windshield.

There it was. Just across a patch of blue sky. A sleek little Gulfstream six-passenger jet. Crammed full of FBI agents and US Marshals, he'd been reminded. And at least one cool-as-ice female with a voice like a chilled smoothie and thousands of hours in big jets. Hoping to hell a few of those hours would rub off on him, he keyed the mike.

"Ready as I'll ever be, sweetheart."

"The name's Delachek," she replied with a composure that acted like a long, soothing swallow of milk on the acid churning up his stomach. "Suzanne Delachek. Can you get someone up there in the cockpit to help you read the instruments?"

"Marshal Cantrell's sitting right here beside me."

"We understand Cantrell took a bullet."

Ryder started to reply, but the dark-haired marshal with a bloody bandage wrapped around his upper arm answered for himself.

"It's just a flesh wound. The flight nurse patched me up."

"Get someone else up in the cockpit," Delachek ordered flatly. "Someone who won't be distracted by pain."

Ryder and Cantrell shared a quick look. They'd met for the first time a short while ago. One was a convicted felon. The other, a law enforcement officer dedicated to hunting down any fugitives who might try to escape the punishment due them. Yet the bond they'd forged in that brief time was stronger than the steel manacles Ryder had worn during the first part of this flight into hell.

"I can help Hamilton," the marshal said tersely. "And I'll be damned if I'm going to let anything else happen to Kelly Jackson while I've still got a breath left in my body. I'll read the instruments."

"Just tell us what to do," Ryder snapped.

A long, even sigh filtered through his earphones. She didn't flap, this Suzanne Delachek. But then again, he reminded himself sardonically, she wasn't flying in a jet with an instrument panel shot all to hell.

"All right. Cantrell, you're there for backup. Hamilton, you and I are going to get real tight, real fast. I'm going to get inside your head. You won't have a thought we don't share, or make a move we don't make together. We'll think as a team, act as one unit. Together, we'll bring Flight 407 home."

Twenty minutes later, Ryder had almost—*almost*—begun to believe her. For every one of those endless, stomach-twisting minutes, his rational mind had screamed there was no way he could fly this behemoth, let alone land it. But the stubbornness bred into him with the dust and heat of West Texas shut out everything except Suzanne Delachek's voice. Cool. Confident. Smooth as glass.

She talked him through a visual of every instrument. Read the gauges with him. Made sure he knew the location and purposes of the switches on the overhead panel. All the while, the Boeing jet punched a big, endless circle in the late afternoon sky.

They were out over the Gulf. Whenever Ryder blinked the sweat from his eyes and dragged them away from the instruments for a second or two, he could catch a glint of the late afternoon sunlight on the waves. He refused to think about going down in that shimmering water. Even at its slowest speed, the jet would smash against the flat, unbroken surface of the sea and disintegrate into a million pieces.

Not that he liked the idea of trying to put this hummer down on a runway any better. But the fuel level had dropped almost a thousand gallons since he'd scrambled into the cockpit and he didn't need Suzanne Delachek to figure out how long they had left. Flight 407 would run out of sky and Ryder out of options in less than four hours. The thought of bringing this big jet down through a dark April night popped fresh beads of sweat on his brow.

"We're going to check the flaps now."

There she was. In his head. Just as she'd said she would be. Putting the airbrakes on his skittering panic with that cool-as-snow voice.

"They're triple-slotted on this model," the ice maiden advised, "with leading-edge slats."

"Whatever the hell that means."

"That means you have low-speed takeoff and landing capability. Do you see the switches to the left of the altimeter? In the upper instrument bank?"

"Left of the altimeter," Ryder muttered. "Upper instrument bank. I've got 'em. Lowering flaps—''

"No! Wait until I—"

The 727 bucked like a bee-stung bronc. The right wing tipped up. The nose went down. The plane dropped into a plunging spiral. A hundred feet. Two hundred. Three.

"Pull left, Hamilton! Pull left! Retract the flaps."

He could barely hear her over the roaring in his ears.

"Hamilton! Listen to me! Suck up those flaps! Now! Do it now!"

The jet shuddered. Metal groaned. Cantrell braced both

boots against the deck and helped wrestle the shuddering controls. Cursing and praying at the same time, Ryder pulled left, saw the sea tilt away.

"That's it. Level her out slowly as those flaps roll up. Slowly, I said!"

Inch by tortuous inch, the sky and the sea shifted into horizontal planes again. A lifetime later, Ryder slumped against the seat. Shudders wracked him. His white prison T-shirt lay plastered to his chest.

"Nice recovery, Hamilton."

He almost hated her at that moment. He couldn't move, could barely breathe over the terror pumping through his veins. Yet she sounded as though she hadn't even broken a sweat.

"The right flaps are gone," he snarled, as if she and everyone else listening in hadn't already figured that out. "It's anyone's guess about the left. How the hell am I going to land without flaps to slow us down?"

"We'll find you a nice, long runway. Maybe bring you in at Cape Canaveral, where the space shuttle lands."

Ryder clutched at that straw with everything in him. Hope flared anew, only to die an agonizing death not five minutes later.

Following her instructions, he tested the landing gear system. A red light flashed on the instrument panel.

"I've got a system malfunction."

"Yes, you do. Your right main gear didn't come down. Retract the left and we'll figure out where we go from here."

He flipped the switch, frowning when the red light continued to flash. "The right gear won't come down."

"Try again."

His chest squeezed by iron bands, Ryder toggled the switch. The red light flashed obscenely.

''Nothing.'' He dragged in a painful breath. ''So what do we do now, coach?''

''Give me a minute,'' she replied with unshakable calm. ''I'll get back to you.''

Switching the radio to receive only, Suzanne squeezed her eyes shut and swallowed frantically to keep the panic rising in her throat from ripping free.

What would they do now? he'd asked.

What *could* they do now?

She opened her eyes, locked them on Mason Taggart. The FBI agent looked like a short, nervous bear, she thought on a near-hysterical note. Thinning brown hair. Brown eyes. Rumpled brown suit. His throat worked once. Finally, he forced out the truth they both wanted to deny.

''They're going to crash, aren't they?''

Suzanne looked at him for long moments. A dozen scenarios flashed like summer lightning in her head. She discarded them all. Searched her mind. Came up blank.

No, there was no way Ryder could land a 727 with only one main gear. No way anyone could. That single set of wheels would become a pivot point as soon as the plane touched down. Best case, the jet would spin off the runway. Worst case, it would cartwheel wildly and burst into a fireball. Shuddering, she pushed that horrific option right out of her head.

Maybe...

No, the passengers couldn't bail out. Even if Suzanne could get parachutes aboard in time, the 727 wasn't designed for emergency egress while in flight. If the passengers tried to exit through the left door, the airstream would smash them back into the wing. Exiting via the emergency hatches over the wings would send them right into the tail-mounted engines. After the D.B. Cooper incident, when another hijacker had parachuted from a plane with several million dollars and was never seen again, a mod to commercial aircraft sealed the aft stairs so they couldn't be opened during flight.

Suzanne didn't even consider bringing the jet down low enough for the passengers to jump into the Gulf without parachutes. The slowest speed the 727 could maintain without stalling was ninety knots, which translated to over a hundred miles an hour. The odds of anyone hitting the water at that speed and surviving weren't even calculable.

The single option—the *only* option—was a water ditching. She stared at Taggart, unseeing, while she searched her memory bank for every scrap of data. The first 727 went into service in 1964. In all the years since, no one had ever attempted to take one down in the water. No one even knew if the hundred-ton jet would float. Even Boeing's computer models were inconclusive. They couldn't predict with any certainty what would happen, either.

But...

She only needed to keep the body of the aircraft afloat long enough for the passengers to egress. And if she brought it down in shallow water... Shallow, *swampy* water. Weeds would break the water's surface tension, soften the landing. A water ditching would be a dicey proposition at best, given the problems with the right flaps, but if she compensated by working the left and—

Suzanne's racing thoughts skidded to an abrupt stop. An experienced pilot might be able to pull it off. Ryder Hamilton would plow Flight 407 right into the swamp.

With a fierce effort of will, she dumped every thought, cleared her mind completely, took another tack. Moments later, she blinked and brought Taggart's face into focus.

"Okay, here's the deal. We're going to bring Flight 407

down in the Everglades. No one's ever ditched a 727 in the water before, but that doesn't mean it can't be done.''

A frown carved a deep V in Taggart's forehead. ''Do you really think Hamilton's up to something like that?''

''Not Hamilton. Me. I'm going to be at the controls.''

Taggart's mouth dropped. Before he recovered his powers of speech, Suzanne was back on the mike.

''Flight 407, this is Chase One.''

''Go ahead, Chase One.''

''I'm going to direct Chase Two up and into position right here beside you. I'll keep this net open and remain in constant contact if you need me, but—''

''Bailing out on me, Delachek?''

He'd buried the terror she knew he must be feeling under a thick layer of cynicism. Someone had done a real number on this guy, Suzanne thought. A woman, if she could believe his snide crack about how he ended up in leg irons.

''No, I'm not bailing out on you. I'm going to see if I can borrow a transport plane, arrange a midair transfer, and join you in the cockpit.''

''A midair transfer?'' He sounded as incredulous as the FBI agent still looked. ''You're crazy, lady!''

Everyone Suzanne talked to in the next half hour echoed exactly the same sentiments. Taggart. The FAA. The Department of Defense Emergency Coordination Center. The tower at Sam Houston International Airport, still monitoring Flight 407's every transmission. Even the commander of the Air Force Special Operations unit at Hurlburt Field in the Florida panhandle, where the Gulfstream swooped in for a landing. As Lieutenant Colonel ''Howie'' Howard acerbically pointed out, midair transfers only happened in the movies.

Despite his very vocal skepticism, however, Howie had a C-130 Hercules waiting for her with engines running. Suzanne jumped out of the Gulfstream jet the moment it rolled to a stop and raced across the runway to the squat, four-engined workhorse that performed such varied air force missions as hauling cargo, suppressing enemy fire, and combat rescue.

"We put a flight suit aboard for you," the pilot shouted over the roar of the 130's four turboprops. "Along with a helmet, an oxygen pack, and boots. The crew chief will show you how the harness and hoist work once we're airborne."

"Roger that."

He cocked a look over his shoulder as she strapped herself in. "You gotta be nuts to even think about doing this."

"So I've been told," Suzanne drawled. "Let's go."

To everyone's complete astonishment, Suzanne's included, she pulled it off.

It took two nerve-wracking hours to bring Flight 407 down in ever-widening circles to a safe altitude to depressurize the aircraft and blow the left passenger door. At the same time, they edged the 727 closer and closer to Florida's southwest coast.

It took another twenty minutes to position the C-130 above and to the left of the jet. That was followed by agonizing minutes of terror when the forward passenger door flew off and everyone in the watching aircraft prayed they wouldn't see bodies being sucked out or the 727 going nose down into the sea.

Then Suzanne was swinging at the end of a steel cable, buffeted by the brutal wind and the 727's jet stream, convinced that this insanity would shave five, maybe ten, years off her life…if she didn't end it in the next few minutes.

The only thing that kept her from signaling the crew chief to winch her back up was the man at the big jet's open hatch. He had anchored himself to the inside galley by a harness fashioned of stainless steel shackles. Wind tore at his hair and clothes. Desperate hope twisted his face.

Shuddering, Suzanne waved to the crew chief to drop her down another ten feet. Fifteen. Twenty. When she was eye level with the open door, she swung out, then in. She missed the hatch and slammed against the fuselage with bone-jarring force. Bouncing away, she twisted like a puppet on strings. Stars pinwheeled behind her eyes. Nausea from the wild spin threatened to choke her. The jet's engines deafened her.

Gripping the cable with gloved hands, she waited for the nausea to pass, sucked in a breath and signaled for another try. This time she got close enough for the man at the open hatch to grab at her boot before the wind and centrifugal forces dragged her away.

Two tries later, she smashed right into the guy. They tumbled backward, clinging to each other while the C-130's crew chief frantically slackened the cable to keep from pulling them both back out.

Wild cheers erupted throughout the cabin when she stumbled to her feet and tore off her helmet and oxygen pack. The man who'd hauled her in, a marshal, she guessed, since he wasn't wearing the prison-issue tan pants and white T-shirt, wrapped her in a huge bear hug.

"You're the most beautiful thing I've ever seen in my life," he shouted over the wind screaming through the cabin. "You and that bird up there. Is it going to take us all out?"

Suzanne shot a glance down the long passenger cabin, stripped to the bare essentials for prisoner transport. Faces stared back at her. Frantic. Joyful. The woman in a middle row caught her eyes.

The hijacker's ex-wife. Kelly Jackson. She'd saved Flight 407 once by helping Spence Cantrell bring down the murderous bastard who shot the pilot. Suzanne would have to save it a second time. Whipping her glance back to the marshal still shackled to the galley, she shook her head.

"I'm sorry. Flight 407's running out of fuel fast. At most, the C-130 could winch up one soul, maybe two. They've got a doc on board with a portable heart crash kit to help O'Connor if he's still hanging in there. The rest of you…"

She speared a glance around the circle of marshals who'd crowded forward to listen to her words.

"Unshackle the prisoners and get them ready for an emergency landing."

When she wrenched the cockpit door open, the injured Spence Cantrell scrambled out of the seat and squeezed past her with a shouted welcome. The door banged behind him a second later, shutting out the roaring wind. Suzanne climbed into the vacant seat and turned to the convict at the controls.

Before she could get out so much as a word, Hamilton wrapped a hand around her neck, hauled her halfway across the throttles, and laid a kiss on her that knocked the wind right out of her for the second time in as many minutes.

Chapter 2

In the few seconds it took Suzanne to gather her scattered senses, she registered several pertinent facts about Ryder Hamilton.

One, he kissed like no man she'd ever met, including her ex-husband, and Jack's all-too-skilled lovemaking had kept Suzanne in her marriage far longer than either common sense or her ex's lack of commitment dictated.

Two, Hamilton was the handsomest devil she'd come across in a long time. Gunmetal gray eyes glinted at her from a rugged, square-jawed face. His black hair had just enough of a curl in it to resist a comb, although his stubbled cheeks and chin indicated he hadn't been anywhere near a comb or a razor in days.

Three, his white T-shirt stretched across shoulders the everyday, average male would kill for. And the muscled thighs under those tan prison pants...

The prison uniform brought her thoughts slamming back into focus. Ryder Hamilton was a convict. A jury had found him guilty of scamming hundreds of people like her folks out of money they couldn't afford to lose. That was why he was aboard Flight 407 in the first place.

And Flight 407 was the reason—the *only* reason—Suzanne had just hurtled a hundred feet of open airspace. Wrenching her mind back to the urgent business at hand, she reached for the throttles. They felt smooth under her fingers, as familiar as a lover's touch.

"All right, Mr. Hamilton. Here's the drill. I'm going to put—"

"Ryder." His grin kicked up another notch. "You're in my head, sweetheart. You'll probably be there for the rest of my life. I think that puts us on a first-name basis."

She refused to let his combination of heady relief and reckless charm infect her.

"I'm going to put us down at approximately eighty-one degrees longitude, twenty-five and a half degrees latitude."

Her cool tone stripped away his grin. Reality in the form of a crippled plane fast running out of fuel had him doing a quick calculation.

"Eighty-one degrees longitude." His brow creased. "Are we going into Miami?"

"Close. The Everglades."

"The Everglades! You're putting us down in the water?"

From the way he choked out the question, Suzanne guessed he'd figured out their odds of survival if they went down in the Gulf and didn't like them any better than she did.

"In the swamp, Mr. Hamil—Ryder. To be exact, smack in the middle of a saw grass prairie called Shark Valley.

As she talked, Suzanne visually swept the instruments, swiftly translating altitude, airspeed and remaining fuel into air time.

"I spent a summer camping in the Everglades with my folks. Shark Valley is a shallow, slow-moving sea of grass. The reeds will break the surface tension of the water and make it act like a cushion instead of concrete."

That was the theory, anyway.

"Even if the aircraft breaks up when it hits, which is the most likely scenario, the scatter pattern of the wreckage should be contained within a few miles. Search and rescue assets are already en route to the estimated impact point."

"Impact point," he echoed, his jaw tight.

She didn't have time to reassure him any further…or herself. "Hang on. I'm going to activate the flaps. I'll compensate with thrust, but…"

"It's going to get bumpy," he finished grimly.

"A little."

With that magnificent understatement, she brought the 727 out of its wide, low-level circle and applied the flaps. The jet shook and rattled like a tin can kicked down two flights of stairs. Every joint in its frame stressed. Metal shrieked against metal. The wings flexed like an eagle in flight.

But she slowed! Thank God, she slowed.

Suzanne took 407 down, sweating, straining, constantly checking airspeed, altitude, fuel consumption. Every few seconds she'd whip her gaze up, praying for a glimpse of the Florida shoreline in the twilight now purpling the eastern sky.

When the first lights appeared on the horizon, she slowed the jet almost to stall speed and brought her down to less than a hundred feet above the water. Suddenly, a flashing red light on the instrument panel put a kink in her stomach.

The fuel low-level light! Swallowing, she searched the horizon. They'd make it. Barely.

With the warning light emitting a continuous reminder of their precarious situation, Suzanne divided her attention between the instruments and the distant coastline. When the purplish smudge resolved into a more distinctive pattern of inlets and cays, she wanted to weep with relief, although she knew the worst was yet to come.

She keyed her intercom mike. "Five minutes to impact."

Ryder nodded, his gray eyes narrowed on the flickering lights in the distance. There weren't many. This stretch of Florida was inhabited primarily by alligators and egrets. In the midst of her own churning fear, Suzanne noticed that he'd clenched both fists so tight the knuckles showed white.

"Don't wimp out on me now."

"What?"

"I need you." She glanced pointedly at his fists, and forced a confidence she was far from feeling. "We're going to walk away from this."

He stared at her for a moment. Then, unbelievably, the weathered skin at the corners of his eyes crinkled and his mouth kicked up. As grins went, it was pretty puny, but it was definitely a grin.

"Actually, I was just thinking that we're putting down only a few hours drive from my ex-fiancée. If we walk away, I might just look her up."

"You do that. But first get on the intercom. Tell the folks in back to put their heads down, wrap their arms around their legs, and brace for landing. Remind them their seat cushions are flotation devices."

While Ryder did as she instructed, Suzanne brought the shaking, shuddering airframe down so low its belly almost skimmed the waves. Her heart bumped each time she checked the fuel gauge.

The coast rushed at them.

They were flying on fumes.

Water gave way to swamp.

When the swamp became a vast sea of grass dotted with scattered, islandlike stands of trees, Suzanne put the left flaps down full, compensated with a sharp right thrust, and throttled all the way back.

"Hold on!"

The big jet slammed into the watery weeds, glanced off, rose like a silver Venus from the grassy sea.

A second or two later, it hit again with a force that smashed Suzanne back against her seat. The last thing she heard was the agonized scream of metal ripping apart.

Ryder thought he'd been through hell in the past two years. The only woman he'd ever wanted to marry had played him like a cheap fiddle, first by working her way into a position as his secretary, then by worming her way into his heart. He still couldn't quite believe he'd been so damned gullible. Only after the feds showed up at his office and hauled him off in handcuffs did he have any idea Sharon and the "cousin" she'd convinced Ryder to hire had used his stationery, his fax, and his name to milk investors out of hundreds of thousands of dollars in phony oil leases.

But the searing shame of his trial and the long months at a minimum security prison didn't begin to compare with the hell he went through when he shook his head to clear the buzzing and saw watery weeds lapping at the 727's windshield.

Or when he turned his head and found Suzanne Delachek slumped lifelessly in the seat next to his.

"Dammit!"

His throat closing, he reached across the throttles, buried

a hand in her hair and pulled her head back. The skin under her jaw felt warm and smooth, but his own pulse hammered so hard he couldn't find hers.

It had to be there! She couldn't be…!

The faint flutter under his fingertips spawned a whoop of relief. "Atta girl, Delachek! I knew you were too tough to let a little thing like a crash landing take you out. Come on, babe. Wake up."

Groaning, she pulled away from his hand. A moment later, her lids fluttered up. Ryder's stomach clenched at the dazed incomprehension in their blue depths.

He had no way of knowing if she'd suffered internal injuries, and right now she couldn't tell him. But he knew he had to get her out of there. The jet's nose appeared to have augured into mud. The whole plane tilted down at a thirty-degree angle, but the damned thing could flop back at any minute, sink into the water, and take everyone aboard with it.

He struggled free of his shoulder harness. The instrument panel now sat almost in his lap. Grunting, Ryder wiggled out from under the tangled wires and crawled over the throttles. He had to fight his way up the angled cockpit and put his shoulder to the door to shove it open. Pushing through, he climbed over the debris in the galley.

"Hey, is anyone…?"

He caught himself a half step from pitching headfirst into the purple dusk. Stunned, he gaped at the empty hole where the fuselage used to be.

The whole body of the jet had broken off, right behind the forward galley. Only a couple of rows of seats remained. He stared at the darkening sky, trying to estimate how far the nose had traveled in the terrifying seconds after they hit. Trying to remember, too, what Suzanne had said about wreckage and scatter patterns.

The fuselage could be a mile behind them, he thought with a twist of his gut. Maybe more.

A groan spun Ryder toward the right row of seats. One of the convicts struggled up. Blood seeped from a cut on his forehead as he stared in stupefaction at the night sky.

"Wh…? What happened?"

Ryder didn't bother to answer, figuring the empty hole spoke for itself.

A second convict poked his head up. A face decorated with tattoos contorted in disbelief.

"Damn!"

After a moment of frozen immobility, the prisoner ducked back down, wrestled the bottom cushion from a twisted seat frame, and staggered up. He was headed for the open passenger door when Ryder caught his arm and hauled him around.

"Wait a minute! The pilot's hurt. I need you to help me get her out."

"Get her out yourself."

"She saved your ass, dammit."

The tattooed swastikas at the corners of his mouth twisted. "Tell it to the judge, cowboy."

The beefy prisoner had him by a good four inches and fifty pounds. Still, Ryder might have taken the gorilla on if the man hadn't wrenched a dangling shard of metal from the overhead compartment and hefted it with unmistakable menace.

"I ain't hanging around waitin' for no marshals to show up and put me in chains again. I'm outta here, cowboy. If you had any sense, you would be, too."

Still clutching the jagged metal, the prisoner hurtled out the door and hit the murky swamp with a splash. He surfaced a moment later, spitting mud, and waded through the shoulder-high water toward freedom. Disgusted, Ryder turned to the other survivor.

"Don't ask me to help," the man whined, scrambling for the door. "Can't you see I'm bleeding?"

"Yeah, I see."

The reddish trickle had already started to congeal, but Ryder didn't waste time appealing to the man's conscience. Two years in a minimum security facility had taught him most of his fellow inmates didn't own one.

When he climbed back into the cockpit, Suzanne was awake and *not* happy about the fact that the crumpled instrument panel had pinned her right leg. She'd dug her fingers into her thigh and was tugging for all she was worth.

"Hang on. Let me help you."

"Unless...you...have...a jack," she ground out, "you won't...lift that panel."

"You're talking to a guy who used to wrestle drill bits through hard rock. I don't need a jack."

Hoping to hell he could follow through on that bit of Texas-size bravado, Ryder crawled sideways into his seat and got one knee on the floor. An awkward contortion wedged his shoulder under the instrument panel. He pushed upward, grunting with the strain.

"It's moving!" she cried. "A little more. Just a little more."

Gritting his teeth, he heaved again. Suzanne gave a gasp and scrambled free.

"Okay, I'm out."

He let the panel back down and climbed out of the cockpit right behind her, making it to the galley just in time to hear her anguished exclamation.

"Oh, my God!"

Bracing himself against the tilted floor, he stared over

her shoulder at the now dark night. No flames or shooting sparks shot into the black velvet sky. Ryder told himself that was good. It had to be good.

"I didn't hear any explosion when we hit. Or see any smoke when I crawled out here a little while ago. Maybe… Maybe the fuselage just sheared off and is sitting in a few feet of water a mile or so back."

"Maybe," she whispered.

A shudder shimmied down her spine, then she pulled herself together with an effort of sheer willpower that was almost painful to watch.

Ryder's admiration for this woman kicked up another ten or fifteen points. If he hadn't seen her in action, he wouldn't have figured someone with her sugar-spun blond hair, creamy skin and baby-blue eyes could be so tough. But then, he reminded himself dryly, his judgment sucked when it came to the female of the species.

"All the computer models for this kind of a breakup say the main body of the aircraft would keep its wings and remain intact," she told him. "I was counting on that when I brought us down."

"So they could have all walked or waded out?"

Her jaw locked. "Theoretically."

"Hey, any theory is better than none at this point."

She flashed him a look Ryder had no trouble interpreting. She'd been in command of the 727. She was responsible for everyone on that aircraft. She wasn't asking for or accepting any reassurances until she knew the fate of each soul aboard Flight 407.

"What about the passengers in these seats?" she asked, frowning as she swept a glance at the two remaining rows. "Didn't you see anyone when you came back the first time?"

"Two men. Both convicts. They bailed out after we hit."

She arched a silver-blond brow. Ryder knew exactly what she was thinking.

"Why didn't I bail, too? I owe you, babe, and I always pay my debts."

The brow inched up another notch, but she didn't comment on the obvious contradiction of a con with ethics.

"I'm going back into the cockpit to see if the radios are working. If they survived the crash, we can—"

She broke off and grabbed at the galley wall for support as the jet dropped a good foot. Metal groaned. Debris shifted and tumbled. The swampy mud whooshed and sucked.

"This thing's going under at any second," Ryder said grimly, kicking aside a chunk of the overhead compartment. "We'd better get out of here."

"No! We should stay with the plane. Search and rescue will lock on to the transponders and—"

Another sudden drop put an end to that discussion. The floor hit the weeds. Water rushed in, swirling waist high. Ryder grabbed Suzanne and shoved her out the door, then jumped out right behind her. Surfacing, he shook the water from his eyes and spun in a tight circle. He found her a few feet away, floundering.

The water that lapped his shoulders reached almost to her nose. Her heavy boots didn't help matters. Ryder caught her as she sank into the mud and hauled her along with him. They'd barely made ten yards when the swamp claimed the forward section of the jet. With a sucking groan, the nose and galley settled into the mud. The domed roof rose above the saw grass, glinting in the moonlight for a moment, until the waving plants closed around it.

A few more bubbling hisses escaped. A long whoosh. Then an eerie silence descended.

Ryder swallowed a lump in his throat. With it came the taste of mud and a gulp of cool, refreshing liquid. It took him a moment or two to realize this sea of grass was actually some kind of freshwater lake.

Beside him, Suzanne tread water and stared at the spot where Flight 407 had disappeared. When she spoke, the steely note of command had slipped back into her voice.

"Let's move out."

Ryder tightened his grip on her upper arm and started forward once again, dragging her along with him. Utter darkness surrounded them. The tall, waving grass almost blanked out the night sky. His skin crawled when he thought about what might be slithering around beneath the water's inky surface. He hoped to hell the alligators and crocs native to these parts had gone to roost for the night.

"Are you sure you got a fix on those trees?" Suzanne asked after a few moments, panting with the effort of keeping her chin above water.

Heck of a time to ask, Ryder thought, hiding his own creeping doubts in a sardonic affirmative.

"Yeah, I got a fix on them."

More or less.

"They were about a hundred yards off to starboard," he added to reassure himself as much as her.

She didn't say a word, but he could guess what she was thinking. Starboard covered a lot of territory. They pushed forward another few yards, only to jerk to a halt at the sound of a distant drone.

Ryder spun around, searching the night sky. Suzanne wrenched free of his grip and practically climbed up his arm onto his shoulder to see over the grass. The drone grew louder, changing to the unmistakable sound of aircraft engines.

"It's another C-130," she exclaimed. "Search and rescue's on the scene. Oh, God, look!"

Her scream ricocheted in his ear as a red ball arced out of the swamp and shot skyward.

"It's a flare!" Pounding on his shoulder with her fist, she shouted again. "Ryder, it's a flare."

"I see it."

"Some of the passengers survived!"

"Maybe all of them."

He dodged another blow and whipped an arm around her waist to keep her from toppling into the water in her excitement.

"Maybe all of them!" she echoed ecstatically.

She slid back down his body until her boots touched mud, her whole being alive with excitement, and grinned up at him.

Ryder couldn't help himself. Her face was little more than a pale blur in the darkness. Her hair straggled down her cheeks and wrapped around her neck. But her eyes shone with such joy he had to kiss her. Right there. In the middle of the swamp. With the faint reverberation of airplane engines teasing his ears and murky water lapping at his chest.

This time, she kissed him back. Hooking both arms around his neck, she threw herself into the fusion of wet mouths and wet bodies with an exuberance that rocked him back on his heels. Ryder felt himself going under, literally and figuratively.

The lust that slammed into his belly almost knocked him off his feet again. It rushed at him out of the darkness, hot and hard and fast. Stunned by the sexual punch, he jerked his head up, yanked Suzanne's arms down, and put a few watery feet between them.

She looked as surprised as he felt, but, true to form, pulled herself together a whole lot faster than he did. "That was a mistake."

"One of many I've made lately," he agreed dryly.

Trust him to get a bad case of the hots for a female as wrong for him as he was for her. He'd traveled down that road once. He wasn't heading down it again...even if Suzanne wanted to, which wasn't likely given their respective circumstances.

When they got out of this, she'd go back to flying.

He'd go back to prison.

Locking his jaw, Ryder gripped her wrist again and turned his back on the incandescent white flare arcing down through the night sky.

They stumbled onto a slippery limestone ledge ten minutes later. Spiky palmettos crowded right to the water's edge, scraping Ryder's arms as he half pushed, half dragged Suzanne onto higher land. Only after she'd gained solid ground did he notice her limp.

"My ankle got caught under the instrument panel," she said, shrugging aside his concern.

"Take your boot off and let me—"

"I'm okay."

Hobbling up to the edge of a forest of twisted mangroves and tall, straight hardwood trees, she grabbed a branch for support and turned to search the swamp behind them.

"Look at that!"

Her exclamation swung Ryder around. The sight that greeted him sucked every molecule of air from his lungs.

A mile or so away the swamp was lit up like a Broadway theater on opening night. A half dozen planes circled, their strobes flashing red and white. Powerful searchlights sliced downward. Loudspeakers sent amplified voices wavering across the sea of saw grass.

Ryder's stomach clenched with each faint echo. Panting from the arduous slog, he stood beside Suzanne and strained to decipher the distant voices.

"We have you. Hang on."

"Just hook the harness under your arms."

"This is Search Three. We've got—" the voice wavered, cut out, came back on "—on board and are bringing up another."

"Wrap your arms around the hoist, ma'am."

Suzanne jerked upright. "Did you hear that?"

"I heard it."

"That 'ma'am' must be Kelly Jackson. She made it!"

"And if she did, I'm betting Spence Cantrell is right there beside her."

Ryder allowed himself a slow, sloppy grin. They pulled it off after all! Then Suzanne matched his grin, and he felt himself going under again.

Well, damn it all to hell and back! When the woman shed her icy control and let loose with both barrels, she packed more punch than the beer and whiskey chasers Ryder used to down like rusty water after a day wrestling pipe.

He was just experiencing a few adrenaline aftershocks, he decided. Some sort of survival syndrome. He'd beat the odds. Taken a bite out of death, chewed it up, and spit it out. He wasn't feeling as randy as a goat just because Suzanne Delachek aimed a grin his way. Hell, he'd feel this way about anyone who'd shared the past few hours with him.

Well, maybe not anyone. Just blue-eyed blondes with

more courage than common sense and bodies that filled out a flight suit in ways that were probably illegal in fourteen states.

"We might as well pull up a rock and have a seat," she suggested, thankfully unaware of the tight ache she'd started in his belly. "Odds are search and rescue won't locate the rest of the wreckage until morning."

"Morning, huh?"

Not a problem. He'd survived a midair shootout and a plane crash. He figured he could survive another seven or eight hours without making a total ass of himself by tugging down the zipper on Suzanne's flight suit and devouring her whole.

Unfortunately, his figuring didn't take into account her little cry of pain when her leg buckled under her. Or the way she fit against his body when he scooped her into his arms to break her fall.

Chapter 3

Suzanne didn't think of herself as a particularly big woman. Five-six and one hundred-nineteen pounds hardly qualified as huge. But most of the males of her acquaintance would have herniated a disk if they'd tried to swing her up in their arms the way Ryder just did. The mere fact that he'd gathered her up with such ease aroused the heck out of her.

With her body tucked tight against his and heat sizzling in her belly, she tried to rein in her galloping hormones. Sternly, she told herself to throttle back. Like, now! Hamilton was even more of a loser than her ex. She was just turned on because she was alive and Hamilton was a genuine, world-class hottie.

Really. This was all just delayed situational reaction. It didn't take a genius to figure out why her throbbing ankle, soaked flight suit and weedy hair had all dropped right out of her mind. She'd successfully ditched a 727. Flight 407's passengers seemed to have survived. And she'd just shared the most intense hours of her life with the sexiest man she'd stumbled across in a long, long time. Of course she'd feel aroused.

Her mind worked it out with perfect logic. Unfortunately, her body didn't seem the least interested in logic at that moment. Little pinpoints of heat burned just under her skin everywhere she connected with Ryder's lean, hard frame.

"I'm okay." She tried to hold herself away from the flat, muscled belly bumping against her hip. "Really. You can put me down."

"I will, as soon as I find us a comfortable spot to watch the show."

Hefting her higher in his arms, he searched amid the tangle of palmettos and mangoes lining the shore. Suzanne had almost forgotten how to breathe by the time he hunkered down on one knee and placed her on a tuft of spongy grass, with her back resting against a twisted tree root.

"Let's take a look at that ankle."

His hands went to the zipper on the leg of her flight suit. When his fingers connected with bare flesh beneath, Suzanne's stomach executed a double back flip. Sucking in a swift breath, she decided she'd better get his hands away from her before she did something monumentally stupid…like suggest he play with the rest of her zippers.

"I don't think I should take the boot off," she protested. "I might not be able to get it back on, and I'm not walking through any more of this swamp barefooted."

"I'll carry you."

Suzanne didn't think so!

"I'm okay. The throbbing's already eased."

Actually, the pain had gotten lost amid several other, far more immediate sensations.

"Be sensible. If you've broken or sprained your ankle,

a tight boot could cause it to balloon up worse than a dead armadillo in July.''

''Oh, charming image.''

A grin slashed across his face. ''A man's gotta call it like he sees it. Besides, that's considered just plain talk where I come from.''

She was still recovering from the whammy of that grin when his fingers went to work on the wet bootlaces. Planting both palms on the spongy ground beside her, Suzanne leaned back. Enough moonlight filtered through the mango's branches for her to look at him—really look at him—for the first time.

She forced herself to see past his rugged, square-jawed handsomeness to the intelligence in his smoky gray eyes. Past his ropy muscles to the gentleness in his hands when he eased off the boot. Past the convict to the man under the now tattered white T-shirt and tan pants.

''Where *do* you come from?'' she asked, driven by a near insatiable curiosity to know how Ryder Hamilton had made the transition from corporation president to convict.

''A little town no one's ever heard of, just south of Midland, Texas.''

''How did you get into the oil business?''

He flashed her an amused look. ''You ever been to Midland, sweetheart?''

She wished he wouldn't call her that. Her heart fluttered idiotically every time he rolled out one of those drawling ''sweethearts'' or ''babes.''

''No.''

''I didn't think so.''

Gently, he rotated her ankle. His palms were warm and leather tough against her skin.

''If you had, you'd know it's smack in the middle of the Permian Basin, one of the richest fields in the West.

Folks around Midland eat, sleep and drink oil. Literally. The underground water tables are so contaminated, they have to truck in drinking water.''

"Isn't Midland where you headquartered your corporation?''

The grin stayed in place, but the look he shot her wasn't quite as amused. "I guess the marshals filled you in on my background. Or was it the FBI?''

"The FBI.'' She made no apologies. "I wanted to know who was in the cockpit with O'Connor.''

He said nothing, just rotated her foot with the same easy touch. An errant bead of water dripped from his hair onto his cheek. Suzanne traced the quicksilver drop down to the line of his jaw. Swallowing, she tried to remember what they were talking about.

"I'll admit my heart skipped a few beats when they told me you'd never flown anything bigger than a bug smasher.''

"Yeah, well, mine skipped a few beats, too, when I got a look at that shattered instrument panel.''

"You did good, Hamilton.''

Her gaze shifted past his shoulder to the searchlights slashing through night sky.

"Real good.''

He swiveled on his heel, still holding her foot in his hands. His thumb made little circles on the indentation behind her ankle bone while he took in the distant lights.

"We did, didn't we?'' he said softly, his eyes on the search and rescue effort.

Suzanne couldn't believe what she was feeling right now. She'd fallen head over heels in love with her husband, had ached inside as that love slowly died. She'd hung on stubbornly for two years, determined to make the marriage work despite Jack's unique interpretation of the concept of monogamy. She'd also learned more than she'd ever wanted to know about the politics of sex from her ex-husband, who'd considered himself an expert at all things erotic.

But she'd never, *ever,* experienced anything like the heat Hamilton branded into her skin with each lazy circle of his thumb. She almost mewled in disappointment when he swiveled back around and gently lowered her foot.

"I don't feel any broken bones or swelling."

"I...uh...probably just pulled too hard when I yanked my leg free of the control panel. The pain's gone now. Really."

She tried for a little humor to cover the fact that she was melting inside her flight suit.

"If you aren't going back into the oil business when you get out of prison, you ought to think about becoming a masseur. You give great ankle, Hamilton."

"Yeah?" His gray eyes glinted. "You ought to try my knee sometime. I have it on the best authority that it's even better than my ankle."

She cocked a brow and couldn't resist another probe. "The 'best' authority being that ex-fiancée you want to look up in Miami?"

His mouth twisted. "Sharon didn't care much for my knee-work."

"She must have been dead from the neck down, then."

"Let's just say I was dead from the neck up." He settled beside Suzanne on the springy turf. "Like a fool, I never saw that the only thing she *did* care about was how much she and her so-called cousin could extract from unsuspecting dupes using my name."

There it was again. Every convict's lament. He was innocent. He'd been set up.

Suzanne waited for disdain to sweep through her. Reminded herself yet again that Hamilton was no different from the sleazoid roofer who'd milked twelve thousand dollars from her parents' savings. And yet...

She wanted to believe him.

Absurdly, illogically, she wanted to believe him.

Against all odds, he'd kept Flight 407 in the air after O'Connor's heart attack. He'd been right there beside Suzanne when they went into the swamp. He'd climbed back through the wreckage to pull her out of the cockpit when he could have bailed out, like the others. What had he said?

I owe you, babe.

And I always pay my debts.

The dichotomy between the convict and the man fascinated her. No, fascinated wasn't the right word. It went deeper than that. The past hours had forged a bond of tensile steel between her and Hamilton. She wanted to know what made him tick. Understand what fed the streak of fair play and decency that his years in jail hadn't wiped out.

"Why do you want to look up this...? What's her name?"

"Sharon."

"Why do you want to look up Sharon? You've already been tried and found guilty. Obviously, the jury believed her and not you."

"I was guilty. Of sheer stupidity, if nothing else. But the jury didn't believe her. They never even heard her testimony. She skipped town just hours before the FBI knocked on my door."

"Couldn't the feds find her?"

"I doubt they tried very hard." The Texas twang slipped back into his voice, as tough and blistering as barbed wire baking in the summer sun. "They nabbed the man whose name was on the phony oil leases. They got who they wanted.''

For reasons she didn't stop to examine at that moment, Suzanne wouldn't give up.

"If the feds couldn't find her,'' she said doggedly, "how do you know she's in Miami?''

"Convicts talk, sweetheart. That's about all we have to do most of the time. The prison communications net would put the Pentagon's to shame. I pinpointed Sharon's location months ago. She and Pauly-boy are fencing stolen goods in a pawnshop in South Miami.''

His voice hardened. He stared at the searchlights sweeping the swamp a mile away. "I've only got six months left on my sentence. I plan to pay them a visit when I get out.''

"And do what? Beat the truth out of them?''

"If I have to.''

"Sure you will, Hamilton,'' she shot back scornfully. "I can see you roughing up a woman. Particularly one you loved enough to get engaged to.''

He swung around to face her. The glint of moonlight in his eyes made them hard as steel.

"How the hell do you know what I'm capable of? I'm a con, remember? Scum that had to be put behind bars for the safety of society.''

"*I owe you, babe.*'' She threw his own words at him. "*I always pay my debts.*''

His jaw squared. "This is one debt that's owed me, and I'm dammed well going to collect on it.''

"You sure talk a good game.''

"Back off, Delachek.''

"If you're so tough, why didn't you leave me? Why didn't you escape with the others?''

"Back off.''

"Why, Hamilton?"

"You want to know? You really want to know?"

"Yes!"

He wrapped a hand around her nape, just as he'd done in the cockpit of the 727. His thumb, his so-skilled thumb, slid under her chin and tipped her head back.

"You got into my head, woman. Just like you said you would. Every move I've made over the past hours, you've made with me. I haven't had a single thought that didn't include you."

Her breath caught.

His roughened.

"Watch yourself, Delachek. The thoughts I'm having right now would curl your toes."

She wet her lips, half flustered, wholly aroused. He looked so fierce with his eyes narrowed to slits behind those ridiculously thick lashes, his chin and cheeks whiskered like a pirate's. The words tumbled out on a husky laugh before she could stop them.

"You're in my head, too, Hamilton. I'm having exactly the same thoughts."

He tipped her chin farther back. Those gray eyes challenged her, warned her. "You couldn't possibly be thinking what I'm thinking."

Alarms started pinging like mad in her head. All systems flashed a warning. Ignoring every dictate of reason and common sense, she followed her instincts.

"Wanna bet?" she said softly, rising up on her knees.

All it took was a little lean forward, a touch of her mouth to his, to short-circuit the warning systems completely. His lips were warm and still wet and incredibly delicious. Suzanne took her time, tasting, touching.

"You want to know what I'm thinking?" she murmured, sliding her tongue along his lower lip. "I'm thinking that you give great ankle. That I'd like to take you up on your offer of knee. Maybe test your navel technique. Or even…''

He jerked his head up, his entire body so taut it quivered. ''You're crazy, you know that?''

''So everyone keeps telling me.''

''Listen to me.'' He caught her face in his cupped hands. ''It's the crash. The adrenaline rush of beating the odds. You'll hate yourself come daylight if you give in to this insane impulse.''

She would. She knew she would. Yet calm, rational, always-in-control Suzanne could no more keep from sliding her palms over his slick, wet shoulders than she could keep Flight 407 in the air.

His muscles jumped under her touch. Hers jumped at the feel of his smooth, supple skin. Leaning forward, she dropped little kisses along his collarbone where his T-shirt had torn.

''Daylight is a long time away,'' she whispered between kisses.

He groaned. Or maybe he laughed. She was too busy drinking in his taste and the fresh-washed scent of musky male to pay much attention to the sound rumbling from his chest.

Ryder made a last attempt to convince her of the utter insanity of this moment out of time. Grasping her shoulders, he held her at arm's length.

''Think about this, Suzanne. Just think! I don't have any condoms. They don't issue them for con-air flights. What if I got you pregnant?''

''I'm on the pill. I was married for a while and got used to protecting myself.''

''That doesn't sound like much of a marriage.''

''It wasn't.''

Funny, she couldn't even remember what Jack looked like right now. Ryder Hamilton's face filled her vision and her mind. Frowning in concern. Tight with desire.

His stark hunger sparked her own. Emotions she'd kept under rigid control since she'd climbed in the chase plane boiled over. Need swept through her, so raw and urgent her womb clenched and her hands curled into tight fists.

"Dammit, Hamilton, are we going to make love or not?"

He stared at her for long moments. Then the slow, wicked grin she was coming to identify as his alone tugged at his mouth.

"Yes, ma'am. We surely are."

Ryder had never undressed a woman wearing a flight suit before. He decided he liked all those little zippers on the green uniform. One for each arm. One for each leg. Then that long, slow slide of the middle zipper that bared her breasts, her ribs, her hollowed stomach.

When she shimmied out of the wet suit and knelt to face him, Ryder's throat went as dry as a played out well. Her white cotton bra and panties were more functional than provocative, but they clung to her like a second, transparent skin.

"Oh, baby."

The hoarse croak earned him a smile.

"I'd take that as a compliment, but you probably haven't gotten this close to a woman in two years."

An answering smile glinted in his eyes as he stripped off his shirt and tossed it aside.

"I've *never* gotten this close to a woman like you, darlin'."

She would be a complete and utter idiot to fall for a line like that, but Suzanne figured she'd passed the point of idiocy sometime around the first stroke of his thumb on her ankle. Ridiculously, she felt flattered. Even more so when she unhooked her bra and let it fall, then peeled her panties down her hips.

He didn't touch her. Just knelt on the springy grass a foot or so away, naked to his waist, his tan pants riding low on his hips.

"Do you have any idea how beautiful you are?"

He made her feel beautiful. Despite the mud, the reeds no doubt clinging to her hair, the total absence of anything faintly resembling makeup. His eyes devoured her.

He reached across the small space separating them to cup her breast. As mammary organs went, Suzanne considered hers to be fairly average. But Ryder worshipped the soft mound, first with his hands, then, wrapping an arm around her waist to draw her close, with his mouth. Before he finished, her nipple was hard and tight and on fire.

So was Ryder. His skin burned wherever she touched him, and she made a conscientious effort to touch him everywhere. His flesh strained, hard and insistent, pressing into her belly when he tightened his arm and pulled her down atop him. They rolled together on the spongy grass, tongues tangling, legs twisting.

In the distance, planes and choppers still hovered. Loudspeakers still blared. Searchlights still cut through the night.

But here, on this island of palmetto and mangoes and buttonwoods rising above the saw grass, they were out of reach of the searchlights, and hours away from the reality that awaited them with the dawn.

Right here, right now, there was only the feel of his body hard on hers, the heat of his mouth, the urgency in his hands when he parted her legs, positioned himself between her thighs, and sank home with a sure, smooth thrust that left Suzanne gasping.

The man knew how to pleasure a woman. This particular woman, anyway. He buried his fists in her hair. Covered her mouth with his. Drove into her. Slowly at first, then faster and harder and deeper.

All too soon, she felt the first, tight waves spreading from the center of her body. Desperately, she tried to push them away. She wasn't ready. She didn't want this impossible moment to end.

"Not yet. Ryder, not... Oh!"

She arched her back, let the sensation lift her, spin her through a universe of pure pleasure.

"Ooooooh!"

She was still riding the waves when Ryder stiffened. He stayed rigid and unmoving until she'd gone boneless beneath him. Only then did he pick up the rhythm again. This time the strokes were shorter, the lunges tighter.

He entered her a final time, lifting her half off the grass with the force of his thrust. For a moment...maybe an hour...Suzanne lay beneath his taut, slick body. Only half aware of what she was doing, she traced tiny circles at the base of his spine.

When he rolled to one side, he took her with him. She cuddled next to him on a bed of grass and discarded clothes. She was hoping that they didn't share this particular piece of real estate with anything creepy or crawly when Ryder gave a grunt of utter male satisfaction.

"Now that," he muttered, drawing her closer into his side, "was what I'd call one hell of a landing."

The giggles started somewhere inside Suzanne's chest. She tried to hold them back. Told herself it was absurd to feel so happy, given the fact that she'd just put a 727 down in a swamp and made love to a complete stranger.

No, not a stranger.

Ryder.

He could never be a stranger to her now. He was in her head. A piece of him was in her heart. Burying her face in the hollow between his neck and shoulder, she let her bubbles of laughter float on the night air.

Chapter 4

Day 5

"So tell me about the jerk you were married to."

The deep drawl drifted toward Suzanne in that hazy state somewhere between deep sleep and almost awake. She pried open one eyelid and squinted at the shadowy figure leaning over her, his head propped in one hand, his beard looking even more scruffy in the faint light of predawn than it had in the cockpit yesterday.

Good Lord! Was it only yesterday? Just... She scrunched her forehead, forcing her sleep-muddled brain to count backward. Just nineteen hours since she'd climbed into the chase plane? Twelve since she'd ditched Flight 407 in the swamp? Eight since...

Since Ryder.

She forced the other eyelid up.

Nope, she hadn't hallucinated him. He was right here beside her, his gray eyes lazy on her face, his black hair sticking up in spikes. Wearing nothing, she saw with a sudden tightening in her belly, except the tan pants.

It took her a moment to realize he'd draped his ragged T-shirt over her chest and upper arms, the flight suit over her lower body.

"Mosquitoes," he said when she fingered the cotton, a question in her eyes. "I didn't want them feasting on your succulent flesh."

"What about your succulent flesh?"

"I'm tougher than old horsemeat, sweetheart. Not even our homegrown skeeters can get through this hide."

Or through the thin coat of mud he'd smeared over himself, she noted wryly, more awake and observant now.

"So what about him?" he asked, reaching up with his free hand to twist a strand of her hair around his finger.

"The jerk I was married to? He was…just a jerk."

"How long were you married?"

"On paper, four years. In fact, probably about three months. Jack had a short attention span, but it took me a while to recognize that fact. Even then, I refused to give up on our marriage. I hung on long after I should have. I, ah, tend to get a bit tenacious at times."

"I noticed that about you."

"You did, did you?"

"Yep. I also noticed that you're smart as hell, braver than a Saint Bernard, and have legs that won't quit."

"Anything else?" she asked, a smile dancing on her lips. "I might be able to use some of this on my résumé."

He gave the strand curled around his finger a little tug. "You make love with a joy that takes my breath away just thinking about it. You crinkle your nose when you laugh. And you're cooler than dry ice when the chips are down. I like that about you…now."

"Now, huh? What about yesterday afternoon?"

"Yesterday afternoon..."

His teasing expression faded as memories of the day before crowded in on him. On both of them. Suddenly, the dark pewter sky held not the promise of morning and rescue, but the remembered residue of terror.

Reality seeped back, curling between them like the cool mist rising from the saw grass. Suzanne shivered and started to draw the thin cotton T-shirt tighter around her shoulders only to realize she'd feel a lot more comfortable in her flight suit. More comfortable, and far more prepared for the rescue aircraft that would widen their search patterns come dawn.

The thought of rescue brought with it another dash of cold reality. In another hour, two at most, they'd go their separate ways. Suzanne back to Oklahoma City and her job with the FAA. Ryder to whatever prison he was headed to when he boarded the ill-fated Flight 407. Without moving a muscle, she could feel the chasm they'd bridged so briefly begin to widen once more.

She'd known it would happen. So had Ryder. He'd warned her last night that she would regret giving in to the insane impulse that had propelled her into his arms. She didn't regret it, exactly. She could never regret these stolen hours. She'd carry the memory of this brief, incredible interlude with her for the rest of her life.

But it was time to face the dawn. To rejoin the real world. To reshoulder her responsibilities as pilot-in-command of a downed aircraft. She knew she'd feel a heck of lot more prepared for those responsibilities once she got dressed and splashed some water on her face.

Yet the mechanics of getting dressed in front of Ryder Hamilton now seemed a whole lot more complicated than getting *un*dressed had a few hours ago. She caught her lower lip between her teeth, wondering how to suggest she needed a little privacy, a little space.

She didn't have to suggest. Ryder must have read the withdrawal in her eyes, or experienced the same dash of cold reality. He stared down at her, his own eyes shuttered, then released the strand of hair he'd been playing with and rolled away, taking his warmth with him.

Suzanne missed him instantly.

Turning his back, he pulled on his socks and boots. She ached to lay a hand on that broad expanse of skin and somehow reconnect. Before she could decide whether that was wise, or even what she wanted to do, he pushed to his feet and raked a hand through his hair. His gaze swept the dense stands of mango and tropical hardwood before coming back to her. Whatever he saw in her face tightened his own. Under the prickly three-days' growth, his jaw squared.

"I'm going to scope out our little island. Maybe scrounge up some fruit or something for breakfast."

She nodded, oddly hurt and relieved by the guarded note in his voice. She could have told him that their "little" island might well stretch for miles, that she and her folks had spent weeks that long-ago summer exploring the limestone ridges called hammocks that rose above the seasonally wet saw grass prairie. Instead, she chewed on her lower lip and kept silent. The time for sharing bits of personal history had passed…along with the soaring joy of beating the odds. Now they both needed to get on with the business of survival.

Suzanne waited until he disappeared into the stand of trees to crawl out from under her makeshift coverings. She'd better get dressed and pick out a handy tree to duck behind herself. With luck, she might even stumble across a freshwater pool to sluice off in. Grimacing at the clammy dampness of her underwear, she tugged them on, then slithered into the flight suit. Her hand faltered when she reached for the front zipper.

Images of the previous night danced before her eyes. Ryder had made inching down that little plastic tab a sensual experience Suzanne wouldn't forget in this lifetime. Probably not in the next, either. Her throat went dry at the memory of the kisses he'd dropped on her throat, her breasts, her—

Whoa! She needed to focus here, to get both her clothes and her head on straight before the choppers started circling. Forcing her mind from the erotic to the immediate, she tugged on her boots and picked her way through the palmettos in the opposite direction from the path Ryder had taken.

As it had so many years ago, the Everglades' unique beauty pulled at her senses. The verdant richness of damp grass drifted through the pinkish dawn. Shady buttonwoods garlanded with air plants vied for space and sunlight with black mangroves, royal palms and the twisted little tree called gumbo-limbo. A much younger Suzanne had delighted in the silly name, just as the sight of a stately heron wading near the edge of the hammock brought a gasp of delight from the woman she'd become.

She paused for a moment, watching the bird silhouetted against the still-shadowed river of grass. He moved so slowly, as if just awakening to the new dawn, until something in the dark water caught his eye. Quick as a bullet, his head shot down. After a short, furious thrashing, the heron emerged with a flapping fish scissored in its long mandibles.

Suzanne's stomach rumbled in appreciation of the hunter's skill. She tried to remember the last time she'd eaten. Yesterday morning. At Sam Houston International Airport, right before she climbed into the chase plane.

"I don't suppose you'd care to share your breakfast, would you, buddy?"

She didn't have any way to light a fire to bake or roast a fish, but a little sushi would certainly help fill the hollow pit of her stomach.

Evidently the heron wasn't into sharing. He tossed back his head and guzzled the fish down whole.

Sighing, Suzanne moved on.

A little farther along the shore she found a break where rainwater collecting in the limestone had formed a stream-like channel. Suzanne plunged into the trees and followed the trickling water to the collection point. She attended to her basic needs, then stripped off the flight suit again and knelt beside the limestone basin.

Even without soap, she managed to do a credible job of removing all traces of yesterday's tumultuous events. A bit of bark scraped most of the night's fuzz from her teeth, making her feel almost human again. She had just zipped herself back into the green uniform when a crunch in the undergrowth jerked her head around.

The palmettos a few yards away rattled.

"Ryder?"

The papery rattle ceased, but Suzanne's mind had already taken off. Her heart in her throat, she recalled in vivid detail the snub-nosed crocodile that had waddled into her parents' campsite early one morning. Or had it been an alligator? She could never keep the two reptiles straight, and wasn't particularly anxious to come face to face with either one right now.

Another crunch brought her surging to her feet.

"Hamilton? Is that you?"

The palmettos shook again. Suzanne backed up. She was

all ready to beat a hasty retreat when a hulking convict with a shaved head and water dripping from his torn, muddied clothes crashed through.

"No, it ain't Hamilton."

Suzanne's first reaction was relief. Even crocodiles possessed more attractive faces than this tattooed creep, but at least he wouldn't have her for breakfast. Then she noticed the jagged shard of metal in his meaty fist.

Relief tripped instantly into wariness, but she'd dealt with enough uncertain situations in her career to know the last thing she should show was fear.

"Are you off Flight 407?"

His mouth twisted, distorting the swastikas inked into the corner of each lip. "Whaddya think, I got these rags on Fifth Avenue?"

"I'm glad you survived," she said for lack of anything else.

"Survived, my ass." He swiped a beefy forearm across his face in disgust. "I almost drowned tryin' to punch my way through that grass, then I got lost in the dark and spent all night goin' in circles."

Suzanne let out a secret sigh of relief. The thought that he might have lurked in the trees, watching her and Ryder, had made her skin crawl.

"Anyone else with you?" she asked coolly.

He took his time answering. She didn't like the way he played with the glistening metal shard, testing it over and over on the ball of his thumb.

"No, I ain't got no one with me. What about you? Who's this Hamilton you was calling to? One of them marshals from the plane?"

"No, a convict."

The word tasted bad in her mouth.

Recognition clicked behind the prisoner's eyes. "Big

guy? Black hair? The one what flew the plane when the copilot crapped on us?''

''That's him.''

''Well, well. He went back and pulled you out, huh? Accommodatin' of him.''

He rocked back on his heels, thinking. Suzanne could almost hear the clank of wheels turning inside his shaved head.

''You hear them rescue planes circlin' over the grass last night and this mornin'?''

''Yes, I did.''

''They gonna find us?''

''Any minute now.''

''That's what I'm thinkin', too. The marshals are gonna drag every inch of this swamp until they round up all the prisoners from Flight 407.''

He stared at her, his black eyes calculating.

''I figure I'm gonna need me a ticket outta here,'' he said slowly. ''That might just be you.''

The hair on the back of Suzanne's neck lifted. Swiftly, she calculated her chances of taking this guy down. He was big, maybe six-four or five, and packed solid with tattooed muscle. She'd tossed enough men on their backs during her self-defense and survival training to feel confident in most situations.

This wasn't one of them.

There was no way she was going to let herself be used as a hostage, though. Not without a fight. She'd try reason first, though.

''You saw what happened to the man who tried to hijack Flight 407. You don't think the marshals are going to just fly you out of the swamp to a destination of your choice, do you?''

''No, but you will.''

''The hell I w—''

For a goliath, the man moved with lightning speed. He was on her like a hyena on fresh kill.

Even then Suzanne might have gotten in a swift kick or a knee to the groin if a mango root hadn't tripped her up. She stumbled backward, off-balance but fighting him with fists and nails. He ended the uneven contest with a single slice of the serrated metal shard.

Frowning, Ryder squinted at the western horizon, just turning a flamingo pink. The drone of aircraft engines cut through the slowly brightening sky. He thought he caught the whap of rotor blades a couple of times. Once, the clang of ships' bells.

Dammit, where was Suzanne?

The guards had removed the prisoners' personal effects before they marched them onto the 727. Without a watch, Ryder could only guess how long it had been since he'd returned to find Suzanne gone, but he was sure at least twenty minutes had passed. Maybe more. He'd give her another five, he decided, then go looking.

Not that she couldn't take care of herself. He'd never met a more self-possessed woman. Man, either, for that matter.

His gut still twisted when he remembered watching that C-130 Hercules creep into position above Flight 407. He hadn't pulled in a whole breath the entire time the slender figure in the helmet and green flight suit had spun like a wind-tossed top at the end of a thin steel cable.

Thinking of that flight suit put another kink in his gut. Who could have imagined that he'd ever see what lay under the green fabric? Not just see. Touch. Taste. The mere thought of her smooth, silky flesh balled his fists.

He had to stop thinking about last night! He'd drive

himself crazy if he didn't. He still had to get through a lot of empty hours before he tasted freedom again. Six months of empty days, restless nights. He couldn't tantalize himself with fantasies of meeting up with Suzanne again when those six months had passed. Or torture himself by wishing he'd met her before a pouty redhead had sashayed into his heart and right out again, taking his company payroll, his reputation, and a good chunk of his pride with her.

For a man everyone round Midland touted as the next Donald Trump, he'd sure been thinking with the wrong body part when he'd locked on to Sharon's radar signal that night at the Rusty Derrick. Funny how easy it was to confuse lust with love.

Hooking his thumbs in his pockets, Ryder scowled at the sun. Okay, so he lusted for Suzanne, too. What man wouldn't? The ice maiden packed a giant-size wallop of heat under her seemingly frigid exterior. She could cut a man off at the knees with one flash of those blue eyes, and the body that went with them took him down another six inches. Hell, her voice had turned Ryder on even before he'd met her, and he'd been expecting to ride a 727 out of the sky at any minute!

Yet...

He couldn't remember mere lust kicking him square in the gut like this before. Or feeling this tight, desperate knot at the idea that he might never see Suzanne again. Maybe after he got out he'd give the FAA a call, get her number.

Yeah, right. Like he had anything to offer her. He'd liquidated all his assets and sold everything he owned to pay back the purchasers of the phony oil leases. He'd walk out of prison with the shirt on his back, one change of clothes courtesy of the government, and enough money for a bus ticket to nowhere.

No, better to put her out of his head right here and now.

Despite the bleakness that settled like a lump in the pit of his stomach, he had to smile. As if there was any way he could get Suzanne Delachek out of his head. After all they'd been through together, the woman was imprinted on his soul.

The distant whap-whap-whap of a helicopter jerked him out of his thoughts. His head whipped up. There it was, a tiny gray dragonfly with orange coast guard markings, heading their way. His pulse jumped with eagerness, with relief, with a stinging regret. Time to go find Suzanne and get back to the real world.

"Ryder."

The cool voice spun him around. He took a single step forward, then froze.

Suzanne walked toward him, her pale hair glinting in the golden dawn. A shard of glistening metal indented the skin just under her chin. Blood trickled down her throat.

"What the hell…?"

The tattooed gorilla who'd refused to help Ryder free her from the wreckage ambled along behind her, his fist bunching the neck of her flight suit. A thin sneer that might have been meant as a smile traced across his face.

"She gave me a little trouble, but I convinced her to be nice."

"So I see," Ryder forced out through a jaw clenched so tight it cracked.

"You give me any trouble, cowboy, and she's dead. I'll slice her up right before your eyes." The sneer broadened into a vicious grin. "I ain't got nothing to lose. I'm already doin' three life sentences."

In the space of two or three heartbeats, Ryder considered every option. The shard pressed so close to Suzanne's jugular eliminated all but one.

Lifting his shoulders, he surrendered to the inevitable. "I won't give you any trouble."

Chapter 5

Suzanne's heart stopped. She'd anticipated a dozen different reactions when Ryder spun around to confront the bastard holding the razor-edged piece of metal to her throat.

That careless shrug was *not* one of them.

"You're givin' up easy, cowboy," the man behind her growled suspiciously. "If you don't care nuthin' about her, why'd you risk your ass to go back and haul her out of the cockpit?"

Ryder strolled forward a pace or two, pitching his voice to be heard over the thud of an approaching chopper. "Maybe I was thinking then exactly what you're thinking now."

"Yeah? What am I thinking?"

"That she's our only guarantee out of this swamp."

Her pulse hammering, Suzanne stared at him, then wrenched her gaze toward the helicopter buzzing toward the hammock. The coast guard bird was following the watery trough she and Hamilton forged in the saw grass last night, from the partially submerged nose section, right to their little island.

"Damn! They're comin' straight at us!" The razor-tipped shard of metal pricked into her flesh. "Don't try nuthin', hear me?"

She set her teeth against the burning pain. "They can't land here, moron. Too many trees. When they spot us, they'll radio for a seaplane or a boat and—"

The tip gouged deeper. Gasping, Suzanne writhed to twist out of his hold. He yanked her back with a jerk on her flight suit, his breath foul against her cheek as he leaned over her.

"Who you callin' moron?"

"Hey, go easy on her!"

"You tellin' me how to handle things, cowboy?"

Ryder moved closer, shouting now to be heard over the whap of rotor blades. "If she bleeds to death, neither one of us will get out of this mess alive. She's the only card we have left to play."

When he saw the expression on Suzanne's face, his shout twisted into a snarl.

"Don't look at me like that! I was ready to serve out the rest of my sentence. But after yesterday, I figure life's too short and too uncertain to spend any more time staring at gray walls."

"Now you're starting to think like a con," the bastard behind her sneered.

"Wave." Ryder rapped out the command, closing the last of the distance between them. "Act like you're eager for rescue. That way they'll only send one seaplane to pick us up instead of a whole damned armada."

A beefy arm hooked over Suzanne's shoulders in a parody of a friendly embrace. The deadly shard withdrew from her jugular and disappeared behind her back.

"Wave, bitch."

The chopper hovered over them.

Suzanne lifted her arm and caught Ryder's almost imperceptible nod. With the same lightning move as the heron she'd spotted earlier, she swung her elbow back down and rammed it into her captor's ribs with everything she had in her.

The blow didn't do any serious damage to the goon behind her, but it surprised him for just the half second Suzanne needed to break his grip. She dropped like a stone, and was still on her way down when Ryder hit him with a flying tackle.

Arms flailing, legs thrashing, the two men crashed into the palmettos. Panting, Suzanne scrambled to her feet. The chopper hovered right above her, its rotor wash beating at her head and shoulders, the engine's whine deafening. Someone shouted over a loudspeaker. Suzanne paid no attention, every particle of her being focused on the gleaming metal shard still gripped in a meaty fist.

She swung her boot at her former captor's wrist with vicious accuracy. Bone snapped. The tattooed con howled. The jagged piece of metal went flying into the saw grass.

Enraged by the pain, the convict wrapped Ryder in python-size arms and squeezed for all he was worth. The two men rolled over and over. Suzanne followed, swinging her leg back for another kick, this one intended for the brute's skull. Before her boot could connect, the thrashing combatants rolled right off the hammock and into the water. They went under with a splash, still grappling, Ryder's face twisted in a rictus of pain and savage determination.

Suzanne started to dive in after them. A hard hand wrapped around her arm and yanked her back.

''Stand clear!''

She whirled around, stunned by the sight of two men in jeans and navy blue windbreakers stenciled with U.S. MARSHALS on the pocket. Even more stunned by the rifles they had trained on the men thrashing around in the saw grass.

They'd rappelled out of the chopper, she saw in a sweeping glance. The line still dangled from the hovering helo.

''We saw them attack you,'' one of the marshals shouted. ''That murderous bastard is Joey Herndon.''

''He was on his way to death row at Marion when Flight 407 was hijacked.'' The second marshal hefted his rifle and squinted though the scope. ''Be wonderful if he saved the taxpayers the expense by drowning. I'll cover them, Alex. You wade in....''

Suzanne slapped aside the rifle barrel. ''You can't shoot. You might hit Ryder!''

''Ryder Hamilton? Is that him wrestling with Herndon?''

''Yes, dammit! He needs help!''

The marshal lowered his weapon with a lack of concern that curled Suzanne's fingers into claws.

''Doesn't look to me like he needs any help.''

She spun around, her heart pounding, as a creature from the deep rose out of the swamp. Wet saw grass drooped over his head. Mud oozed down his neck and shoulders. Chest heaving, he slogged through the waist-high water, dragging a dazed whale behind him. As he neared the hammock, all Suzanne could do was swallow convulsively and offer him a stupid grin.

''Nice recovery, Hamilton.''

White teeth gleaming in a muddy face, he panted out a

reply. "I wasn't sure...I was going to beat the odds...this time, Delachek. That's quite an elbow you've got on you."

She was still grinning when one of the marshals waded into the swamp and slapped a pair of handcuffs on Herndon. She turned to the other marshal, a question burning in her heart.

"What about the rest of the passengers aboard Flight 407?"

"As far as we know, they all made it. Now that we've got Hamilton and Herndon, we've accounted for everyone on the manifest, along with a female passenger and another marshal not on the list."

Kelly Jackson and Spence Cantrell.

Suzanne let out a long sigh of relief. Her relief evaporated in the next instant, however. To her dismay, the marshal she'd questioned waited only until Ryder had gained dry land to pull out another pair of cuffs.

"Hey, what are you doing?"

The steel bracelets snapped into place. "He's a prisoner in transport, ma'am. Federal regulations require—"

"To hell with federal regulations! This man helped save your aircraft and everyone aboard. He also pulled me out from under a crumpled instrument panel."

"I'm sure that will be taken into account when he comes up for parole. But for now—"

"For now," she interrupted fiercely, advancing on the man with fists balled, "you'd better take off those handcuffs."

"Sorry, ma'am. I can't do that."

Ryder smiled wryly. "It's okay, sweetheart. I'm used to them."

At the casual endearment, the two marshals exchanged glances, then carefully wiped all expression from their faces. When they turned neutral looks on Suzanne, heat crawled into her cheeks.

She could guess what they were thinking. She'd heard all the stories about women who became pen pals with convicts and got sucked into relationships. How some even married men they'd never met outside of a prison visitors' center. The sickening realization that she was no better than any of those desperate groupies curled in her stomach for a moment.

Only a moment.

All she had to do was shift her glance to Ryder to shatter the stereotypes. He wasn't just a nameless, faceless number in a prison computer. She wasn't a bubble-headed female so hungry for love she'd enter into a relationship with anyone who stroked her ego and her heartstrings.

Ryder Hamilton had shown more courage in the face of extreme danger than anyone she'd ever met. He also held to a personal code of honor that allowed for mistakes, but not for criminal activity.

Her back stiffened. Icy determination flowed through her veins. Ryder must have recognized the signs. Before she could let loose with both barrels, he stepped forward a few paces and spoke quietly, without rancor.

"Let it go, Suzanne. We both knew this was going to happen."

Last night she knew it would happen. Even earlier this morning. Now, she was damned if she'd let the system swallow him again.

"Listen to me, Hamilton. Everyone aboard Flight 407 owes you. I owe you. You're not the only one who always pays their debts."

"Suzanne…"

"You're not going back to Whiskey Springs in handcuffs,'' she said fiercely. ''In fact, you're not going back at all until we make a little detour.''

''Detour?'' His black brows snapped together. ''Where?''

The scheme had popped into her head only a second or two ago. Her mind raced, spinning out the details. It might work. It *had* to work!

''South Miami.''

Stunned, he stared down at her. Hope flared in his eyes, only to die as swiftly as it was born.

''You're crazy.''

''So everyone keeps telling me,'' she shot back, grinning. Spinning on her heel, she stalked over to the nearest marshal.

''Is that radio clipped to your waist tuned into the search and rescue net?''

''Yes, ma'am.''

''Get on it. I want to talk to FBI Agent Mason Taggart. Now!''

Three hours later, Suzanne gulped down hot coffee on the deck of a coast guard cutter and waited impatiently for Taggart to transfer from the launch bringing him across the swamp.

A fresh white bandage covered the cut on her neck. She'd changed out of her soggy flight suit into a pair of jeans and a soft cotton ''swabbie'' shirt borrowed from one of the female coast guard officers, but Taggart still wore the same rumpled brown suit. Stubble shaded his cheeks, and his thinning brown hair badly needed a comb. Yet Suzanne could have kissed him when he climbed onto the cutter's deck and greeted her with a nod.

That was all she needed. A single nod. Whooping, she

tossed the coffee over the side, flew across the deck, and hugged him for all he was worth.

Red singeing his cheeks, he grinned at her. "I had to call in every favor owed me and then some to get Washington to agree to this."

"They're going to get the bugs in place today?"

"One of the FBI's technical squads is on their way to the pawnshop at this very minute."

"Hot damn!"

Pulling a crumpled paper bag out of his pocket, he offered its contents. Suzanne shook her head. She hadn't eaten in twenty-four hours, but macadamia nuts were the last thing on her mind right now.

"It helped considerably that the locals have been watching that particular operation for some months now," Taggart told her between crunches. "They're pretty sure this Sharon Smith and her friend have been fencing stolen goods. That was the only explanation the locals could come up with for the matching BMWs Smith and her friend drive and their twelve-room shack with an ocean view."

Suzanne knew what had paid for those flashy cars and the ocean view. Ryder's payroll and the hundreds of thousands of dollars Sharon Smith and her friend had raked in from the sale of phony oil leases.

She didn't stop to question the fact that she believed Ryder implicitly now. He said he was innocent. He *was* innocent. Period. End of argument. Now it was just a matter of proving it.

"Marshal Cantrell wants in on this sting, too," Taggart informed her. "He was transported to a hospital in Fort Myers last night, but he's checked himself out and will rendezvous with us in South Miami."

"All right. Let's get those blasted cuffs off Ryder and go to work."

Taggart stilled her with a hand on her arm. "Cantrell's put his career on the line by convincing his superiors to let Hamilton walk into that pawnshop alone. The place is a near arsenal, with enough guns on display to outfit a small army. Hamilton could walk right out the back door armed to the teeth."

"He won't."

"Or he could put a bullet through this woman he claims set him up."

Remembering the way Ryder's eyes had gone so hard and flat when he talked about collecting on the debt his ex-fiancée owed him, Suzanne swallowed.

"He won't shoot anyone."

"You got that in writing, Miz Delachek?"

"I don't need it in writing. He won't hurt her. If this plan works, he won't need to. All he has to do is scare the truth out of her by showing up without warning. Your tech squad gets it on tape, the tape goes to the judge, and Ryder goes free."

"It's not that easy. *If* she confesses—and that's a big if—he'll have to file a motion to reverse his conviction. A federal judge will have to..."

Suzanne swept the minor details aside with an impatient hand. "We'll work all that out later. Let's go get those cuffs off him."

To everyone's complete astonishment, Ryder's included, he pulled it off.

Wearing borrowed jeans and a white shirt, he strolled into Doc's Pawnshop two hours later. The pouty redhead filing her nails behind the counter took one look at him and went pasty white.

"Ryder! Wh…? What are you doing here?"

"Looking for you, Shar."

"I thought…" She sidled toward the register, her shaking hand groping along the counter's edge. "I thought you still had another six months to serve before you came up for parole?"

"I got time off for good behavior. You don't need to hit any silent alarms," he told her as her fingers curved under the counter. "I'm not planning to wring your neck. Not that I didn't think about it," he added with a sardonic smile. "More times than you want to know."

"Then—" she wet her lips "—what do you want with me?"

"I had a lot of time to hash things out in the past couple years, Shar. We were good together, before Pauly got between us. You were the only woman I ever…"

He couldn't force out the word "loved." He knew now that whatever he'd felt for Sharon all those months ago didn't come anywhere close to love. Suzanne had taught him the difference in one night.

"You were the only woman I ever asked to marry me," he finished.

Incredibly, she seemed to take his hesitation for emotion and looked at him with considerably less apprehension. He forced himself to bait the trap with a shrug and a smile.

"We were good together, weren't we?"

Thinking back, he could barely keep from shaking his head at his own stupidity. Why hadn't he seen past the black spandex, the 36D cup, and the dark roots under that mahogany hair? Suzanne was everything this woman wasn't. Honest. Courageous. Sharp and clean as a winter morning.

Still wary but thawing fast, Sharon kept the counter between them. "Look, none of that business in Midland was my idea. Pauly thought the whole thing up."

"Yeah, right."

"He did! After I told him about meeting you at the Rusty Derrick, he started asking around. Found out how much you were worth. He was the one who thought I should get a job as your secretary."

"And I suppose you didn't know anything about the forged signatures on those lease agreements?"

"All right, I signed your name," she admitted, "but I was going to find you when you got out and share my cut of the money with you. I swear!"

"What about Pauly?"

She abandoned the counter and moved toward him, emboldened by the possibilities she read in his face.

"He doesn't treat me like you did. I...I missed you, Ryder." Sliding her palms over his pecs, she lowered her voice to a husky whisper. "Like you said, we were good together. We could be again."

"I don't think so."

Turning on his heel, he walked out the door.

Spence Cantrell climbed out of the nondescript van parked two doors down and greeted Ryder with a grin. "We got it, Hamilton. I'm having a copy of the tape made for you as a personal keepsake."

Two FBI agents hustled out of the van as well and made a beeline for the pawnshop. Mason Taggart swung open the front door and descended more slowly.

Ryder ignored them all, his eyes locked on the silvery blonde who joined the small crowd on the pavement. He reached her in three long strides. There were a hundred things he wanted to tell her. Only one he could say with law enforcement officers flanking her on either side.

"Thanks, Delachek. I owe you. Again."

Laughter, excitement, and an emotion Ryder wouldn't let himself believe danced in her blue eyes. "Saving each other's butt is getting to be a habit with us, Hamilton."

"You've noticed that, have you?"

"So how are you going to repay me for this one?" she wanted to know.

He clenched his fists at his sides to keep from hauling her into his arms. "I'll come up with something appropriate. I expect I'll have some time to think about it until that tape gets before a judge."

"Maybe not as long as you think," Cantrell put in. "Four weeks, maybe six weeks max. Don't forget that uncle I told you about. I've already called him."

Ryder refused to release the reins of the wild emotions galloping through his chest. Yesterday, six months had seemed like a lifetime. Today, six weeks stretched even longer. If he thought Suzanne might be waiting for him at the end of those six weeks, however, he'd do them standing on his head.

He couldn't ask her to wait. The words wouldn't come. Not in front of Taggart and Cantrell. Not until he could say them right, with a reversal of his conviction tucked in his pocket and no shadows hanging over him.

He might have known cool, confident, always-in-charge Suzanne would take command.

"Well," she demanded impatiently. "Are you going to kiss me or not?"

Something warm and wonderful knifed into Ryder's heart.

"Yes, ma'am," he drawled. "I surely am."

Epilogue

A small welcoming committee awaited the sleek Gulf-stream jet when it swooped in for a landing at Whiskey Springs just past ten o'clock that night.

Christine Logan stood beside Quinn Buchanan in the star-kissed April darkness. Most of the debris left by the tornado that had almost destroyed her airport had been cleared, although plywood still covered the shattered windows of the passenger terminal.

Christine couldn't help a little thrill of pride as she swept the lighted runway with a proprietary eye. The portable tower was fully functional. Commercial traffic had resumed regular schedules. Streams of approach lights shone a steady blue and white path for the small jet returning the last of Flight 407's passengers to its point of origin.

"You brought them home."

She glanced up to see Quinn's eyes on her face. More than anyone else, he knew what she'd gone through to get

Sam Houston International Airport back up and running. Even more, how close Flight 407 had come to taking her life.

She slipped her hand in his. "*We* brought them home."

The smile he gave her melted her knees. "We make a hell of a team, Slim. Too bad it took us so long to figure that out."

"We know it now. That's all that matters."

"Here they are!"

Kelly Jackson's eager voice floated on the soft night. She'd refused all treatment and counseling at the hastily organized trauma center and insisted on being at the airport tonight. She, like Christine and Quinn, wanted to be on hand when the last of Flight 407's passengers and crew returned to Whiskey Springs.

Her slender body quivering in anticipation, Kelly pressed her fingertips to her ears to shut out the Gulfstream's whine as it turned onto the taxiway and headed for its designated parking space. The ground crew had no sooner set the chocks than the small jet's side door raised and a set of steps folded down.

Kelly's heart thumped painfully when a tall, broad-shouldered marshal ducked his head through the door and edged sideways down the stairs, using his unbandaged arm to steady himself.

Had these past days been a dream? Or had she really found a man like Spence Cantrell, as gentle as he was tough? As loving as he was good?

When he started across the tarmac, his smile for her alone, Kelly had her answers. The ordeal of the hijacking, the horror of the crash, all faded away. Only Spence remained, filling her heart with hope and the first stirrings of something so deep and sure she ached with it. He took her hand, not saying a word until a clatter of boots on the stairs turned their heads toward the Gulfstream.

The gorgeous female pilot Kelly had glimpsed for only a moment or two after the extraordinary midair transfer climbed out, followed by Ryder Hamilton. He looked so different in jeans and a red knit shirt, with his face clean shaven…and no handcuffs.

For a moment, the six people whose lives had been bound so inextricably by the terror in the skies had no words to say to each other. The joy of being alive spoke for itself in the silly smiles that spread across their faces.

Then Ryder thrust a hand through his gleaming black hair and aimed a grin around the small circle.

"Helluva flight, wasn't it?"

* * * * *

For more pulse-pounding,
heart-stopping romantic suspense
from USA Today *bestselling author*
Merline Lovelace, read

THE SPY WHO LOVED HIM,

Intimate Moments 1052, part of
THE YEAR OF LOVING DANGEROUSLY,
on sale January 2001.

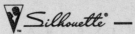

where love comes alive—online...

eHARLEQUIN.com

your romantic
books

♥ **Shop online!** Visit Shop eHarlequin and discover a wide selection of new releases and classic favorites at great discounted prices.

♥ **Read** our daily and weekly Internet exclusive serials, and participate in our interactive novel in the reading room.

♥ **Ever dreamed of being a writer?** Enter your chapter for a chance to become a featured author in our Writing Round Robin novel.

your romantic
life

♥ **Check out** our feature articles on dating, flirting and other important romance topics and get your daily love dose with tips on how to keep the romance alive every day.

your
community

♥ **Have a Heart-to-Heart** with other members about the latest books and meet your favorite authors.

♥ **Discuss** your romantic dilemma in the Tales from the Heart message board.

your romantic
escapes

♥ **Learn** what the stars have in store for you with our daily Passionscopes and weekly Erotiscopes.

♥ **Get** the latest scoop on your favorite royals in Royal Romance.

INTIMATE MOMENTS™

presents a riveting 12-book continuity series:

A Year of loving dangerously

Where passion rules and nothing is what it seems...

When dishonor threatens a top-secret agency, the brave men and women of SPEAR are prepared to risk it all as they put their lives—and their hearts—on the line.

Available January 2001:

THE SPY WHO LOVED HIM
by Merline Lovelace

Although headstrong Margarita Alfonsa de las Fuentes was mesmerized by Carlos Caballero's fearless courage, she wasn't about to bow to *any* man. But now that a murderous traitor was hot on their trail deep in the Central American jungle, the beautiful secret spy struggled with the raw emotions Carlos's fierce protectiveness stirred in her!

*Available only from Silhouette Intimate Moments
at your favorite retail outlet.*

Where love comes alive™

Coming in January 2001 from Silhouette Books...

ChildFinders, Inc.:
AN UNCOMMON HERO

by

MARIE FERRARELLA

**the latest installment of
this bestselling author's popular miniseries.**

The assignment seemed straightforward: track down the woman who had stolen a boy and return him to his father. But ChildFinders, Inc. had been duped, and Ben Underwood soon discovered that nothing about the case was as it seemed. Gina Wassel, the supposed kidnapper, was everything Ben had dreamed of in a woman, and suddenly he had to untangle the truth from the lies—before it was too late.

Available at your favorite retail outlet.

Silhouette®

Where love comes alive™

#1 *New York Times* **bestselling author**

NORA ROBERTS

brings you more of the loyal and loving,
tempestuous and tantalizing Stanislaski family.

Coming in February 2001

The Stanislaski Sisters

Natasha and Rachel

Though raised in the Old World traditions of their
family, fiery Natasha Stanislaski and cool, classy
Rachel Stanislaski are ready for a *new* world of love....

And also available in February 2001 from
Silhouette Special Edition, the newest book in the
heartwarming Stanislaski saga

CONSIDERING KATE

Natasha and Spencer Kimball's daughter Kate turns her
back on old dreams and returns to her hometown, where
she finds the *man* of her dreams.

Available at your favorite retail outlet.

COMING NEXT MONTH

CMN1200